BROKEN STERN

Ellie O'Conner Coastal Suspense Series | Book 1

JACK HARDIN

First Published in the United States by The Salty Mangrove Press

Copyright © 2018 by Jack Hardin. All rights reserved.

This is a work of fiction. Names, characters, businesses, places, events, locales, and incidents are either the products of the author's imagination or used in a fictitious manner. Any resemblance to actual persons, living or dead, or actual events is purely coincidental.

No part of this book may be reproduced in any form or by any electronic or mechanical means, including information storage and retrieval systems, without written permission from the author, except for the use of brief quotations in a book review.

To Mom
I miss you

FOREWORD

Hello, Dear Reader,

The first four books of the Ellie O'Conner series all form one larger story arc, with all subplots resolving at the end of book four (Vacant Shore).

Broken Stern does end in a cliffhanger, and the story continues into book 2.

Books 5 and onward are standalone installments.

Happy reading!

CHAPTER ONE

No one had told her time could be compressed, that experiencing the phenomenon almost made one dizzy.

Ellie O'Conner closed her eyes and saw their faces. Her heart rate ticked higher. She was always calm, composed. Only an IED could shake her up. But today. Today was different.

The ring of the phone snapped her from a nostalgic trance, and she snatched it up.

"Tough waiting like this, isn't it?"

"What?"

"The wait. It sucks."

"What? Who is—" She was cut off by sharp laughter that came through the phone's receiver and drifted across the room from behind her. She turned to see Kurt "Buck" Rogers with his field boots on his cluttered desk, clearly pleased with his own antics.

She turned back to her desk, slamming the phone back on its cradle. Buck. He would never learn the meaning of tact, timing, or keeping a phone line clear.

One day it was going to get him killed. If not by a hostile, then certainly by a co-worker who'd lost patience with him.

The phone rang again.

Ellie rolled her eyes and looked back over her shoulder. Kurt's desk was vacant, and he was headed toward the cold coffee pot. Her body straightened. She closed her eyes, took a deep breath, and grabbed up the receiver.

"Go. Fifteen minutes."

She jumped to her feet, grabbed her canvas rucksack, and set her sunglasses on the bridge of her nose as she thrust her hip against the heavy metal door that opened to the bright Afghanistan afternoon. Her Sig Sauer P320 was tucked away at the small of her back, ten rounds nestled patiently in the magazine. She pulled open the door to the desert-colored Humvee where her driver sat with the engine running. The vehicle was moving before her door slammed shut, leaving a cloud of fine desert dust billowing in the rearview mirror. Within thirty seconds they were speeding past Camp Phoenix's checkpoint where two heavily armed soldiers in sunglasses nodded at them.

"How long?" her driver asked.

"Fourteen."

He glanced at his watch and flicked his sober eyes back on the road ahead, taking a sharp left onto Kabul-Nangarhar Highway. They sped east toward the outskirts of the capital city and the snow-tipped Hindu Kush mountains, which loomed far ahead of them.

Ellie slid in her earpiece. There would be no chatter until their arrival at the predetermined pickup. She steadied her breathing and looked out the window at the small buildings set off the highway. It still intrigued her that so many chose to make their homes in the middle of the desert. Almost four million people out of every ethnic group in the region lived in Kabul. But today, for Ellie, there were only four.

She was rounding out her second year in the province, eight months longer than she or her superiors had projected, the weight and effects of which would all be compressed into the next fourteen minutes.

Seven hundred and nine days squeezed into the next quarter hour.

The events of the last two years came into focus as Ellie stared out the window: Murad was one of the finest men she had ever met. He was the reason she was here. A career dentist who, because of Ellie's patient massaging, had become one of the CIA's most important and trusted assets in the region.

Ellie had transferred here from Europe for the sole purpose of recruiting Assam as a tool for American interests, coming to him as a patient and with a cover as a journalist with Reuters. She slid her tongue against the back of her lower incisor, remembering the first procedure he performed on her. Ellie had always possessed good teeth, and that was the primary hurdle in finding a reason to go to Assam's office as a patient. Her co-workers joked early on that they wished he had chosen chiropractic as a profession. Ellie could have recruited him much faster. As it was, a cleaning once every five to six months meant one needed to get creative in order to increase touch points without setting off any psychological or municipal alarms.

It was unusual in this area of the world for a female to play such a leading role with a male informant.

Women were often viewed as socially and spiritually inferior to men, making it difficult for a female on the front lines of counter-terrorism to be taken seriously. Getting close enough to a male asset could quickly raise suspicion, seen as inappropriate at best, provocative at worst. Simply donning a wig and sunglasses to meet in the dark corner of a café or pub wasn't possible like she had done in Paris or Dublin. Converting Assam had been the challenge of her career, and she had succeeded.

The planning and patience had finally paid off. Assam had given the CIA what they had wanted for years now: his highest-profile patient and distant cousin, Fahad Sarkaui. Sarkaui was ISIS's third in command in the country, and up until then the CIA had yet to get near him. Assam had finally provided Ellie with information that led to a perfectly placed drone strike nearly two days ago—one that sent his cousin's teeth and skull scattering in thirty different directions. Ellie's primary task these last thirty-six hours was to get Assam and his family safely out of the country.

He gave the signal ten minutes ago: a yellow cloth placed in the far left window of the flat. Assam and his family had gone to visit his mother where she lived in a rundown area on the outskirts of the city. It was where she had grown up, and Assam had been unsuccessful in convincing her to move to a nicer area of Kabul, though he offered to pay for it himself.

The driver turned his watch toward his face. "Three minutes."

Ellie's breathing was perfectly tuned to her slow heartbeat, a testimony to the level of control and discipline she had over her body. Nothing rattled her unless she allowed it to. But now, with one hundred seconds until the extraction, an unusual sensation settled beneath her skin. Her nerves were crawling, her stomach sour. One of the first rules of the game was to not get attached to anyone on the outside. You tilled the ground of your assets until they became a fictional family - never the real thing - always keeping them at an arm's length. But Ellie had quietly broken that rule with this family over six months ago. It had been a decision where her heart followed her mind and, not as one might expect, the other way around. She knew that if this was going to be her life, then she was no longer going to live simply as a calculating machine. She had done enough of that for the six years prior to her Afghan tour. She was in the people business, and at the right times, one had to care about the right kind of people.

Assam's family were the right kind of people.

His wife, Vida, was gracious and kind. Assam's ten-year-old son, Ibrahim, had a sober and contemplative personality that contrasted with his little sister, Khalida. The six-year-old girl was fully energetic, and her spirited personality poured out of her. Ellie still kept a little straw doll on her pillow that Khalida had made for her. In the last ten years, Ellie had been back home to Florida to visit only twice. Her role with the Agency afforded her no other opportunities to do so, as much as she would have liked it. In many ways, the Murads had become a second family to Ellie. She would go for dinner at their home a couple times each month and sit with them until late in the evenings talking about the war, their culture, and their collective hopes for the future of their country.

The Humvee exited the highway and turned left under the darkened underpass. Its two passengers bounced up and down on the uneven road as it dodged potholes and split asphalt. Ellie reached into her sack, pulled out a black hijab, and wrapped it loosely around her head. She looked into her side view mirror and saw their escort pull in behind them, another Humvee carrying four armed soldiers.

"Arrived," her earpiece chirped.

They pulled up hard at the corner, and Ellie stared out her window at the rusty metal door nestled on the side of the old, five-story, plastered building. "Come on," she muttered. Nothing. The driver looked at his watch and lowered his head as he swung his eyes around and surveyed the windows and roofs of the buildings around them. "Come on," she said again to the door, as if the words had magical powers to accomplish her bidding.

Ellie's earpiece came to life. "Zero tango," a man's voice whispered. "Negative thirty seconds."

Her eyes were glued to the door. "Eagle, how's it looking up there?" she asked firmly.

"Clear," a deep voice crackled. Two armed CIA snipers were on surrounding rooftops, keeping watch for unwelcome activity.

Suddenly, the metal door flung open, and Ellie shot out of the Humvee. Three doors belonging to the vehicle behind opened, and as many men in desert fatigues and helmets poured out with their HK416 automatic rifles drawn. They stepped onto the sidewalk and scanned the landscape. A tall, bearded man wearing a grey perahan tunban emerged from the doorway carrying a little girl across his body. Her arms and legs were wrapped tightly around her father. Ellie wanted to smile and tell the girl it was going to be all right, but there was no time. Her father was trailed by a middle-aged lady with her hand resting protectively on the head of her young son. Like his parents, Ibrahim's pupils were dilated wide with fear and urgency. The foursome moved quickly, their heads held low. "This way," Ellie said. "Quickly." Her eyes darted from the family to the buildings surrounding them. It was only fifteen feet from the metal door to the escort.

Suddenly, two loud "pops" filled the air. Vida's hand came off the head of her son as her body lifted violently off the ground and was flung into the side of the building she had just exited.

"Vida!" Assam screamed and turned toward his wife.

"Assam, no!" Ellie yelled. "We have to go!"

"Mama!" Ibrahim screamed. Another "pop" and Ibrahim's body crumpled to the ground. His father turned to him in horror. "No!"

The American soldiers behind them scanned their surroundings in vain for the shooter, then moved in to cover Assam.

"Do you have eyes?" Ellie yelled angrily into her mic.

"Negative."

Assam swiveled toward Ellie and shifted his daughter into her arms. He turned and ran back to the bodies of his wife and his son lying lifeless on the concrete, dark blood pooling underneath them. "Vida!" Assam yelled again, squatting over her and shaking her shoulder. He turned to his son as a full round of bullets hit the building, spraying pieces of concrete into his face. He ducked and turned a face filled with horror toward Ellie. "Go!" he choked out. "Take Khalida. Go!"

"Assam, you have to—"

"Go!" he yelled. "Go now! Save her, Ellie!"

Ellie's earpiece was squawking with furious commands. Instinctively, Ellie knew the proper decision. Take the girl and go. Now. But the smallest of moments kept her staring into Assam's eyes, wanting to scream at him one last time to come, to get in the escort.

A soft hiss quickly grew loud and filled the air.

No, she thought. *No*.

She didn't need to turn to know what was coming toward them. Assam's eyes grew wider as they found the rocket flying through the air behind Ellie and the Humvee. He shifted his vision to his youngest child clutched in the embrace of his American friend. His eyes met Ellie's. They were not angry. Only darkened with sadness, confusion, and questions that would never be answered.

A man's voice was screaming through her earpiece. She held Khalida tighter, turned, and darted toward the vehicle just as the missile struck behind her. The blast twisted Ellie's body around and tore the young girl from her arms. Ellie landed with the small of her back pressed against the passenger seat cushion of the Humvee.

A soldier darted toward her, the butt of his gun still wedged into his shoulder, his eyes frantically scanning the area. "Ellie!" he screamed. She felt a strong hand reach around her upper arm and forcefully pull her onto the seat and into a sitting position. She leaned back, and the door slammed shut. Ellie shook her head, clearing her mind, and flung the door open. "No!" she yelled. Her head was spinning. Ellie watched the soldier pick the girl up off the pavement. "Give her to me," she said and reached out. He quickly but gently slid her into Ellie's arms and shut the door. Her driver was too professional for her to need to scream at him to go. No sooner had Ellie's door shut than he floored the pedal, and they darted off just as the sound of another missile hissed through the air above them. The atmosphere rocked around them as a second explosion found its mark where they had just been sitting.

Ellie's mind was clearing by the second, but her ears were still ringing. The world sounded muted. Like she was underwater in a calm serenity while chaos ensued above.

She looked down at Khalida who was limp in her arms. "Khalida?" she said. "Honey?" The girl's hijab had been torn off in the blast, and her small face was peppered with dirt and small bits of concrete. Ellie sat her up on her lap and let the girl's head rest back on her shoulder as she assessed her condition.

She looked down and saw it. Her small white shirt had bloomed red. Ellie tore against the buttons, and the fabric moved away from Khalida's body. Ellie's breath stopped. A long piece of twisted shrapnel three inches wide was lodged just below her navel.

"What happened? Report!" her earpiece squawked. She reached up and yanked it out. Her driver looked at the fifty-pound body lying across Ellie, and the vehicle lurched forward as he accelerated. With her left hand, Ellie unzipped her backpack and grabbed an embroidered scarf. It was to be a gift for the girl's mother. She had packed something for all of them for the fifteen-minute drive back to base, the gifts intended to distract their troubled minds until they were safe inside the American compound.

Ellie carefully laid the girl across her lap to slow the drain of blood, then gently wrapped the scarf around the metal and pressed on the outside of the wound to mitigate the flow of blood. The girl's face was pale and clammy.

"Hurry, Ron."

A HALF-HOUR later Ellie stood in the small operating room at Camp Phoenix and watched the doctor pull down his blue surgical mask. His latex gloves snapped as he pulled them from his hands. He looked at the clock and sighed.

"Time of death, fourteen thirty-seven."

Ellie blinked against the impossibility. How had this happened? All four of them were gone. Gone. For what? Why? Rage overcame grief as Ellie pushed at the door and stepped into the painted cinder block hallway. She threw open the outside door and was blinded by the mid-afternoon sun while she crossed the sandy street. She quickly passed a few shipping containers and stormed through an entrance leading to another cement building. Her hands were clenched and her shoulders stiff. She walked to the end of the hall and threw the door open, her shoes moving from the bare concrete of the hallway to carpet.

Ryan Wilcox sat behind his military-issue desk with his narrow face looking fatigued and heavy brown eyes set on his case officer.

"Ellie," he said. "I'm sor—"

"What the hell happened, Ryan?" she snapped. "Who was it?" Her small nostrils flared, and she loomed over the desk with the energy of a panther who had found its dinner.

"I don't know yet."

"What do you mean you don't know?"

"Come on, Ellie! You know I'm looking for answers. As soon as I hear back from Langley or Berlin, you'll be the first to know." He ran a hand through his hair. "We did everything right. It wasn't us."

She pointed toward the building across the street. "There is a dead six-year-old girl on a cold metal table in the building next door. You want to go have a look at her?"

"Oh no," he said softly. "She didn't make it?"

"Or we can take a short ride, and I can show you the pieces of her parents and her brother?"

Ryan took a long, slow breath. "I know you're upset - you should be."

"Upset?" Her tone was incredulous. "We are the damn CIA, Ryan! This kind of thing isn't supposed to happen. Someone didn't keep a tight enough lip about this, and they knew. They knew when and where we were coming. This was a mistake on our side. *Our* side, Ryan. Some moron in a tie is to blame for...for this." She shook her head and set her jaw tight, blinking hard to keep back the tears.

She plopped into a wide upholstered chair in front of Ryan's desk and slicked a hand down her face. She closed her eyes and immediately recognized the mistake. All she saw was blood. Not her own.

She opened her eyes and stared at a fixed spot on the floor. Assam and his family were just another number in this American crusade. Besides her and the few people involved in today's mission, no one on this side of things would even remember them. No one ultimately cared that a husband, a wife, and two innocent children had been murdered today. Ryan did. The soldiers out there with her today did. But the suits behind mahogany and walnut desks did not. This family had been murdered because someone made a deal where it was beneficial for them to let Assam's name slip. Not just his name. His time and place of extraction too.

Her boss stood and walked to the front of his desk. He sat back on the corner. At forty-eight, Ryan Wilcox was almost fifteen years her senior. The short hair on his temples was beginning to show gray, and the crow's feet stamped around his eyes were deepening. He looked down on his agent. The blood on Ellie's shirt was darker now that it was dry. The skin on her knees was gone, the side of her face littered with tiny cuts.

"Are you okay? Have you been looked at?"

"I'm fine, Ryan."

"Ellie, look. I know this is hard on you. You were close to them. It's hard for me too." Ryan brought his fingers up and slowly rubbed his temples. "I hate that this happened, and I'll do whatever I can to find out who's to blame. Your training doesn't exempt you from feeling shock. Just go get checked out and get some rest. We can talk about it in a couple—"

"No, Ryan." Her voice was icy now. She paused, allowing a heavy silence to fill the room. "I'm done. I'm done with whatever it is that you think we're doing."

"Ellie, Assam made his own choices. He knew the risks."

Ellie's head snapped up, and her eyes burned into those of her boss. "He trusted us. He trusted *me*. There is no good reason why this happened. None. We've got billions of dollars and thousands of the world's finest behind us."

"Ellie. You're the best officer I have out here. Your experience and training are unmatched. I can't just make a call and replace you."

"Replace me? Why would you need to do that?" she hurled back. "The very reason I was brought out here is in a hundred pieces in a back alley across town. You don't get it, Ryan. I'm not quitting." She paused again and lowered her voice. "I'm opting out."

Her superior lifted a brow.

"I came into the Agency because I love my country and wanted to make a difference. I moved into handling assets because I no longer believed what I was doing for the Agency was the right thing to do. I believed in what I was doing here. But the bureaucracy and the incompetence comes with a price I'm not willing to pay any longer. What happened today should never happen. Never. We both know that. But it did, and it's happening all over the Agency with more frequency than ever. This wasn't a technological mistake or a training failure, Ryan. Somebody, somewhere on our side, leveraged that family to get something in return." She shook her head. "I'm not going to do it anymore. I'm not going to ask good people to put their lives and the lives of those they love at risk just so they can further some fat suit's agenda in Washington or wherever they happen to be. Some moron who's going to kiss babies and shake hands and never really know about what happened here today because he doesn't really care."

Ryan stood up and went back to his chair. "Where will you go?"

"Home. I've been gone for too long anyway. I'm

thirty-four. It's time I learned what it's like to live a normal life. I want a dog. I want to get back out on the water. I want to breathe again."

"So my best trained and most experienced officer is going to move to South Florida and spend the rest of her life fishing? You can't be serious."

"I haven't figured all that out yet." The tinny smell of drying blood drifted into her nose. "I just know I'm out."

Her boss calmly searched her eyes. He had never known Ellie to make any decision driven by emotion. This was personal, that much was obvious, but he knew well enough that it wasn't the primary factor in her decision. He tossed his hands up. "What can I say? I'm not going to convince you. To be honest, I respect you too much to try."

"Thanks, Ryan."

"Your renewal is coming up in three weeks. I'm guessing that's when you're stepping out?"

She nodded.

"Okay," he conceded reluctantly. "Well, you know the drill. I'll have to restrict your access and bury you in exit reports." He raised his eyebrows. "You're sure about this?"

She winced as she rose from the chair and headed toward the door. "I have to take a shower."

CHAPTER TWO

Pete Wellington throttled down on his NauticStar 22XS, and the Yamaha 200 four-stroke that powered it eased the spin of its rotor. He brought the boat to a stop, dropped anchor, backed down on it, and set it. He shut off the engine, grabbed his YETI coffee cup, and sat on the flip-down bench positioned at the stern, then closed his eyes and breathed in the cool air sitting over the waters of the Sound. This was his respite, his blood pressure medication. At his old age, some people went on walks, bike rides, or to those group workout sessions at the local gym, but Pete's battery was recharged by being the only person out on the water. It was only him all alone in the vastness, producing an intimacy with nature that couldn't be bought with a charter or an African safari.

Each Friday Pete's alarm went off at three-fifteen in the morning. He would be out on the water within thirty minutes, when the shrimpers were still a couple hours from coming back in and before the deep sea boats headed out to their favorite spots. Times like this, out here alone in the inky blackness, it felt like the world was his. Sometimes he would throw a hook in and see if he could come up with a snook or a snapper, but most Friday mornings he would just sit here on the bench seat, close his eyes, and listen to the wind blow gentle sheets of air across the water.

He took a sip of his coffee and felt the hot liquid run down the back of his throat. The preferred choice was black: no cream or sugar. If he didn't drink it all, the YETI would still have it warm at dinner. But he would finish it within the next hour.

A fish - he guessed a mullet - flipped out of the water behind him and made a loud splash as it re-entered. He waited and listened. They usually jumped out two or three times before moving on.

Voices. He heard voices. Murmurs, too far away to make out, but in a cadence that wasn't English. Spanish, perhaps. He opened his eyes, and his brows lowered. The sounds were coming from behind the darkened shape of a small cluster of mangroves on his port side. Pete stood up and walked to the bow, stopped and listened again.

"...*date prisa!*" It was all he could make out. The Spanish voices were muffled and spoken in low tones. Curious, Pete moved back to the console and turned on the single outboard motor. He gently moved the throttle and, after backing over the anchor and pulling it, idled his way around the vegetation. He hit the switch that turned off the LED canopy lights and the green underwater lights, then killed the engine as the coastal shrubs slid away from him.

He could just make out a speedboat bathed in soft red light a hundred yards out. What looked like a barrel was floating in the water next to it with dim yellow light streaming out of the top. Pete didn't know enough of the language to make out any of it. A crease formed between his brows. He squatted and pulled up on the ring to the deck's small storage compartment. Looking in, he found his binoculars and drew them out, then walked back to the stern. Setting the glasses to his eyes, he squinted and slid a finger across the focus knob. The scene in the water sharpened. Several men were scrambling around the speedboat carrying black packages. One man was leaning over the side, looking into the barrel. The boat was thirty-eight to forty feet in Pete's opinion. He couldn't make out the brand etched onto the side, but by its size, outline, and the three outboards locked onto the transom, he guessed it to be a Nor-tech. If he was right, he was looking at a half-million-dollar boat.

He looked back to the barrel and blinked hard. A man's arms appeared at the top of it, coming up from the inside. The arms pushed a black package up to the man looking down from the boat. Pete's stomach clenched. That was no barrel. He took a couple steps toward the stern, set the binoculars back to his eyes, and focused on the tube coming out of the water. He could see water slightly displaced on two sides of it, as if something was just under the surface of the barrel. He removed the field glasses and brought a hand up to his forehead. He rubbed his brow, and his heart beat a little faster. He swallowed hard as he realized what he had just stumbled onto. Something he'd heard distant stories of somewhere far out in the real world and had seen plenty of times on television shows. It was a drug exchange. And the barrel was no barrel. It was a small, privately-engineered narco-sub. Semi-submersibles could carry several tons of product worth one to two hundred million dollars. He knew they had become popular with Mexican cartels as another covert means to avoid U.S. radar and sneak their cargo into the States. Most of the waters in the Sound would be too shallow for even a small submarine to get through. Whoever these guys were, they knew these waters well and were exactly where they wanted to be.

He swallowed again and stepped back into the console. His favorite place on Earth had just become the last place he wanted to be. As far as he could tell, no one had seen him. All the lights on his boat were off, but the white powder-coated paint of the canopy was reflecting the light from the quarter moon. All he had to do was slip back behind the cover of the mangroves and he should be all right.

He placed the binoculars on the seat and stepped over to the keys that protruded from the ignition. He held his breath and turned them, keeping his eyes on the scene ahead. The engine growled to life and began to churn water behind him. Pete turned the wheel and brought the throttle up an inch. The motor growled louder and pushed the boat forward, and he turned the boat around and slowly retraced his previous wake.

He was still holding his breath.

The boat did not have a marine radio, and Pete never brought his cell phone out with him on a Friday morning. There was no need to. At least, not the last five hundred times he'd come out here. Now, all he could think of was getting back to the marina and calling the Sheriff's Office. The back of his neck warmed as his anger grew within. Drug dealers in his own backyard.

Every few years you heard rumors of the Coast Guard reportedly finding a rogue package of drugs floating on the water somewhere around. Drug movement on a scale that required a narco sub was unheard of in these quiet parts. At least, he thought so. Apparently it was happening right under their noses while Pine Island slept and dreamt of fish and piña coladas.

A muffled drone hit Pete's ears, one above the noise of his own engine. He turned and saw the shiny glint of a boat hull and the whitecaps made by its high wake. The hair on his arms stood up, and he shot the throttle up as high as it would go. It was another seven miles to his slip at the marina. The bow tilted upward as the boat shot forward and quickly reached its top speed of eighteen knots, a speed that was impressive for an engine of this size yet no match for the three outboards strapped to the boat behind him, each of them likely running at four hundred horses. They would be on him in thirty seconds.

His fishing tackle was back home, most importantly the fillet knife that accompanied it. Pete's handgun was resting quietly in his nightstand drawer. He had nothing with which to defend himself if it came down to that.

He looked over his shoulder. The boat had already covered half the distance. Somehow a serene morning had turned into the run of his life. This couldn't be real. Not here.

A voice yelled out to him. He kept on. It yelled again. The speedboat gunned up to his starboard and matched his speed. Four Hispanic men were staring at him, one waving him down. He smiled politely, nervously, but didn't slow, kept his hands on the wheel. The men called out again, their tones becoming increasingly angry. Pete could see the lights atop the Matlacha Pass bridge about a mile out. He didn't have to make it back to the marina. He just had to make it to Matlacha. There he could shoot into one of the canals off Island Avenue, jump out, and run for his life.

The speedboat eased down, and Pete's NauticStar was alone once again. He felt some tension exit his muscles, and he turned back to see where they had gone. Panic filled his chest as he heard their engines roar again, and the other vessel shot forward to his boat's port side. The boat blazed past him and turned hard directly in front of his bow. He threw the throttle down to prevent a head-on collision, and the speed boat moved out and around his stern.

They were doing circles around him, leaving him stationary, their furious wake spraying a fine mist of salt water into his face. They were willing to risk a collision with the knowledge that their boat would take an impact better. Pete grimaced and turned the engine off, tossed his hands up in defeat, and brought them back to rest on the wheel. The speed boat slowed and came in swaying at his starboard. The NauticStar bobbed hard in the high wake their antics had created.

A thin man with a thin mustache grabbed the speed boat's gunwale with one hand and raised another toward Pete. Another man shined a spotlight on Pete. "Hey, *mi amigo!*" the man yelled over their engines. "*Podemos hablar?*"

Pete's bushy eyebrows lowered, and he raised a fist and extended a middle finger. The four men laughed. He was seventy-two now, and there was one of him, but Pete Wellington wasn't going down without a fight. He had seen what he had seen. They had seen him see it.

"Eh, Mister!" the man called out again. "You talk, yes?"

"No!" Pete growled back.

"What you doing? It...is dark...early, yes?"

"That's none of your damn business," he snapped.

"We talk." The man nodded like he had made a decision. He stepped onto his gunwale and jumped off, landing on the deck of the NauticStar, which now drifted over the other boat's wake.

"Get the hell off my boat!" Pete stepped out of the console and faced the man. A chill went down his back. The man seemed amused, indifferent to the anger in the eyes of the older man before him, anger generated by the fact that he had boarded another man's boat without consent. His eyes twinkled with a pleasure that made Pete feel like a mouse before a herd of cats.

Pete didn't hear the second man jump off the speedboat and land nimbly behind him. He didn't see the gun tucked in the small of the man's back nor did he see the man grab it. He had no time to process the cold steel making contact with the back of his head before everything went dark.

CHAPTER THREE

Ellie looked patiently through the Nightforce scope and tuned in to her breathing and heart rate. Her desert brown McMillan Tactical was chambered in a .338 Lapua, ready for her final shot of the morning. She had adjusted from her previous shots and had most recently dialed in a degree on her scope's external windage knob to take into account the growing breeze coming off the ocean a mile to the west. Her target was eight hundred yards downrange, a sixteen-inch gong made of AR500 steel, painted white with a small black dot to indicate center. It hung from a railroad tie using transport chain. She slowly pressed the two-pound trigger. The trigger was light, one pound less than the factory or tactical standard, but she liked to be surprised when the bullet discharged. It made for a crisp execution that minimized the chance of pulling the shot and contributed to greater accuracy.

The gun jumped into her shoulder as the bullet exploded and slid out of the twenty-seven-inch barrel at three thousand feet per second. Ellie waited less than a second, and the target jerked and swung back and forth on its chains.

"You shoot like a girl," a deep voice said behind her.

Ellie smiled but didn't look back. She took her hand off the gun and waited.

"Eight inches, left."

Her lips tightened. Not bad. But not her best either. At this distance anything within ten inches was golden.

"Overall groupings were wide on me by one and a quarter inches. That means that today, compared to me, you lose. How does that feel? Losing to me again?"

Ellie rose up from her prone position and came to rest on her knees. She smiled back at Tyler Borland, who, at six feet two inches, stood four inches taller than she when she was on her feet. A red, sun-faded ball cap with gray stitching reading *Hornady* was pulled low over his forehead and served as a permanent fixture on his body. Ellie had never seen him without it, and he was unmoving in his conviction that the hat had been there when his mother brought him into the world.

"Seeing that you generally set the bar so low, it feels terrible," she countered.

"Ouch. If I respected you more, that would have hurt."

She leaned over, grabbed her pencil, and scratched down her final numbers. As a safety precaution, Ellie slid the bolt through the empty chamber, then lifted her gun. She gathered up her mat and gear and came to her feet. She slung the gun strap over her shoulder and looked at Tyler. His eyes were a deep green, like they were made from tiny strips of woven palm fronds. His sandy brown hair fell just over his ears, and he kept a couple days' worth of stubble over a square, cleft chin that looked like a child had poked him at the edge and the skin had never folded back out.

"If you respected me any more, I would own you," she grinned. "Come on. I've got to get back."

She grabbed her bag and stepped onto the dirt path whose center was worn clean of any grass. It led to Reticle's offices and training center a quarter mile away. Tyler slid the Vortex Viper spotting scope into its canvas case, zipped it up, and handed it to Ellie. The two had met six months ago, less than a week after her arrival in Florida. They shared a mutual passion for shooting long-range precision rifles, and it didn't take them long to establish a standing meeting each week where they shot their chosen rifle and acted as a spotter for the other. Tyler had moved to Lee County from West Texas only two years earlier and secured the land and licensing to open up Reticle, the only long-range shooting range in the area. If fifty women in Lee County had been interested in long-range shooting then, it doubled almost overnight when Tyler showed up. Everyone knew it didn't have much to do with precision shooting as much as it had to do with precision fishing. The ladies were drawn to him the way a redfish was drawn to a swimming lure, but Tyler wasn't interested in their advances. He had been married back in Texas but wasn't now. Ellie had yet to get him to talk about what had gone wrong. Whatever had happened back in Texas was painful enough for Tyler to close up like a gun safe with the hinges welded shut.

Ellie took in a deep breath of the thick, humid air.

Being back home was a surge of moisture to her dry, saltwater veins. After twelve years with the Agency, she was finally on the edge of what was beginning to feel like a normal life. She had arrived stateside six months ago, spending the first three weeks at Langley in exit interviews, debriefings, and paperwork. As soon as she was given the nod to walk out the door for good, she went straight to the airport and boarded the first flight to Fort Myers, then took the forty-five minute drive west.

Being back home didn't require as much of a psychological adjustment as her exit shrink at Langley had informed her it would. Up until her decision to leave the United States' most clandestine organization, she had spent her entire adult life as one of the Agency's most efficient and lethal undercover operatives, running covert operations all over the globe. At twenty-two, two months before she had graduated from the University of Florida with a degree in linguistics, she'd been approached by the CIA to come work for them. Three months and four rounds of interviews later, she had accepted an offer to work at headquarters in Virginia as a wire analyst. In that role she reviewed recordings from the field, detecting hidden meanings in foreign voice inflection before filing them away or sending her notes back to those who needed them in the field. It was mundane and uneventful, but she understood the game. *Stay true to what's in front of you, and new opportunities will open up.* It's what her father had always taught her. And open up they did. Her second year in, she had been tapped to enter a new program, one that would take her onto the international stage and slip her into the darkest shadows of geopolitical conflict.

She'd entered a vigorous training program that

lasted eighteen months and brought her into the extreme heats of Dead Valley, the bitter colds of North Dakota, the frigid waters of Alaska, and the Daintree Forests of Australia. When it was complete, she and the six others that made up TEAM 99 - a total of five men, two women - were considered among the seven deadliest assassins the Agency had produced on this side of the Cold War. No one outside of their immediate management knew of the team's existence. Even their trainers, while given precise instructions for the team's maturation, were not privy to the team's purpose or mission. They were black-ops and belonged to the darkest corner of the CIA's Special Operations Group. For six years they'd carried out hits on the most sensitive of targets and covertly gathered intelligence on foreign troublemakers. Ellie had been surprised by the offer to train for such an elite team, but Langley had hired her for such a role from the very beginning. Between high school and college, Ellie had learned three languages fluently: French, Portuguese, and Russian. Her SAT score was three missed answers less than a perfect 1600, all of them in math. She had spent her teenage years achieving the level of black belt in Brazilian jiu jitsu and had consistently ranked on top in national youth tournaments for sharp shooting. By the time she was fifteen, she could regularly hit a matchstick at a hundred yards with a .22 rifle. Langley had only given her the desk job to keep her under watch and to test her patience and analytical skills.

Everyone on the new team had come in with prior military experience - everyone but her - each of them already elite fighters in their own rights. But her specialized skills and brilliant mind had kept her from appearing or feeling inferior to her teammates. During their year-and-a-half of training, she quickly rose to the top, and, when they were finally deployed, she was second in command to the brilliant and fully apt Voltaire. Voltaire had formerly been a Captain with the Army Rangers and led the team with a humble intensity that was fueled by his need to execute each mission cleanly and bring each member of the team back home safely. The team operated well together, and, for six years out of their home base in Brussels, they carried out mission after mission, successfully eliminating threats to national security and to the U.S.'s foreign operations. They were finally disbanded. Budget cuts was the formal reason, but Ellie knew it went deeper than that, although she wasn't exactly sure what. The timing, though, had been uncanny. Her last mission, an assassination scheduled in Saint Petersburg, Russia, was disrupted when she discovered an envelope on the nightstand of her hotel room earlier that evening. Who had placed it there and how they had gotten access to the room, Ellie never did find out. The contents of the envelope were, upon a cursory review, alarming but quickly moved to disturbing. The majority of the time, Ellie's team had not been given full reports on their targets. Faces, locations, transportation habits, associations, but rarely exhaustive details that were unnecessary to the mission. They got in, they got out, satisfied that they had scored a small but true victory for their country. But, that evening in Saint Petersburg, Ellie had spent over an hour cross-legged on her bed, reviewing new intel - papers, photos, sound recordings - on her target. His name was Boris Sokolov, that much she knew, an aspiring oligarch who had spent the last fifteen years consolidating his wealth into controlling interests in bioenergy corporations. Ellie had also been advised that he was a primary backer of Mother Russia's broad and audacious attempts at hacking America's national security systems. But, if the information in front of her was correct, he was being targeted by Ellie's government for putting in a competitive bid for oil contracts in Iraq, which had amassed considerable support with his people at the UN. Ellie had reviewed the new intel until she was confident it was accurate, that she wasn't being duped by misinformation or someone with allegiances different from her own.

That night, when Ellie had Sokolov in the center of her sights, she had pulled the shot - an easy three hundred yards with minimal crosswind - and the bullet landed in the wall five inches in front of his face. It took two months for the damage caused by the concrete chips to fully heal, but he had gotten off with his life. Ellie never found out if the disbanding of her team was the doing of whoever had provided her with the information. The older she got, the less she believed in coincidences.

Over the course of their six years together, only one member of TEAM 99 had been killed. Faraday, the only other female on the team. She had been hit by a sniper round while exiting a building in Mogadishu. The subsequent investigation had revealed that her exit from the rooftop had been sloppy, and they made her before she slipped back into the stairwell. While in Afghanistan, and through diligent digging, Ellie had discovered Faraday's true identity. Sarah Cornish. Outside of her relationship with Voltaire, Ellie had grown the closest with Faraday, close being a highly relative word seeing as they couldn't reveal much about their true selves. After the failed mission in Saint Petersburg, their team leader, Mortimer, called her back to Brussels into his mahogany-laden office and presented Ellie with two choices. She could exit the CIA with a thank-you and a pat on the back, or she could request reassignment into a role that was more traditional. She chose the latter and moved into her new position as a case officer, a role that would require more interpersonal relations and challenges. She left Brussels two days later and was sent back to Langley for three months of training, much less than what was typical but shortened because of her previous experience in tradecraft and espionage. Back in Virginia she became proficient in asset recruitment and handling and was immersed into a study of the local customs and culture of Kabul. Then, before her first assignment in her new role, she had come home to Pine Island to visit for two months before shipping out to Afghanistan, where she remained until choosing to step away from it all that fateful day in Kabul six months ago. Being back home underneath the generous Florida sun and gently bobbing on its water had been healing these last six months. Paradise had a way of helping you forget your guilt.

Just not all of it.

Now, as her feet pressed into the sand-washed path back to Reticle's offices, she looked over at Tyler and asked, "Tomorrow's Friday night. You want to come hang at The Salty Mangrove or go see a movie?"

"I can't tomorrow. I promised Hank I would go to the gun show with him up in Tampa. You could come too, you know."

"You guys have fun. Maybe another time."

"I'd have you back before bedtime," he said. "And bring you home sober."

"Right..." she laughed. "I'm going to lay low this weekend. You should come fishing sometime. There's a lot of good snapper in the Sound right now."

"Fishin'," he said, slowly shaking his head. "I've told you a hundred times, Ellie, I don't do boats. Not unless it's tied bow and stern to a piling and has a mound full of dry dirt underneath it."

"I'll never understand how you can live in Florida, be five minutes from the ocean, and never get out on the water. You might as well live on Mars."

He wagged his finger toward her. "Now you're talking. See, I was going to wait to tell you this, but I've been spending my evenings building a spaceship in the back office. You're welcome to come back and take a look. I put a couple really cool engine deal-ies on it. Even started on a spacesuit, but I ran out of duct tape and superglue."

"You sure are a scaredy cat for a man who likes guns and gravy."

"I like to know what's inside things. That's why I don't enjoy hot dogs, ocean water, or all those energy drinks that everyone seems to like so much. I have it on good authority that one contains pig rectum, the other definitely has sharks, and the last I'm pretty sure is only slightly filtered monster pee."

Ellie raised her brows. "Monster pee?"

"Indeed. I saw a documentary about it on Hulu, so it has to be true."

"Still doesn't mean you're not a scaredy cat."

"I'm not scared. I'm wise. But if you want to catch me some fish, I'll eat them. I'm just not going to go look for them on purpose outside of a restaurant or a grocery store. The water gives me the willies."

Ellie looked down the path and saw a large man approaching. He had thick arms and a lineman's neck. A duffle bag was slung over a shoulder and a rifle clutched in his meaty right hand. "Ellie, Tyler. How are you two?" he asked. The man was Augie Smith, a Lieutenant in the U.S. Coast Guard and posted at the USCG's station at Fort Myers Beach. He was one of Reticle's first monthly charter members and could be seen somewhere within the boundaries of the training facility at least a couple times a week. He was a good marksman, getting better, trying to make good on a promise to himself that one day he would best both of the people now standing in front of him.

"Hey, Augie. You're here early," Tyler said. "You working the late shift today?"

"Yep. They have us running night patrol the next couple of weeks. Word on the water is that Border Protection surveillance has spotted a few runners lately. One of them was intercepted last week. Nabbed a few kilos."

"Where?" Ellie asked.

"Cape Haze. Just across Charlotte Harbor. Little rats were tucked in at Turtle Bay unloading."

"Was that in the news?" Tyler asked. "I didn't hear anything about it."

Augie repositioned his duffle strap on his shoulder. "Yeah, well, you won't. Someone on the city council wants to keep it hush. Drug dealers running in these waters?"

"You don't easily come back from that," Tyler finished.

Augie snapped his fingers. "Boom. Give the man a prize."

"I've already got the prize," Tyler said, grinning. He nodded toward Augie's rifle. "You haven't beat me with that yet."

"I will. I will. Give it time." He smiled and nodded with a polite urgency. "Anyway, I'll see you both later. I don't have a lot of time out here today."

They said their goodbyes, and Ellie and Tyler continued charting down the path.

"I hate that," Ellie said.

"What?"

"Drugs. Running around a place like this. I know every place in the world has an underbelly, but I don't like hearing about it being in my own backyard."

"I'm sure it's not much," Tyler said dismissively. "If it was, they would have to notify the public for safety reasons. You heard Augie. They caught the guys. That'll dissuade them, and they'll look for cleaner entry points."

Somehow that failed to relieve a nagging at the bottom of Ellie's stomach. "Yeah, maybe."

They came to Reticle's main building and stopped. It was a one-story, stucco structure that housed small locker rooms for ladies and men, a gun shop, and a smith shop in the rear. Besides the eight-hundred yard range they shot at today, Tyler's setup boasted two five-hundred yard lanes, three three-hundred yard lanes, and twenty outdoor handgun stalls. Ellie swung her rifle off her shoulder and clutched it between her fingers. "I'm going to head inside and give this girl a cleaning."

Tyler sighed, almost reluctantly, and started walking away. "And I have a class to teach with ten women who I'm pretty sure aren't all that interested in shooting."

"Quit complaining. You enjoy it."

"I enjoy it more than hot dogs."

Within twenty minutes her rifle was clean, reassembled, secured in her personal locker, and she was in her truck headed home.

CHAPTER FOUR

Reticle was situated a few miles north of Florida State Road 78, at the southwest corner of Yucca Penns Preserve, just two miles from the Gulf of Mexico lining Florida's western edge. The air whipped through Ellie's long, honey-blonde hair as she turned her dark grey Chevy Silverado west onto Pine Island Road, named after the long stretch of land that Ellie called home.

Pine Island, Florida was the largest island in the tropical state and began its northward ascent just above its more famous cousin, Sanibel, ending seventeen miles later in Charlotte Harbor. It stood apart from Sanibel and neighbors like Captiva Island and Cayo Costa in that it had no beaches to speak of. Their sugar-sand beaches so attractive to tourists were noticeably absent on Pine Island. The locals considered such a topographical anomaly a major contribution to the island's perpetual charm. Instead of beaches, its circumference was fringed with generous mangrove forests whose branches were teeming with roseate spoonbills, wood storks, and pelicans, its underwater root systems swarming with snapper, snook, and redfish, making the Sound the perfect environment for dolphins and manatees.

The Old Florida feeling of Pine Island was maintained by the continued resistance to any major development or construction projects that would indubitably replace the warm and trusting atmosphere of the island with cold, impersonal progress. Hiking trails, kayak and canoe waterways, and ancient Indian shell mounds added to its charm in a state that was quickly becoming over-commercialized. The tourists came and locals stayed on for the island's secluded, small-town atmosphere, and, outside of seasonal tourism, the locals supported themselves by fishing, fruit and palm farming, and a funky art community. Stepping onto Pine Island was like entering into the kind of story you would hear while sitting at the feet of a benevolent grandfather, listening to him talk of the old days when life moved slower and stress wasn't a thing. It's where Ellie had grown up and where, for her entire adult life, the best parts of her had longed to return.

Ellie eased down on the brake, and the truck slowed at the four-way stop sign where Pine Island Road and Stringfellow Road came together, the intersection where all roads in and out of the island found their source. Pine Island had not one stoplight and wouldn't be getting one anytime soon; its ten thousand inhabitants saw no need for one. Outside of weekends hosting one of several festivals, "traffic" just wasn't in the local vocabulary. Ellie pressed down on her blinker, pointed the truck south, and began the seven-mile stretch of road to St. James City, the southernmost community on the island and where Ellie spent most of her time.

She filled her lungs with the fresh, salty air that swirled through the truck. The drive south never got old; it never got boring—miles of near-empty land filled with wild grass, pine and palm trees, and dotted infrequently by turn offs and small island homes. The last mile the breeze coming off the water cooled the air another five degrees and created an anticipation for the destination that was never disappointed by the reality.

Ten minutes later, Ellie arrived at the southern tip of the island and turned the steering wheel slightly right and into the narrow, crushed-shell parking lot that lined the edge of the road and butted up against Henley Canal. She turned off the engine and stepped out, the broken shells crunching underneath her sneakers until they hit the upward slope of the boardwalk, where visitors were greeted with a large red sign that told them, in case there was any doubt, that *Island Time Begins Here*. She walked up the protracted incline and faded right when she got to the top and it leveled out. It was another twenty feet to The Salty Mangrove, another hundred beyond that to the marina.

The Salty Mangrove was the island's favorite restaurant and watering hole and had been owned by Ellie's uncle Warren for the last nineteen years. The small wood-lapped building had a kitchen squeezed in between a tiki hut that faced the full-service marina and an indoor seating area for the restaurant that was encircled by a wooden railing with rolled patio curtains that would be lowered when it rained. The Norma Jean Pier, like a long pointy finger, began just south of the bar, jutting eighty yards into the southern waters of Pine Island Sound.

When Ellie wasn't having fun at the range, sleeping in at her house, or out fishing on a boat, she could be found here. She spent half her week helping her uncle take orders, pour drinks, and clean up, sometimes helping scrub boats and fill out order slips for boat and tackle rentals. She had yet to get what Tyler called a "real job." The truth was, she didn't need one. Not yet anyway. Her work at the CIA had her crisscrossing Europe, South America, and the Middle East for the better part of a decade. All her assignments had been fully funded by the Agency. Ellie rarely needed to spend her own money on anything, which meant that, between her salary and a few worthy investments she had made, she had enough to live on cruise control for the foreseeable future. For now, her new life of relaxation and ease was fully funded.

Ellie stepped behind the bar and poured herself a glass of water over ice, then tossed in a lime and planted herself on a barstool.

"There she is," a woman said. "You went shooting this morning?"

"I did," Ellie answered. "Just got back."

The woman was Gloria Wang, and she sat under the edge of the palm frond roof perched next to her husband on their usual bar stools, their backs to the marina. They were permanent fixtures at The Salty Mangrove and, in some strange way, contributed to its charm. They were as unlikely a pair as one would could find. Fu was a small man, just over five feet, and had a flat face, flat nose, and a neck that was too thick for his small frame. He had a leg and a third, his left possessing nothing but a nub four inches above where his knee should have been. The prosthetic leg attached to the stump never seemed to fit right, making him waggle from side to side like a reverse pendulum when he walked. The original leg God had given him had been unwillingly donated to the hungry teeth of a Chinese rice harvester when Fu was eight. He hadn't seen the machine, the driver hadn't seen him, and his leg was promptly surrendered to Yunnan's fertile soil.

Gloria was a wide woman with thick bones and a double chin that looked like it might be entertaining a third. Her only attire appeared to be a straw sun hat that was redundant underneath the outer shaded edge of the tiki hut and a black one-piece swimsuit which barely contained her heavy, flaccid breasts. Her thick brows hung low over deep set eyes, and she wore an unfortunate nose that would have looked better on a bird of prey than someone made in God's image. Fu had been stateside on a visitor's visa five years ago when he and Gloria were seated next to each other during a boating tour of the Keys. Struck by a surge of lust, he was immediately taken with her, she with him. They married soon after, bought a Gibson houseboat fitted for salt water, and slid around the coasts of Florida for a year until they experienced the slow, secluded Old Florida way of life that was Pine Island. Their houseboat was the only home they had and for the last three years had been tethered to a slip in the marina, making them the only liveaboards at the south end of the island.

"Did you best Tyler again today?" Gloria asked.

Ellie sighed. "Not today. He's a natural at it. I'll get

him next time." In a subtle way, Tyler getting the best of her at the range really did bug her. She had been trained by the world's most advanced government agency; Tyler had taught himself in the dry, windswept grasslands of West Texas. Ellie had been one of the CIA's best marksmen for the six years she was in her role as a covert operative. Tyler had never been formally trained, nor had he ever tried his trigger finger at any competitions, local or otherwise.

Gloria wagged her eyebrows. "Tyler...he's a hottie, Ellie. Are you going places with him? You really should snag him up."

"No, Gloria. He's a friend, and I think we'll be keeping it that way." It all sounded quite high schoolish, but, at least for now, it was true. "Have you seen Major this morning?"

"About an hour ago," Gloria said. "He was behind the dry dock washing down a couple skiffs."

Fu nodded, agreeing with his wife. Ellie had never heard Fu speak one word of English besides the word "yes," "good," and possibly "sexy," but she wasn't sure about the last one. He spoke only Chinese to Gloria who had somehow taken the effort to learn his language and not the other way around. Anyone trying to begin a conversation with Fu without the presence of his wife was doomed to futility and would have him smiling large and nodding politely like he understood. "Yes...yes," he would say, and his eyes would squint hard, smiling in their own right along with his mouth. If Ellie had ever seen him without a smile, she couldn't remember. Fu was a happy man, had a disposition that said he was just glad to be here, wherever that happened to be at any given moment.

"Are you guys still thinking about going up to St. Pete next week?" Ellie asked. The Wangs were—or rather, Gloria was—always talking about picking up anchor and visiting somewhere else for a few weeks. So far it had all been planning and talk, and they had not yet gotten around to making the actual trip. They just stuck around Pine Island as if an invisible force field was keeping them in.

Gloria shook her head. "Fu is thinking he'd rather wait a while. At least until after the upcoming hurricane season."

"I think you should do it," Ellie prodded. "At your age you should be off seeing the world. Besides, hurricane season won't be here for a few more months."

"There's my favorite blonde-haired niece."

Ellie smiled at the deep voice behind her, then felt two strong hands on her shoulders. Warren Hall leaned in, kissed her on the back of the head, and then walked behind the bar.

She grinned. "Silly man, I'm your only blonde-haired niece. How's everything going in Marco?"

He turned his back to the bar, opened the lid to a refrigerated cooler, and rummaged around. "Need more shrimp," he muttered to himself. He made a jot on a yellow legal pad in front of him. "Good," he answered. "Now that it's May, and the snowbirds have migrated back north, slow season is upon us. But we just added a few more slips, and I hired one more mechanic."

Marco Island lay fifty miles to the south, and six years ago Warren had purchased a marina down there. Old Ed Wright had owned the place since around the time boats were invented, and he finally sold it over to Warren before dying three weeks later. Warren hadn't wanted it when Ed first approached him, said he had enough on his hands managing The Salty Mangrove and the accompanying marina. But Ed was persistent, said he didn't want to just hand off what he'd spent most his life at to just anybody. Warren finally conceded. He bought the place, made some updates, did some advertising, and brought in a couple charter boats. The acquisition changed his lifestyle, and ever since, like clockwork, he spent two weeks out of every month in Pine Island and the other two at Marco Island. Fourteen days there, fourteen days here. He had just returned from his most recent stint down there.

By all accounts Warren was a handsome man. At just under six feet, he came in at average height, and broad shoulders and thick forearms gave him a stocky appearance. His face was square, eyes set back under low brows, and his graying auburn hair was kept short. His face held the deep, weathered lines that years on the water carved into a man. He wore cargo shorts and a white, short-sleeved, button-down shirt and double-banded Birkenstocks. Without question, he was a long stitch in the fabric of the local community. Warren Hall sponsored Little League teams, chaired the Rotary Club, and contributed both time and money to the local Meals on Wheels. More than once he'd been prodded to take a run at the mayor's chair, but he valued simplicity too much to go along with it. He was a businessman and a philanthropist, he would retort, not a politician.

Biologically, Ellie and Warren were not related, and yet he stood in all of Ellie's earliest memories. Warren and her father had been best friends - like blood brothers - going back to their early college days. He had always been her uncle. The years had absorbed the reason Ellie called him Major; she just always had.

Warren called for his cook, his bartender, and his waiter - all the same man - and handed him the legal pad when he appeared out of the small kitchen. "Ralphie, go ahead and order some more shrimp from Glen. There's a couple more things on there too."

"You got it, boss."

Warren turned back and pressed both his hands into the edge of the bar. "You ready to get out on the water, kiddo? I've got it all ready."

"Let's do it," she said, and then stood up.

"But Ellie and I were just getting started on a good conversation," Gloria said, smiling and feigning frustration.

"No," Major corrected. "You were talking. All the good conversations happen out on the water." He looked at Ellie. "I'll grab the bait out of the cooler and meet you down at the Contender in a couple."

Ellie said goodbye to the Wangs and walked across the open deck and down a strip. She unconsciously frowned when she passed Pete Wellington's boat, tied up in his regular slip. His NauticStar was found three weeks ago, bobbing anchorless on a sandbar in Buzzard Bay. Everyone feared the worst. It was found on a Friday afternoon, the day of the week Pete would go out in the early morning. Something had happened; that much was clear now. A water-loving seaman didn't abandon his boat and not show up for nearly a month. An investigation led by the Sheriff's Office had as yet yielded nothing. There were no signs of foul play - no traces of blood or damage to the boat, no note - Pete had simply vanished. Conclusions ran wild as they tend to do in small communities. Some said he may have gone for a swim and ended up a hammerhead's dinner. Others guessed he had a heart attack, fell overboard, and still ended up a hammerhead's dinner. Gloria said Fu thought Pete had possibly been abducted by pirates, and Ellie couldn't tell if Fu was joking or serious. Pete was a good, kind man. Ellie, and the whole island for that matter, still held out hope that he would turn up soon with a rational explanation. Her gut told her not to hold her breath.

Twenty minutes later Ellie and Warren were nestled between Pine and Sanibel Islands, bobbing in the boat, the anchor set, lines in the water. The heat from the mid-morning sun was tempered by a soft breeze drifting across their skin, its light glinting off the water like tiny flashes of fire escaping from underneath the surface. It was moments like this, when a light breeze rocked the boat and Ellie was out here with one of her favorite people in the world, that she wondered why she had ever left at all.

"You know," Major said. "Summer days out here in the Sound make me miss your father. We came out here a thousand times together if we came out here once."

The words tore at the loose stitching of a raw and mending heart. "I know," she said softly and stared at the water where her line disappeared. Two years ago Ellie's soul was splintered by a phone call from Major, informing her that her father had died in a car accident. Frank O'Conner had been driving back from a game of poker at a friend's house in Cape Coral when a gas tanker slid into his lane on Veterans Parkway and sent both vehicles into a fireball that incinerated everything, even melted the metal.

At the time she was entrenched in Kabul, almost a year into her commitment to flip Assam, and was unable to come home for the funeral lest she blow her cover: a journalist with Reuters. In any other situation, she could have taken a military hop out of the city and gotten here in time for the funeral. She hadn't asked to come. She knew the Agency wouldn't have let her. It was one of the gambles you took within that line of work. And just like that, Frank O'Conner's death left her without a parent. Ellie was five years old, her sister, Katie, three, when their mother had died on the table undergoing an emergency appendectomy. Her mother was Russian and met her father when he was on a student internship in Moscow. Now she and Katie were without the man who had raised them and loved them as well as any man who had ever raised two girls alone.

Katie had yet to forgive Ellie for her absence at the funeral and hadn't spoken to her older sister since the day their father's ashes were laid in the ground. Or what was left of them. Katie now lived in Seattle with her five-year-old daughter, Chloe. According to Major, her sister couldn't handle the memories of the island any longer. Chloe was only two years old when Ellie had come for her last visit. It was the first and only time she had ever seen or spent time with her niece. Having just stepped out of her role with TEAM 99 and finished with her training at Langley, Ellie had spent the two months of leisure time back home with those she loved: her father, sister, niece, and Major. Since moving back home, Ellie had regularly sent Katie and Chloe letters, all of them unanswered.

"I still have to remind myself that he's gone," Ellie said. "Like sometimes I think he's going to come back from a trip or walk up the dock and join us out here on the water."

"Me too, kiddo. Me too."

Ellie felt a pull on her Intercoastal rod and watched it bow quickly toward the water.

"Look at you," Major said. "Got one already."

Ellie flicked her wrists up to set the hook in the fish's mouth, then used her left hand to spin the reel. She pulled back on the rod and reeled in again, repeating the motions three more times before the snapper broke the surface. Its scales sparkled like tiny diamonds against the sunlight. Ellie brought it into the boat and unhooked it. "It's over a foot. A keeper," she said, and tossed it into the live well.

"Not bad," Major said. "I got a twenty incher last week inside Gullivan Bay."

"I bow to you, O, Great One."

Major smiled. "And I let you."

She worked a fresh shrimp onto her jig and cast it back across the water. Major brought his line back in, checked it, and sent it back out.

Ellie loved these times on the water with Major. There would always be long stretches of silence where no one felt the need to speak and it didn't feel awkward. Some days they might be on the water for an hour and say ten sentences the entire time. It wasn't about the conversation. It was about being with a person you were free to be yourself around and felt no obligations to please.

Over the next half hour, Ellie snagged four more fish, and Major brought up three of his own. After baiting his hook again and casting back out, he dug into the side pocket of his shorts.

"Almost forgot," he said. "Here. I want you to have this." He pulled out a switchblade with a black rubber grip and flicked it open and shut a few times before handing it to her.

"What's this?" she asked, taking it.

"It was your father's. Probably not anything special or super sentimental, but you should have it. I was going through some boxes of his in my closet a few weeks ago and found it. He probably got it at the hardware store or some random tackle shop."

She looked it over and flicked the blade out. The sound - that quick metallic click - was one of the most distinct and recognizable sounds in the world, like the pump of a shotgun or the yearning call of a seagull. She slowly ran a finger down the side of the blade and was rushed back to the first time she had ever taken someone's life with a knife. It was in Mauritania, one of the largest countries in West Africa. Her entire team had been sent in to grab Yahya Azid, a virulent man connected to the bombing of the U.S. embassy in Kazakhstan. They snuck into the courtyard of his two-story compound under the shroud of darkness. Ellie had been the first one in and snuck in behind a guard armed with an AK. Her thigh holster lightly scraped the wall, and he, hearing it, started to turn. But action is always faster than reaction, and her knife was already clenched in her fingers. She stepped up behind him and brought the knife around, puncturing his larynx and unlacing his throat. Killing with a knife was fully unlike shooting someone. With a knife, you had to be up close - it was rare that a blade was thrown in the midst of combat. It looked good in the movies but was impractical, rare that a throwing knife would find such a mark on someone's body that they would make no noise of pain or protest as they fell to the ground. Killing someone with a knife was an intensely personal experience...feeling the slice of the blade through their skin and muscles, feeling their body tense and then relax as their life ebbed away. Ellie preferred killing with a gun every time.

She returned to the present. The knife was four inches long and razor sharp. It bore no nicks or scratching showing wear. She folded it back. "Thanks, Major." After her father died, Major and Katie split up his possessions - he took whatever she didn't want and bartered with Katie for items he knew her older sister would want to have. When Ellie arrived back home six months ago, Major had her come over to his garage and work through the boxes. Of everything that remained, three things were her favorites, one of them a pink, soft plastic My Little Pony that Ellie had given her father when her mother died. Five-year-old Ellie had woken up to her father's sobs one night. She took the doll off her bed, walked down the hall, and pressed it into his wet hands. For the last twenty-some years, that pony had sat on top of his clothes dresser, next to a small framed picture of her mother. Her second favorite item was the white fedora, which he wore anytime he was off work. It gave him a relaxed, distinguished look that went well with his personality. The third had been an old edition of Hemingway's collected short stories, a volume her father had passed through cover-to-cover many times. It had been healing, working through the memories her father's possessions divined back up. Ellie slipped the knife into her pocket with the intent of making it a permanent fixture in her tackle box.

"You know, Cindy Gershwin lost her mother two

years ago and still has an entire storage unit she hasn't gone through."

Ellie looked at Major and smiled. "That's the third time you've mentioned her in as many weeks." She wasn't in the mood to think about someone else losing a parent, so she said, "Something going on there I need to know about?"

Warren had never married. Every couple of years, he would find a new girlfriend to chum around with, and then, like always, they would part ways after having their fun. For whatever reason, being alone seemed to fit his personality. Warren Hall liked to do things his own way, in his own time. Cindy Gershwin was Major's age, divorced ten years. She had come up to Pine Island one weekend supposedly to go fishing in Gasparilla Sound, but everyone keen enough knew she was interested in the owner of The Salty Mangrove and Marina.

"Not a thing," he answered glumly.

"You're about due for a relationship, aren't you?" she teased.

He shrugged. "Maybe. I'm in no hurry for that kind of thing. You know that." Now it was Warren's turn to want a change of topic. He looked at Ellie. "How are you doing?"

"How do you mean?"

"It's been half a year now since you dropped your career. Any regrets? Do you ever feel like you made a preemptive decision?"

Ellie turned her reel a couple revolutions and stared at the spot where her line disappeared below the water. She waited half a minute before answering. "It still feels like I'm on vacation. Like in a few days I'll be flying back over the Atlantic to get back in the game."

"Do you miss it?"

"Parts of it. I miss the challenge, the thrill. I was good at it." Being careful with her words, she said, "I was good at both of the jobs I had. I didn't think adjusting would be this hard."

"How so?" Warren came to his feet and worked on bringing up another catch. Something heavy was on his line. He tightened his body and started working against it. The snook broke the surface, flopping and gyrating on the hook. "Good one there," Ellie said. The fish was close to three feet long. Warren got it into the boat, and Ellie held it down while he worked the jig out of its mouth. The fish had a long, silvery body with a black line down the middle of it, like a child had taken a black Sharpie and drawn all the way to its tail. Its fins were a bright yellow.

"There," Warren said. He tossed the hook to the side, grabbed the fish with a firm grip, then heaved it overboard. He wiped his hands on a towel then worked more bait onto his hook. Warren was a stickler for falling in line with Florida's fishing regulations. His license as a marina owner almost necessitated it. Eyeballing it, he knew the snook would measure a few inches too long to keep. Beyond that, snook season was still a few months away which meant that, for now, the catch had to go back. He cast back out and settled back into his seat. "Sorry for the interruption. You were talking about the adjustment being hard?"

"Yeah," she said softly. "What I did...what I was a part of...had a way of mastering you. Several of my..." She wanted to say *team members*. Instead she said, "...co-workers started to live on the adrenaline rush. There was a real thrill to what we were doing." *A real power too,* she thought. That was the most thrilling part about all of it. You came into an area, scouted it out, perched yourself, and became an indifferent executioner with no consequences. You pulled the trigger, confirmed the kill, and went back to your daily routine of exercise, training, and favorite television shows. Or, if the mission was simply to garner surveillance, you inserted yourself, stayed for a couple months, and blended into the cultural landscape of the locals. Accents, dress, mannerisms. All-in-all you were always pretending to be someone else. And that was the hardest part of being back. Major was the one person she could be completely honest with. "I think somewhere along the way I forgot how to be myself."

He said nothing, but she knew he was thinking. Major was a good listener—always had been. Ellie could remember vividly when her shoe heel broke at the junior prom and her father had been in D.C. on a work trip. She had called Major and asked him to come get her from the prom. After his failed attempts to get her to stay, he whisked her away and landed them both in a hard booth at Dairy Queen. He listened to her pre-adolescent dramatization of the humiliating evening while they both worked down a ginormous Oreo Blizzard. When her father died it had been Major who called to tell her the news. She hadn't said much that night, but she called him in tears two weeks later, and he just listened.

Ellie had come to learn that after you circle through one of the most intense training programs ever concocted by the U.S. government you don't come out with a better knowledge of yourself. No, you lose yourself. The *me* dissolved into the *mission*. You were a biological weapon—

a warm, highly skilled body to get a job done in service for your country. Your favorite books, movies, colors, paintings, people, wine; your beliefs, religion, philosophy; all became irrelevant. You were trained to do a job where your personal preferences did not factor in. Only your ability to flawlessly carry out a mission. It was pure ability created, shaped, and perfected by the government for the government. Ellie still loved an aged merlot while listening to Dylan or Coltrane, still loved Hemingway and Sean Connery. And the salty waters of the Gulf made her feel like a part of her she had suppressed for so long was beginning to stir beneath. It wasn't that these preferences became non-existent when she was on the team; they just stopped being important. They were not necessary and had no place to bloom.

Even the members of her team were, by all accounts, all unknown to each other.

All but one.

Voltaire.

From the first hour of training to the day their team was dissolved, they were never allowed to speak of their origins or their pasts. The reasons for this were clear and obvious. If someone were captured and tortured, they could not give away personal information about anyone on the team.

Where is their family from? *I don't know.*

Where do they like to vacation? *I don't know.*

Who are their oldest friends? *I wouldn't know.*

They knew the trivial things about each other, and the more missions they went on they came to know who was the clown of the group, who always forgot a piece of equipment, who would smack their gum with their mic turned on. They knew what TV shows each one liked and what kind of food. But the important specifics were never discussed. Not with anyone.

Except for Voltaire.

She adjusted her ball cap over her eyes.

Major finally spoke up. "If it helps, I haven't forgotten who you are. And these last six months have been a great reminder for anything I may have forgotten about you. As a matter of fact, you were barely an adult when you left. Now you're a mature woman, and I can't think of anyone I would rather be out on the water with."

She looked over at him. "Thanks, Major."

"But that's not the whole of it, is it?"

She smiled in unbelief and shook her head. He just always knew. "No. It's not."

"You're wondering if you made a difference."

How did he know?

"Yeah. Yeah, I do."

"Does that matter?"

The question surprised her. "I think so. Don't we all want to put our mark on the world, no matter how small? To get to the end and know that we did something good with our lives?"

Warren started to reel his line in for a recast. "Ellie. Most all of us live our lives according to our conscience. We do what we believe in, and we think it's right. Outside of the few with no moral compass, we all go to work believing, to some degree, in what we do, even if we happen to be stuck in a dead-end job we don't like. I know you, Ellie. You believed in what you were doing. You're not one to compromise. If you thought that what you were doing at the time was wrong or unhelpful, you would have quit."

He was right. He was so very right. That night, sitting atop a gold and burgundy bedspread in a fifth-story Saint Petersburg hotel room, Ellie spent hours poring over the information she had been given. She had almost thrown up that night, but the anger overwhelmed the nausea. She had decided to find a way to confirm that the unexpected intelligence was legitimate, that it wasn't misinformation. If it was, she was out. But it didn't come to that. She botched the mission, and, after being recalled back to their operational base in Brussels, the team was told collectively that there was no longer a need for what they were doing. That they had served their country well and that funding had been cut and...(*white noise*). She had stopped listening. The reasons were concocted. Ellie had been in the game long enough to detect BS. If she had her guess, she was not the only one who had received the information given to her in Russia. The leak had spooked someone at the top, and they turned on the faucet, soaped up, and were washing their hands of it all. The swiftness and vitality in which the team was disbanded only served to confirm that this new information was correct. How many missions had been executions and takedowns for someone's monetary or political agenda? She didn't know, and even now it turned her stomach.

Major flicked his line back out. "Plus, you're not old like I am. You're still a young little thing with the rest of your life ahead of you to go and make a difference."

"You're not old, Major. Geez, you're barely sixty."

"But I'm not thirty-four either."

"Maybe it would be easier on this side of things had

I been able to see more good that I accomplished. Instead I just see a trail of ruins that leads nowhere."

Ellie had filled Major in on the general reasons why she had left the CIA, but she didn't have the authorization to speak with anyone about the specifics. She still wondered about the people she had killed. During her time in Afghanistan, she'd had little opportunity to access the proper databases. Most of her time was spent in a flat in the city with no access to the servers that might give her answers. In the event her flat were broken into and she were robbed, there would be nothing amiss on her laptop that would point back to her undercover work. The few times she had been covertly bussed back to Camp Phoenix for debriefing, she had searched and found some information on her past targets. Some of them had proved to be legitimate. Others, however, were ghosts. She couldn't find anything on them. How many of her kills had truly been for the security and better interest of her country? How many had been assassinations for a suit with an agenda? How many innocent fathers, mothers, sons, daughters had she killed? Assam's confused eyes flashed across her vision. She blinked it away and checked her line again.

They were quiet for the next few minutes. The breeze kept the sun's growing heat off their skin and gently rocked the boat. Major's voice broke the calm. "I called Katie last week."

The name stung like a hot poker on raw meat. She closed her eyes. Last summer Katie took a low-level tech job in Seattle. It was literally as far away as she could get from her childhood home, the furthest corner of the contiguous states.

Ellie opened her eyes again, blinking against the sunlight. "How is she?"

He sighed, reeled in his line a couple feet. "I don't know. She doesn't say much. I don't ever hear from her. If we talk it's because I call her. Sometimes I wonder if she's mad at me too."

"Why?"

He shrugged. "Why not? She had to blame someone, right?"

"How about the driver of the tanker?" Ellie suggested hotly.

"But he's dead too. Much easier to blame someone still breathing."

"I guess," she conceded, then sighed. All her memories of Pine Island had her father and her sister in them. Now she was making new ones without them. It was like painting on a new canvas without your favorite colors. "Everything's changed," she said. "Everything but *this* place." She looked out at the west side of the island, dark green leaves of the mangroves flanking it. Tall palms stood strong along the edges as if they were the eternal guardians of the island. She blinked behind her sunglasses. "Okay, enough heavy talk for one day."

Major smiled.

"How long are you going to keep going back and forth to Marco? You've been at it for, what, six years now? Is that a forever thing?"

He shrugged. "I don't know. Maybe. I didn't think I would hold onto the marina down there this long, but I kinda like the change of pace it affords. It's turned into a good source of income. Maybe I'll sell it one day."

A white boat hummed loudly across the water a couple hundred yards out from their location, heading in their direction. Several boats had criss-crossed them since they had been out here, but none of them had a course set directly toward them. They both kept their eyes on their lines, and the boat kept on its course in their direction. "I sure hope he turns," Ellie said.

Major raised his chin and squinted through his sunglasses. "DEA," he said.

"You got rid of all that heroin you were keeping on here, right? Major, tell me you got rid of it."

He chuckled. "Funny girl. You get the wrong agent out here, and he'll stay around talking your ear off and waste half your day. I still don't know why they come out in the daytime."

"They're probably tired of pushing paper and want some sun time."

"Bingo."

Two men were in the government boat, and the man at the controls brought the throttle down and idled toward them before pulling up a few feet off Warren's starboard.

The other agent, a tall man in a dark blue wind jacket and sunglasses, spoke up. "Hey, folks, sorry to intrude. We're doing a few rounds out here today." He dug a hand into his jacket, brought it out, and a badge caught the sunlight. "We're with the Drug Enforcement Administration."

"We may have gathered that from your boat decal," Warren said, smiling.

"Yes, well...we just wanted to stop by and see what you're up to today. Out for a little fun in the sun?"

"Just fishing, Officer," Ellie replied courteously. "I—"

The other boat drifted closer. Warren frowned and

pointed into the water. "Ellie, you might want to bring your line in so it doesn't get tangled into their rotor."

She leaned over and started spinning the handle.

"Ellie?" The agent dipped his head forward and focused in on her, forgetting the conversation he had initiated. He set the inside blade of his hand over his eyes. "Ellie O'Conner?"

Ellie darted her eyes toward her uncle, then back at the agent. "Yes," she said slowly.

He laughed, removed his sunglasses, and squinted against the flashing glare coming off the water. "I can't believe it! Ellie, it's me, Garrett. Garrett Cage."

The name brought up dusty images from Ellie's past. "Garrett? Garrett, no kidding!" Her voice perked up. She tilted her head. "You're DEA?"

He laughed. "I am that," he said.

"You get that badge on eBay and steal the boat?"

"Actually, I'm up at the Fort Myers office."

"Wow," she said, genuinely impressed. "It's like you grew up."

"Well, now I wouldn't go that far, but...yeah, maybe." He put his shades back on. "Did you...did you move back? Or just visiting?"

She hadn't seen Garrett Cage in over a decade - not after her first year of college. They had gone to high school together and ended up going to Florida State before Garrett dropped out and came back home. "I moved back in February."

"No kidding." He widened his stance for support as his boat rocked in the water. "Where from?"

"I was abroad for a while." Old friend and with the DEA or not, she couldn't tell him where she had been. "I'm back for good now."

"What are the odds?" Garrett asked out loud. "I just got back myself about eight months ago."

"Hey, kids," Warren interjected, "I hate to break up the reunion, but we are doing what we can to catch some fish."

Garrett shot up an apologetic hand. "Of course. Yes. Sorry to bother you guys." He looked back at Ellie. "Call me at the office sometime. We should get some coffee or breakfast and catch up. Been a long time."

"That would be nice. I'll do that."

He nodded toward her uncle. "Sorry to bother you two. Enjoy your time out here."

"Have a good day, Agent Cage. Thank you both for all your work," Warren said. The boat idled away slowly until it was fifty yards off their starboard when it throttled up and shot away. "What's the connection there?" he asked.

"Old friend from my school years." Ellie looked out toward their disappearing wake. "I never would have pegged him for law enforcement. Funny how things work out."

"Think he would have pegged you for CIA?"

Ellie huffed. "Of course. I look very CIA-ish. Good looks, perfect skin, and out-of-this-world smarts."

He laughed. "Well, I hope he's doing his job right. The world isn't getting any better. Those drug cockroaches are everywhere."

"Has the DEA stopped you out here before?" she asked.

"No. A couple of them came by the marina a couple months ago and got some lunch at The Mangrove. They asked a bunch of questions - have I seen anything suspicious, heard anything, will you call me if you do - the standard stuff. I got the feeling that they were just working a procedural handbook, trying to run the clock down until they could go home."

The sound of water spraying into the air got Ellie's attention. She turned and saw two dolphins swimming calmly past their stern. "Beautiful creatures, aren't they?" Warren said.

"They really are."

"We'd better be getting back," he said. "It will take a while for the fish to come back after your old buddy ran over our spot. I have a meeting over at the Kids Club. Picture day or something like that. They want me over there after lunch."

Ellie set the hook in the fishing rod's eye. "Pictures for what?" Hanging behind the bar at The Salty Mangrove were a couple dozen small, framed pictures of the community events and sponsorships Warren had been involved with over the years. Little League teams, Randall Research Center, Elks Lodge, among others. He was the embodiment of everything that made the island good.

"I donated some wheelchairs to some kids in need, so they want me to come get my face in the middle of them when they give them away."

Ellie took his pole while he got behind the wheel. "You're a good man, Warren Hall." She grinned. "I don't care what Fu Wang says about you."

~~~~~

A half hour later, Ellie stepped off the end of the boardwalk's ramp and back into the parking lot. She'd left her fish for Major to clean and to serve for dinner at the grill. She walked past her truck, up Oleander Street, and turned east onto Fourth Avenue before heading south onto Lime Street. It was early enough in the day that she would eventually make her way back to the bar. She would bring her truck back then. The breeze blew softly into the palm trees, and their lazy fronds generated a rustling sound like dry wheat. A gull squawked overhead before turning right and coasting toward Monroe Canal. Her house was the fourth one on the right. It was a narrow cottage she had purchased from a couple who had rented it out to vacationers for the previous fifteen years. Like many of the cottages on the island, the exterior had been painted with a bright, eye-numbing blue. Ellie had decided early on that she preferred softer, less intrusive colors. She repainted it herself, opting for a kinder gray instead.

Ellie walked down her driveway and punched her code into the keypad on the side of the garage. It beeped, accepting her code, and the door rattled open to reveal a 1968 El Camino. Its royal blue color gave it the appearance of being painted with ocean water, and the two white racing stripes down the hood made it look more powerful than it really was.

The car had belonged to her father. Ellie could remember the day he brought it home. He had taken both his daughters for a drive all the way up the island to Bokeelia, then back down to St. James City. She had loved the vehicle as a child, but now she wasn't as sure. El Caminos were polarizing vehicles that left one either mocking or adoring them. They looked like the poor genetic offspring of a car and a truck, each donating a faulty chromosome that produced something almost unnatural. Next to his daughters, the El Camino had been Frank O'Conner's baby.

Ellie could hear a high-pitched whine on the other side of the pedestrian door that led into the house. "Hold on, I'm coming," she said. She opened the door, and her Jack Russell Terrier shot out, ran twice around the car, then vaulted off a Rubbermaid box and into her arms. Ellie laughed and let the dog lick her neck. "Hey, Citrus." She bent over and set the dog down, then walked into the house.

The cottage was only two bedrooms, and the front door opened to a living room with a vaulted ceiling boasting exposed rafters that Ellie had stained a walnut brown. A small kitchen table sat near the rear sliding door at the end of a shotgun kitchen.

"You want a milkbone?"

Citrus barked and sat up on his hind feet. She reached above the fridge, grabbed a treat from the box, and teased him with it before he snatched it from her hand. Ellie moved over to the rear glass door and slid it down its metal track. Citrus darted out into the small backyard. "I'll be right out," she called after him. She stepped into the kitchen, pulled the small knife that Major had given her from her pocket, and placed it next to the coffee pot. The copper samovar Vida Murad had gifted her sat in the corner of the kitchen counter. It stood there silently, yet screaming. Vida had used it dozens of times to fill Ellie's cup with Kahwa, a tea made from a combination of green tea, cardamom pods, cinnamon bark, and saffron strands. In Kabul, sharing a meal together, even a cup of tea, was an indication of friendship. It was termed "the right of salt," a cultural practice that placed great responsibility on the guest to be faithful and honest with his host. Vida had gifted the serving pot to Ellie the night that Assam had provided Ellie the information she had moved there to attain. It had been Vida's way of telling her American friend that she trusted her with what they had just revealed. There had been a deep sense of soberness in the apartment that evening. Assam had given up his murderous cousin at tremendous risk to his family, and they all knew there would be no turning back from such a decision. Vida had washed the samovar—a family relic her mother had passed down to her—wrapped it, and presented it to Ellie two days before the extraction. Two days before Vida died.

When Ellie moved back to Florida and unpacked the very few things she owned at the time, she chose to leave the pot on display in the kitchen. Its very presence pressed down on something fragile within her and hurt. The pain made her feel less guilty—as if it were a meager atonement for a broken promise and the murder of a beautiful family. A family that should be stateside at this very moment, enjoying each other's company and laughter somewhere in Idaho or Arizona. Assam could have even started a dental practice under a new identity.

Ellie walked out onto the back porch and slid the door shut behind her. The backyard consisted of a small, concrete porch slab and a stretch of St. Augustine grass that extended out eight feet to the railroad tie which formed out the top edge of the concrete canal wall. Her twenty-one-foot Bayliner Element hung out of the water, sitting peacefully on the I-beams of the boat lift. Citrus was staring at her as if pleading, like he was asking her a question to which only he could hear the words. Ellie looked down and smiled at him, then nodded toward the canal. "Go ahead." The dog barked, and a second later its body was suspended between water and sky. When God finished making the world at the end of day six, he took whatever energy he had left and stuck it into the DNA of the first pair of Jack Russells. Citrus fell seven feet and hit the water with a splash, and he paddled his way back to the side. Ellie had built a small ramp that ran into the water so the dog could easily get out of the canal and back into the yard.

Ellie sat at the canal edge and let her feet hang toward the slow-moving sea water that ran through it. Citrus ran and jumped again, then yipped when his head came up. On the other side of the canal, a couple houses down, a neighbor came out of her house with a watering can and waved at Ellie. She returned the gesture. She had good neighbors—folks that made you feel like you were family.

She had grown up in Pineland on the northern end of the island. Over the years, whenever thoughts of coming back home drifted through Ellie's mind, she knew she would settle down in St. James City. Its interconnected canals brought the sea water inland like generous fingers serving up a utopian paradise. Homes sat on lots often no larger than a quarter acre, most of them, like Ellie's, half that size. Many mornings, just as the golden rays of sunshine were touching her rear windows, Ellie and Citrus would idle the Bayliner down the canal and out to the Sound and just let the wind whip their hair and the salty breeze wake them up.

Citrus trotted up to his owner and dug his muzzle underneath her hand. "You hungry?" she asked him. He barked and shook his body free of the water matting his short hair. "All right. I'll go fix us something." She stood up, walked to the back door, and stopped to turn on the sprinkler. It squawked to life, and Citrus darted through it, shaking his head and pawing at the stream. He loved the sea water, but the salt drying on his body was bad for his skin. "Rinse off," Ellie said. "I'll be right back with some cold cuts."

CHAPTER FIVE

Ellie pulled on the door handle to The Perfect Cup, and the smell of sugary caramel mixed with the astringent scent of coffee hit her senses as she walked in. She located Garrett at a small table in the corner and lifted a hand to him, then walked up to the counter and ordered a white chocolate mocha over ice. Two days ago she had called Garrett, and they set up a time to meet and catch up. Ellie gave the barista her name, paid, and made her way to the table that seated only two. Garrett came to his feet as she approached, and Ellie noted that his features were as cool as they had been in high school. He had a high forehead and jet black hair that was finger-combed to the right and blended down into a handsome fade on both sides. His blue eyes were bright and relaxed, his eyebrows thick, and his mouth wide. He was apparently off duty, wearing dark blue shorts, a white V-neck T-shirt, and black loafers. She leaned in and hugged him before taking her seat.

His eyes were sparkling, and he stared at her for a few seconds.

"What?" she asked, grinning.

"I can't believe you're sitting in front of me. It's been, what, thirteen years?"

"Yeah. Seems like it was a just a couple years ago we were all packing into Davie's car and heading to Fort Lauderdale for the weekend."

"You look good," he said.

She smiled. "Thanks. You too."

They spent a few minutes catching up, broadly filling in the gaps of the previous decade. Garrett married a few years out of college and as yet had no kids. His wife was currently in New York, working to get her own fashion line noticed. She would come down a couple weekends a month to see him and relax from the tyranny that New York imposed upon aspiring fashionistas. Garrett was hopeful that by the end of the year things would take off for her and she would be back down here more often than not.

Ellie excused herself when she heard her name called and walked over to the counter to pick up her drink. She returned to the table, sat back down, took a sip, and closed her eyes as the cool, sugary liquid slid down her throat.

"So, DEA, huh? Don't I remember our yearbook pinning you as most likely to polish door knobs? What gives?" she asked.

"What? Hey, come on."

She laughed. "Come on? You were the biggest toker in school. Now you're DEA? You were the Pig-Pen of the school, except your cloud was a very specific kind of smoke, not dirt."

He shrugged defensively. "People change, I guess." His face slowly clouded over. "My cousin up in Tampa had gotten me into the green when I was thirteen. He paused our game of Street Fighter, escorted me to the alley behind his house, and lit a roll for me. You're right. I did get heavy into the green after that, but that's all I ever did. Over time he moved on into the harder stuff. The year after we graduated high school, he started on gremmies."

She curled her brow. "Gremmies? Geez."

"Yeah. A year after I saw you last, he moved on to heroin, and it was lights out after that. My aunt found him dead in the bathtub with the needle still in his arm. I mean, poor lady. She had gone out of town and didn't find him until day three. That whole thing freaked me out so bad I quit cold turkey. I don't think I'm the kind of guy who would do the hard drugs. I went eight years without them just smoking the green. But it scared me anyway, and I left it all behind."

"That's hard," she said. "About your cousin."

He sighed. "He was a good guy. Just hung out with the wrong people. I needed a change and decided on the Army. I couldn't stand the thought of being on the threshold of the rest of my life with no clear path ahead. I'd been cleaning boats for four years in Fort Myers and knew I could do better. After basic I ended up with the 82nd Airborne out of Fort Bragg. I got out after four years, joined the DEA, finished my degree, and moved up to Special Agent before ending up on a FAST team."

Ellie had met several men in the DEA's Foreign-Deployed Advisory and Support Teams as they circled in and out of Afghanistan. As a part of FAST, Garrett would have been trained by Navy Seals, outfitted by the Pentagon, and gone into countries to conduct drug raids on stashes that could potentially end up in the United

States via the black market. FAST had recently been decommissioned and replaced with SRT units—Special Response Teams—to address higher risk tactical operations in the field.

"Airborne and FAST. Impressive. So how did you end up back down here?"

"I finished my time with FAST and got out as First Lieutenant four years ago. They sent me to work at headquarters in Springfield until they offered me my own local division down here."

"Wait a minute...you're at the helm down here?"

His smile was humble. "Yeah."

"Well, good for you, Garrett. That's a big deal."

"Thanks." He nodded toward Ellie. "So, enough about me. What about you?" he asked. "You left the CIA just to come back to sunny Florida?"

Ellie's eyes narrowed.

He raised his hands in defense. "Okay, okay. I made a few guesses and went out on a limb. Made a few deductions and poked my nose around."

"What kind of deductions?"

"You major in linguistics at Florida State, then I hear you've moved to Virginia after you graduate. Then I see you the other day, and you tell me you've been 'abroad.' No one who lives overseas for years on end comes back home and speaks in generalities about where they've been. My sister, she goes to Madrid for three years, comes home, and can't stop yapping on about the food and the culture and the men. Anyway..." Garrett smiled like he knew he was about to be in trouble. "I took the liberty of typing your name into JWICS." When pronounced out loud, JWICS sounded like *JayWicks* and was the acronym for Joint Worldwide Intelligence Communications System.

Ellie looked on him cautiously. JWICS was a top secret network run by the Defense Intelligence Agency and used to transmit sensitive data across agencies.

Garrett's smile was charming but guilty, like a teenage boy trying to explain to his mother what the pack of cigarettes under his bed was all about. "Now, before you go getting upset, know that there wasn't a whole lot on you anyway. Your name popped up, and it showed that you spent your first couple years in Virginia with the CIA's Office of the Inspector General. After that there's nothing but a listing for a few years as a case officer, but it doesn't list the wheres, whens, and whys. All that's either been redacted or just not there. If it makes you feel any better, I was just curious. So call me a curious cat and kill me now if you need to."

Her shoulders relaxed as she realized the information on her was skeletal. "It's not a big deal, Garrett. You surprised me, that's all. Don't worry about it."

"Whew," Garrett sighed, as if he was thankful he would live another day. "So you're done with it all?" he asked.

"I am."

He winked at her. "A better job opportunity present itself on Pine Island?"

"Yeah, you could say that." Ellie looked into her cup, swirled the last bit of liquid around, and then looked back up. "I hit a point where I needed to live on my own terms, to stop doing the bidding of others. I'm in my mid-thirties now. I've worked for the government for my entire adult life."

He eyed her, searching her expression. "What really got you back here?"

She looked out the window. A stray dog lifted its leg on the tire of a car, sniffed at it, and walked off with its head a little higher. "Politics." She turned back toward Garrett. She couldn't say where she'd been or what she'd done, but she was free to have an opinion. "We're fighting this shadow war, this undeclared war that gives us the freedom to do whatever we want all around the world. After 9/11 the CIA migrated from a Cold War espionage service to a paramilitary organization. I did some good; I know that. And I wouldn't change anything. But the Agency is no longer what it used to be." Ellie looked around the coffee shop. People were typing on laptops, earbuds in, laughing with a friend, sipping their drinks, reading books. "Whatever the average person thinks of the CIA is probably informed by pre-Cold War tactics and methods. It's not an espionage organization. It's a global clandestine killing machine, and it was just time for me to make an exit. We're on the front lines of a war-mongering enterprise run by Washington's pimps, and I got tired of doing tricks."

Garrett narrowed his eyes on her, intrigued by the sharpness of her words. "You bitter?"

"Bitter?" She shook her head. "No. I'm not that kind of person. If I were I wouldn't have made it this far. I stayed the course because I believed what I was doing was good. Once I stopped believing that, I stepped out." She tried to smile. "I wouldn't change anything. There are still a lot of good people there doing good in their own way. For all its faults we still need the Agency. I loved what I did, and it will always be a part of who I am. A bloated bureaucracy and weariness of working for someone else's obtuse agenda...that's why I'm back here." She picked up her mug, tilted it up, and finished the last bit of her coffee.

"You said the other day you've been back six months now?" he asked.

"Yeah."

"Do you miss any of it?"

"Of course. I was good at it. One day I might find a different way to serve my country again." She felt a sudden urge to move the conversation away from herself. "So tell me about what you're up to down here. What's it like being top dog?"

"It has its perks," he admitted. "We've cleaned up a lot on the streets since I've come on. But things keep changing at a rapid rate, and it's hard to keep up. The whole world of illegal drugs - cocaine especially - is different than most people think."

"How do you mean?"

"Well, nowadays, mostly because of Hollywood, when your average guy thinks of the cocaine trade, they think of Medellín, Escobar, Cali—the drug lords of thirty years ago. Those guys are legend now, but things have changed. Drastically. Cocaine production has become decentralized and typically doesn't have one or two big men at the top anymore, at least not in Colombia and Bolivia. The Mexican cartels figured out that they could undermine the Colombians by securing the base product, then throw it into their own labs and distribute it themselves." He paused. "Stop me if I'm telling you what you already know."

She shook her head. "Narco-terrorism wasn't my forte."

"The big cartels aren't in South America. They're in Mexico. Colombia and Bolivia and Peru, if they have any trades routes of their own, are throughout Europe, via African ports, but mostly they just sell to the Mexicans. Mexico is the golden trampoline; whatever drugs end up there are bounced somewhere else for a whole lot of money. These guys, Ellie - they're as smart as they have ever been. Their networks are so vast that when you make one good bust you might as well have broken a capillary. They're smart, better funded, and have far more resources than we ever will."

"What's this area look like?" she asked. "You're seeing drugs actually being brought into Lee County or just in from Miami?"

"Oh no, directly. As best we can see, the Mexicans are bringing their product right into our coastlines. They're getting bolder, going farther and farther north, away from their decades-old routes in the Keys, Miami, and the Glades."

"And they brought you in to stop it all?" She smiled.

Garrett's expression tightened, molded into frustration. "Supposedly. That's what I was told, but they haven't come through on it."

"What do you mean?"

"This is where I grew up, and it's the place I love, so when they offered me the helm I accepted with the caveat that I would be able to dig into the routes and sources. That hasn't happened yet. They won't give me the right people for it. You talk about politics; I've got my own to deal with."

"They won't let you dig under the skin? You're joking."

"I wish I were. It looks better for them when they

can show a bust and hold up kilos in front of the cameras. I'm about to circumvent some suits and bring someone in anyway."

"You should, Garrett. Good for you."

Garrett's lips formed a hard line, and he ran an open palm across the back of his neck. "Yeah...so, about that. What would you think about joining me? Coming on my team?"

Ellie blinked a couple times. "Hold on. Wait, you want me to chase down drugs?" She laughed, and, when she saw that Garrett wasn't smiling, she lowered her voice. "I'm not a detective, Garrett." It wasn't completely true. Her first two years with the Office of the Inspector General at Langley meant she sometimes had a hand in finding the early morning shadow of officers that were suspected of unapproved or illegal activity overseas. Beyond that, her time as a case officer in Afghanistan meant that thinking logically and noticing trends could sometimes be the matter of life or death.

"You don't need to be," Garrett answered. "Ellie, I came down here to stop the flow of drugs from coming in at our coastline, not kick down the doors of single moms and grown punks who trade a few ounces here and there. My entire team is busy making raids and arresting bottom feeders who use more product than they sell. I need someone who I can give freedom to step outside the lines a little bit. Someone who has the creativity and the chutzpah to make connections and find pathways that no one else sees."

Ellie wasn't surprised easily, but Garrett had somehow discovered how to do it. She was intrigued, not sold. "So you're telling me that Lee County is bringing in drugs directly - not just bringing it in from other places - and that you're not getting the tools to stop them?"

"That's exactly what I'm saying. I probably don't need to tell you that red is the color of the tape that ties up good ideas and sends them down to the basement to rot. I have good agents at my office, but I also have to record a certain number of seizures on the books every quarter." He made air quotes with his fingers. "'Have to show progress.' That leaves little time or resources to actually track down where it's all coming in at and where it's all moving. Miami has a lot invested in uncovering the logistics of the drugs and working with the other agencies - the Navy, Coast Guard, and the Department of Homeland - but that keeps the focus on what's happening down there. That means a lot of focus is spent on what's coming in around Miami-Dade County and less on the goings-on up here. The entire area from Naples to Tampa is rising as a destination port."

"Is it that bad here?" she asked. "I'm not naive enough to think there isn't an underworld wherever you go, but I haven't seen anything that would tell me drugs are running in and out of here by the boatload."

"That's because they're moving them out quickly. You're right, consumption isn't as bad around here as an inner city, and we don't exactly have the state's most sought after nightclubs either. That's my point. Consumption is average, but we have sufficient evidence to believe that a lot of product is coming into our coastlines and quickly being moved up and out of the state. By my estimate we're not catching ninety-five percent of what comes into and through Lee County. Maybe more."

Ellie ran the tip of her finger around the top edge of

her empty mug, then raised an eyebrow as a warning. "I'm not saying yes, Garrett, but, if I were to even entertain the idea, how exactly would you see me fitting in?"

A twinkle of hope shot from his eye, and he leaned in. "We'd start by running leads on low- and mid-level offenders and go from there. Honestly, Ellie, right now we're basically blind as to the way their networks are structured. We've got a couple top men on our radar, but we know there's got to be more than that. You're a fresh face, and I can't tell you how valuable that is. These drug kingpins, they have their own shared networks of photographs and personal files, and it's filled with cops and agents from every GO under the sun that has ever been involved with drug hunting at any level. Whether it's you or not, I have some discretionary funds in my budget to bring someone like you on. I just can't get my own people on it. You wouldn't formally be with the DEA and would have a lot of freedom to do things your way. You'd have a contractor badge and work for me on the side. We'd issue you a firearm, laptop. I would have to get you vetted, interviewed, and brought up to speed. That process is usually a few months, but with your background I could get it sped up to a few weeks."

Ellie looked out the window again and watched the cars pass. In a moment of honesty, it sounded intriguing. But she had also grown used to the slow pace of her life now. A part-time job with Major that she loved and the freedom to do what she wanted when she wanted. A job like this would not come without stress and political pushback of its own.

She looked back at him. "I appreciate the offer,

Garrett, but I think I'll pass. I'm sure it would be good for the right person, but I don't think it's me."

"Fair enough." His eyes held a gaze like that of a grouper lusting after a lure. He couldn't hold back and asked, "Mind if I ask why?"

"I like the pace of my life right now. It fits me. Everyone runs around this world now like you're wasting away if you're not going a hundred miles an hour. Old Florida is healing, you know? Like magic. The air rustling the palms is almost a soundtrack - always in the background - the gracious sunshine, the call of a gull, the way the water laps at a hull in an eternal quest to find itself way inside. That's what I need right now."

Garrett laughed. "Fair enough. Just so we're clear, no one is asking you to go to Juarez or Havana and get in a shootout with anyone. But just so *I'm* clear...you're completely happy working at a bar part time and fishing the rest?"

"Isn't that what everyone works toward?" She smiled. "I think it's called retirement."

His lips drew a thin line. "You have a point. Okay," he conceded.

"I'll have to find a real job at some point down the road, but I don't think it's now."

"Well, if you reconsider, you know where to find me. Forgive me if I was too direct too soon. I've been told I am not one to smile kindly on patience. After having a vague idea of your past and making a few connections, I thought you might be a fit. Especially with us being old friends."

"No harm," she said. "It never hurts to ask."

"It does hurt to hear 'No.'" He grinned and then stood up. "Come on. I'll walk you out."

CHAPTER SIX

THREE DAYS LATER, AFTER A LONG MORNING OF shooting, Ellie and Tyler had decided to go for lunch and selected Nick's Fish House on Matlacha as the place to do it.

Matlacha was a sleepy fishing village that connected Pine Island with Cape Coral via a single-leaf drawbridge at Highway 78. The bridge, dubbed "The Fishing-est Bridge in the World," hosted generous quantities of mangrove snapper, trout, sheepshead, cobia, redfish, snook, and even small sharks.

The small island was a unique community in its own right and offered visitors such a rare glimpse into Old Florida that many now called it "The New Key West." Its old fishing shacks sat along both sides of the narrow road that ran through it and were splashed in bright energetic colors. Until the mid-1990s, Matlacha had been a famous and vibrant fishing community, bringing in mullet by the boatload for the good of all. In 1992, a pernicious voter referendum led to a ban on net fishing, and, in a punitive response, many of Matlacha's commercial fishermen shot holes in their boats and set them on fire. The heaven-stretched flames could be seen out to Fort Myers Beach and Sanibel Island, a final death knell signaling the end of Matlacha's existence as a commercial fishery.

Over the years the area came to be inhabited by a surplus of musicians, writers, and artists that in more recent years helped Matlacha grow primarily into a funky art community, giving the island its name, The Creative Coast. The locals claimed the relaxed way of life and the fresh, salty air were the perfect concoction for creative juices and imagination to flow freely. Art galleries, small seafood restaurants, and souvenir shops lined the side of the road west of the bridge and together formed a community that lived according to its own relaxed rhythms.

After looking briefly at the menu, Ellie had ordered Gulf shrimp tacos layered with shredded cabbage, garden fresh salsa, and cream sauce. Tyler opted for a steak strip sandwich that came served on garlic herb bread and topped with sautéed onions and Swiss cheese. They talked about rifles and trucks, and Ellie had managed to squeeze a little more out of him about what was back in Texas. Tyler had an older brother by three years who lived in Dallas and drove semi trucks for FedEx. His parents were still together, still lived in the same country house he was born in, and had their own business making custom leather products: wallets, knife sheaths, pens, and belts. Those were all reasons to stay in Texas - not to leave - but Ellie couldn't bring herself to push that bright red button. Not yet.

"So...I've been offered a job," she finally said.

Tyler stopped chewing and eyed her suspiciously,

then finished chewing and swallowed. He took a long sip of his sweet tea and then nodded confidently like he already knew what it was. "It's *The View*, isn't it? They want you to join the cast. Bring on a former CIA agent who is now a part-time bartender in Florida?"

She smiled. "Stop it. I'm serious."

"Okay. So what is it?"

"I was with Major last week and bumped into an old friend of mine from high school. He works with the DEA—"

"The DEA?" Tyler interrupted. He scrunched his face. "As in the Department of Ecological Advancement?"

"Would you stop it? He tossed out the idea of me coming on as an outside contractor."

"And what would you be contracting?"

"I'd help to identify connections between drugs being brought into the area and their sources."

"You mean like find street dealers?"

"More like find the people the street dealers work for."

"Aren't those guys sunbathing in Speedos at the Equator?"

"No. It's not like that. There are these domestic kingpins who control their own organizations. The guys doing the ordering and taking possession. That's who'd I'd be helping to locate. It's not sexy. Mostly just working through a lot of paperwork and asking the right questions of the right people."

He probed the bottom of his glass with a straw and, like a toddler, slurped the remaining moisture out from around the half-melted ice cubes with a noise that sounded like an engine was taking off at their table.

When he stopped he asked, "You mean these kingpins are around here?"

"Seems so. We have a lot of good coastline close to main roads, and I would imagine that makes it attractive to imports looking to avoid the eyes focused in on larger cities."

Tyler patted a trim belly, which sat in front of a now empty plate, then leaned back and locked his fingers behind his head. "So you gonna take it?"

She shrugged. "No. I'm happy with the way things are."

"You'd rather take the position with *The View*?"

Ellie ignored him and took another sip of her tea. "I don't need to work. These last several months have been good for me."

"So humor me for a second. What don't you like about the possibility?"

"I know it would be stressful. Even if I work at it part-time. I have to be accessible and couldn't just pull up and go down to the Keys for three months if I wanted to."

The waitress brought their ticket and set it on the table. "Whenever you're ready," she said.

Tyler grabbed it. "I've got this." He took out his wallet, grabbed a piece of plastic, and set it on top of the ticket. "If you did it, when would you start?"

"Whenever I say 'yes,' I guess. It's weird. Here I am fishing one day, and the next I have an option to step into something like this."

"You're intrigued," he noted.

"Yeah. Yeah, I think that's it. But I'm not sure I really want to do it."

"Well, I think you'd be good at it."

She smiled. "Thanks."

"I also think you should do it."

"Really? Why?"

"Why? Ellie, all the smart people that study people say it's not good for people to do nothing."

"Hey, I don't do nothing."

Tyler dipped his chin and stared at her. "Helping your uncle around the bar and the marina here and there does not classify as something. You keep this up, and you'll be dead in five years. We're not meant to be half idle for long periods of time. You know the stories of retirees who don't find purpose after they leave their careers. They croak within a few years. Shoot, at least go buy a set of golf clubs."

"But I'm not old. And I do have purpose."

"Yeah. I'm not saying you don't. But you can't live the rest of your life on vacation either."

Ellie grabbed her sunglasses off the table and stood up. "Watch me." She grinned.

He winked at her. "I do that already."

CHAPTER SEVEN

The white Suburban moved gently on its suspension as it turned into the large circular driveway. It came to a stop, and the young boy's eager feet were on the concrete before the vehicle's transmission was set in park.

"Mom, can I take my bike out for a while?" he asked through his mother's open window.

She turned off the SUV and opened her door. "I thought you were going to call your grandfather and wish him a happy birthday?"

"I will. I just want to go for a ride. Come on, Mom," he prodded. "I've been running errands with you all day. I won't be gone long."

She stuck out her hand and rubbed the top of his head. "And thank you for being patient. Of course you can ride your bike. Don't be gone for too long."

He darted from the vehicle and ran toward the garage to get his bike. His mother clicked the garage door opener on her visor. "And don't be loud when you come back in!" she called after him. "I'm putting your sister down for a nap!"

"Okay!" he yelled back. He ducked under the door as it shuddered upwards and rushed over to the blue Diamondback Octane he'd begged his parents for—and gotten—for his birthday last week. He walked it out of the garage and jumped on, then adjusted the gears as he gained momentum. He turned out of the driveway onto the main road of their secluded neighborhood. He loved this place, and even more he loved riding through it. His father was an engineer for an aviation company, and that meant they got to live in the nicer area of Ionia. The plots were two to three acres and set well off the road. Trees were thick, and it almost deceived one into thinking you were in a forest far from the ocean and not less than a mile from the water's edge.

The chain clicked against the gears, and he twisted the dial on his handlebar. It locked in, and he gained more speed as he pushed hard against the pedals. The wind whistled around his ears, and he pictured Ben, his best friend, racing behind him, trying to catch up. Ben would be back soon from the family vacation he took to New England last week. They would race down this road like they had hundreds of times; only this time Ben would lose. He hadn't seen the new bike yet. There was no way he could beat it.

∼∼∼∼∼

The man's legs dangled off the pickup truck's tailgate,

and he fidgeted with the suppressor on his .45 ACP. "I can't believe we're doing this during the daytime," he mumbled. "You guys hurry up." Andrés Salamanca and Jared Robinson stopped and stared him down.

Andrés was just at six feet tall and had a high protruding forehead and a sharp nose. His head was shaved down to the scalp on both sides, and the long hair on top was slicked back and shiny under the excessive amount of hair gel he'd folded into it. Andrés had grown up in the sordid streets of Ciudad Juárez, Mexico, a brazen border city that was the main cocaine gateway to the United States. Shoved up against the metal fences of the Texas border, exactly halfway between the Pacific and the Gulf coasts, the city had long been a smugglers' lair: a place where illicit fortunes were made and blown on fast cars, gaudy mansions, and purchasing amoral politicians.

Andrés was smart and quickly moved up in the ranks of the local cartel, but after a few years, his closest friends had all been killed by anti-narcotics efforts or assassinated by rival cartels. He liked breathing, liked the feel of his heart beating, so he transferred to the port city of Tampico and started running product across the Gulf. Over time he'd gotten to know his current boss, the cartel's most respected distributor in Southwest Florida. When Andrés was apprised about coming to work stateside, he cleared it with the Mexican lords and made the switch. Three months later he was furnished with a social security number and an American passport, both legit and above board. The move was good for both parties. The cartel now had someone on the receiving end who knew the routes better than a migrating dolphin, and his new boss had someone who was respected by the runners and who had a reputation for getting things done.

Jared "Chewy" Robinson: Tallahassee born and raised. "Chewy," so called because he was tall and had a condition that made him feel cold all the time, so he wore his light brown beard thick, his hair long, and a wool trench coat that never came off. Not even in the humid Florida summers when it felt more like a steam room outside than a domestic paradise. Sometime, a few years back, someone mentioned that Jared looked more like a Wookie than anything else. Rumor was the man who suggested the nickname thereafter suffered from a broken nose. The new name stuck nonetheless.

Chewy stared flatly at the short, pale-looking man sitting on the tailgate. "You could help," he said, his voice booming deep and low in his chest. He dropped a kilo of cocaine into a wooden crate stamped with the image of a mango formed in black ink. None of them liked what they were doing today. Moving product like this in the daytime was unusually dangerous and greatly increased the chances that they would be seen or caught.

"Someone has to keep an eye out," the man on the tailgate replied. He had a lazy eye. It rolled to the side, and he looked like he might fall over. "Someone comes off that road and through those trees for some reason, we're toast." He was a small man, better at delegation than the actual work, and his name was Scotch. No one knew his last name, and most likely no one cared. He was a good administrator but lacking on the people skills. No one liked to work with him. He was kept around strictly for his utility.

The previous evening a nervous Mexican crew had pulled their boat into the mangroves, dumped a quarter ton of product into them, and taken off. They had been convinced they were being tracked by Coast Guard surveillance. Now the cleanup crew had been sent in to recover the product and render it safe and hidden - where it should have been last night. Andrés and Chewy had spent the last thirty minutes walking to the water's edge, fighting their way through the thick mangroves and walking the thirty yards back through the woods to the small unlabeled moving truck.

"No one comes out here, and you know it," Andrés said with a disgusted tone. "Housing development stops a mile back down the road."

Scotch ignored him and kept his attention on the gun. His wrist folded and unfolded in rhythm as he churned on the suppressor to the end of the barrel. "How much longer?" he asked.

"Fifteen minutes," Chewy wheezed. "Ten if you would get over here and help. The boss doesn't like that we are in a position where we have to transfer bricks in the middle of the day." Chewy huffed and set another couple packages gently into a crate, then walked back to the water's edge.

Scotch sighed and slid off the tailgate until his feet touched the ground. "Fine," he mumbled. He stuck the gun in the front of his pants and followed Chewy through the thick brush. Getting to the water's edge, he held on to the branches of the mangroves and carefully placed his feet onto the slippery root system that poked out just above the waterline. He looked through the branches. Chewy and Andrés were fifteen feet farther, grabbing at packages still hanging in the branches and bobbing in the water against the roots. The crew had chucked the packages in the right place. Punta Rassa

Cove was full of tiny islands and inlets, some inlets almost too narrow and shallow to ride a small boat through. Andrés hunched down, walked over to Scotch, and handed him two packages. "One more," Scotch said. "If I'm gonna help, let's just get this done with."

Andrés shook his head. "Two at a time."

"Give me another one," Scotch repeated.

Andrés looked over at Chewy. Chewy rolled his eyes and nodded out of frustration.

"Fine." Andrés reached over, grabbed another kilo, and set it gently on top of the other ones nestled in Scotch's arms. "Go," he said. "Be careful."

Scotch slowly turned and jammed his chin onto the top kilo so they would stay put while he used his other hand to grab the branches. He precariously navigated his way out of the root system and back onto the grassy terrain of the forest floor. It sloped gently upward, and he kept his eyes on the white siding of the moving truck as it came into view. All of a sudden it was hard to walk, and he felt a pulling tension on the lower package. He frowned and looked down but couldn't see anything.

He heard Andrés's voice behind him. "Stop! You snagged on something."

Scotch didn't stop. He set his chin down harder and swung his hands to the right. The tightly bound plastic wrap punctured and tore hard against the branches, releasing Scotch and his packages. Scotch flew outward, and the kilos went with him. White dust puffed up into the air before quickly settling down into vegetation around him.

Andrés cursed and ran up to him. "What are you doing? I told you to stop!" Scotch rolled onto his side and sat up. He rubbed his head and looked back. A broken branch jutted out of a bush caked in white dust. That was the culprit.

Chewy came up behind Andrés. "Get up. Just get up. We only have a few more left. Clean this up, and get what's left of it all into the truck. The man won't be happy with this. He'll take it out of your pay."

"Big deal," Scotch said. They walked past him, set the packages into an empty crate, and headed back down to the water.

Scotch stood up and brushed himself off. He didn't know what the big deal was. These guys needed to relax a little bit. He stared at the white mess in front of him. It looked like a hurried cook had spilled flour everywhere. All of a sudden and out of nowhere, a tingle drifted across his stomach. Scotch spent the better part of the last four years on the administrative side of things. He hadn't seen the actual product in as many years, nor had he tried it in a very long time. He had kept away from it because he couldn't stop before. Now, temptation tore through his body like a starving dog staring at fresh bowl of chow.

He plucked a small leaf off the bush, jabbed it into the open side of the broken package, and brought it back out with a little mound of cocaine on it. It had been a long time. Just a little bit would be all right. It would calm his nerves and give him the boost to hurry up and get off this boring job site. He tapped the leaf, letting some of the drug fall off. He took his left index finger and pressed hard against the outside of his left nostril. Then he brought the leaf up to his nose and inhaled quickly, almost violently. The effects were immediate as the drug unfurled through his veins. Euphoria catapulted through him, and his heart rate clicked higher. It felt like he had just drunk ten cups of coffee. His nose started to tingle. He shook his head a few times and smacked his lips. It was good stuff all right. And oh, how he had missed it.

"What the hell are you doing?"

Scotch turned around to see his two co-workers staring him down and holding what was left of the previously discarded kilos. His eyes were dilated, and he wiped at his nose. "Nothing. Just...well it was just sitting there. Didn't want it to go to waste. You know?"

Chewy and Andrés looked at each other. Scotch had just broken rule number three. No one ever broke rule number three.

"You are unbelievable," Andrés said. "Get up." He tucked the two kilos he was holding under his right arm and reached down and plucked the untorn packages off the ground. Chewy carefully picked up the damaged one. They walked back to the moving truck and deposited all but the torn one in a crate. Chewy grabbed a roll of duct tape from the cab and wrapped up what was left of the product. He then placed it in the crate, nailed a few brad nails in the top, and pulled the sliding door down.

"We are done here," Andrés said. "You need to clean your mess up over there."

"I will. Come on, guys. I'm not an idiot."

"That's debatable," Chewy said, then got into the passenger seat of the truck.

Andrés opened the driver's side door and turned back around. "You'd better be out of here in five minutes," he said. "The boss is already edgy. This whole thing we had to do here today is unprecedented. Make like a fairy and vanish."

Scotch waved him off. The moving truck started up, and Andrés navigated it through trees and bushes and back out to Shell Point Boulevard. Scotch pulled the gun out from his belt and aimed it at a tree in front of him. He faked shooting it, even letting the tip of the gun kick up. He supposed he'd been lucky that it hadn't discharged into his crotch when he fell earlier. He set the gun on the tailgate and grabbed a bucket from the truck bed. He then walked down to the water's edge and filled the bucket with water. He would toss a couple buckets of seawater on the area and be done. A couple more afternoon showers this week, and it would be like it had never been there at all. It wasn't like anyone would come out here anyway. This was nowhere land. He grabbed the handle with both hands. Water sloshed out with each step he took. He came up on the spot, put a hand underneath the bucket, and stopped. He wasn't alone. A young boy was staring back at him.

The boy had on jean shorts and a white T-shirt with Iron Man's red and gold face on it. He sat wide-eyed on a bike with his right foot planted on the ground.

Scotch set the bucket down and walked toward the truck. "Hey, kid. Whatcha doing out here?" He slid his backside onto the tailgate and moved his gun behind him.

The boy looked a mixture of curiosity and fear.

"Have a seat right here." His patted the empty space of tailgate next to him. "It's okay. No problem at all, all right?" The boy walked slowly to him, darting his eyes around, fear spilling from them. He parked his bike and took a seat, leaving his legs to hang motionless off the edge of the tailgate.

"I'm not going to hurt you. Let's just have a talk."

Scotch smiled. "What uh...what are you doing out here?"

"I...I...am just riding my bike," he said. His breath was short, and his small Adam's apple rose and fell as he swallowed nervously.

"Now, no need to be nervous." He smiled, and the boy's shoulders relaxed just slightly. "I am going to ask you a question, and I need you to tell me the truth."

Pupils dilated, the boy nodded.

Scotch followed the boy's eyes to a space behind him. He looked down and saw the grip of his gun. "Oh." He chuckled. "Don't worry about this." He set the weapon down on the edge of the truck bed. "Never know when you'll see a gator, right? Now then, I think you have a pretty good idea of what I am going to ask you. So why don't you just go ahead and answer it."

"I...I..." he stuttered.

Scotch spit into the grass and then laughed. He felt so good, the fiery rush of energy still riding through his veins.

"Yes?" he urged.

"I didn't see anything, sir."

"Then why do you look so scared?"

The boy tried to cough, but no sound came. "I know you are doing something out here. I know I shouldn't be here. But I don't know what you want me to tell you I saw. I didn't see you do anything."

Scotch pursed his lips and nodded. He look at the kid and, smiling, put a hand on his shoulder. "That's the truth? I've been a Catholic from the time I came out from my mother's legs. You wouldn't lie to a Catholic, would you, son?"

"No...no, sir. Not at all, sir."

Scotch flashed another smile. "Well, good then," he said as he slid off the tailgate. "I'm glad you didn't see anything. That is very good. Now, if you wouldn't mind, I am in fact trying to get a little work done. Maybe you could find another way into the woods a little further out down the road to ride your bike in? You can do that for me?"

The boy's head lifted, his face draining of concern. "Yes, sir," he said emphatically. "Sorry to have interrupted you."

"No problem at all." Scotch put his feet on the ground and walked up to the bike. He turned it around and held it out for its young owner. The boy got up, walked to his bike, and jumped back on.

"Have a good day, mister."

Scotch's eye drifted out again, and he smiled. "You too, kid. You too."

CHAPTER EIGHT

Suds grew like larvae out of the back and forth motion of the scrub brush as it crossed the deck. Ellie pushed down harder on the handle and slid the brush over the last untouched area of the boat. She tossed the brush over the edge and grabbed the hose. She depressed the nozzle handle, and the fresh water rinsed away the salt and the cleaning solution.

Major had pulled the boat out of the water with the marine forklift and set it on a couple boat dollies where they staged boats in need of cleaning. The Salty Mangrove Marina had a small, covered dry dock that could keep up to forty-six boats on a bi-level stack. Once boats came back in off the water, they would be cleaned immediately, the engines flushed, and re-racked. Ellie liked the work. It only took about a half hour to get a boat washed up and ready for storage again. Cleaning a boat was like mowing the lawn; it allowed your thoughts to drift and gave you time to think about whatever came. It contrasted with her working at the bar where you had to engage customers and strike up conversation. She enjoyed both.

This time of year the dry dock didn't see much action. The busy season, when the boats' owners came down from up north to visit and play for a few months, was typically from December to April. Right now, most of the active boats in the marina were wet docked at one of the twenty slips that Major's marina offered. Many of the locals in St. James City had their own boat lifts in the canals behind their homes.

Ellie finished spraying down the deck and vaulted over the side, bringing the hose with her. She grabbed the power washer and started spraying down the hull. She heard a deep voice over the sound of the compressor and the water and turned to see her uncle walking toward her with his cell phone on his ear. He nodded, said something, and hung up. He stepped over to the compressor and turned it off. "Hey, Ellie, listen. Henry just called from the Rotary Club. He said a boy went missing earlier today in Catalpa Cove. The cops over there are asking for folks to come out and help search for him."

"Ugh," Ellie said. She recentered her Salty Mangrove ball cap over her eyes. "What happened?"

"Not clear on that. All Henry knew was that he went for a bike ride a little after lunchtime and never came back. His mother said he's never gone for over an hour and it's been five or six now."

"Did they check his friends' houses?" she asked.

"They've checked all the spots: friends, putt-putt, arcade, fishing dock. The police don't get anyone involved until they've done that."

"Yeah," she said, then blew out a long puff of air. "I can't imagine what his parents are feeling right now."

"About like that time Katie went missing when she was three. We thought maybe she fell in the canal. Took us two hours to find her. You remember that?"

"Yeah. Not much of the details but I remember how scared and panicked I was. Dad just kept crying after she was found."

"We found her asleep in the closet. That whole ordeal took about five years off my life."

"Should I come too? I can help look."

"No. Go ahead and stay here and look after everything. I'm sure we'll have plenty of people looking for that boy before the hour is up."

"Okay. Well, call me if you think I can help."

"Will do. Hopefully, he just detoured to his favorite hangout and we can get him home to his parents so they can wring his neck." He started walking away, then stopped and looked up. The clouds were thickening overhead, the sky a mixture of light and dark gray. "Oh, hey. That storm will be here in a couple hours, so the bar might be a little light on traffic late tonight. Fu and Gloria are the only ones up there right now. If it gets to raining too hard, go ahead and shut down early."

"Will do."

~~~~~

"Ellie, you mind topping me off?" A tall mug came sliding down the bartop. Ellie caught it and smiled. "One day I'm going to miss, John."

"Not a chance. Besides, I always give you a heads up."

Ellie brought the glass underneath the spout and pulled back on the handle for Miller Lite. The golden liquid ran down the side of the glass, and she held it straighter the fuller it got, finishing it off with a frothy head. She walked over to John and set it on the damp coaster in front of him.

"Thanks, sweetie," he said.

It was dark now, and the Christmas lights wrapped around the cedar posts of the bar and the Edison lights strung behind the bottles of liquor on the back wall provided a soft glow against the brighter glare of the television hanging in the corner. There were more patrons tonight than Ellie would have expected. It seemed like folks had been inclined to come grab a quick drink at their favorite watering hole before the storm hit. Several people had planted themselves inside behind the transparent rain flaps of the indoor eating area, and a handful were at the bar. A cool gust came off the water from the pier's direction and was a reminder to all that closing time would be early tonight.

The flat screen television had Jeff Jamison, the local CBS weatherman, pointing to the radar map behind him, showing strong rainbands heading toward Fort Myers, Cape Coral, and the barrier islands. His tie was a bold checkered pattern of purple and orange. Ellie thought he always wore the best ties. He finished and turned it back to the news desk, and Ellie grabbed the blender to fulfill an order for a lime daiquiri.

The Wangs were focused on the television. "Oh my God," Gloria said. "Ellie, turn it up."

Ellie reached for the remote, clicked the volume higher, and gave the screen her attention. The camera panned in and showed an image of two thin legs lying limply in wild grass. The newscaster was saying a boy had been found. Murdered, shot in the back of the head, on the mainland just across the water from them. Out of respect, the camera showed only the legs of the preadolescent body, motionless in the grass. It quickly panned away.

"Oh dear," Gloria said. Her fingers went to her lips.

Ellie's mouth went dry. "Oh my Lord. No," she said. "Where is that?"

"Ionia, right down the blueway from here. That poor boy's family. They said they found traces of drugs not far from him," Gloria said. "Like maybe he stumbled onto something by accident."

A picture flashed onto the screen of a young family sitting on a beach. Father and son wearing khaki pants rolled up at the ankles and matching button-down shirts. The mother and baby girl wore matching yellow sundresses, and they all stared into the camera as if life had only ever blown a sweet breeze across their bows. The newscast slowly zoomed in on the face of the boy, but before the mother's face disappeared Ellie caught a clear view of it and gasped. Visions of long, tan legs standing on top of a cheerleading pyramid and a homecoming queen's crown flitted across Ellie's memory. The newscaster said she was Gina Stark. Back then she was Gina Higgs, the most popular girl in high school, the embodiment of all clichés: head of the cheerleading squad, homecoming queen, straight As. But she was kind, and Ellie had always liked her. She was even prettier now than she had been back then.

Ellie grabbed her cell phone from off the side of the cash register. She had two missed calls from her uncle.

She thumbed over her contacts and selected the one she wanted.

"Hello?"

"Garrett," she said softly.

It took him five heartbeats to answer. "You heard?" His tone was quiet, sober.

"Yeah."

"That's Gina Higgs, isn't it?" she asked.

"Yeah."

Ellie blinked back tears. It was strange how she could feel for a woman she hadn't seen in fifteen years. But no one should have to lose a son. Especially like that.

"They said there were drugs. Did they bring you in on this?"

"Of course. I got on scene a few minutes ago. We're getting samples of the drugs. It was cocaine. A lot of it by the looks of it. There's tire tracks all over here."

"You don't think the boy was in on it, do you?"

"Not a chance in hell. This kid was your upper middle class, baseball playing, 'I want to go to Disney for my birthday' type of kid. Twelve, Ellie. He was twelve. We're not talking about a rich, clean-looking college kid who never had the chance to hear Nancy Reagan tell him to say no to drugs."

Cell phones across the bar started ringing. The news was spreading quickly.

"Yeah. Yeah. Okay," she said.

The news anchor sent the program into commercial, and Ellie stared into the plastic container of lime wedges.

"Hey, I've got to go, okay?" he said.

Ellie blinked. "Yeah. Of course." She hung up

without saying goodbye. She slipped her phone into her pocket and pinched the bridge of her nose. Her eyes were damp, and she did her best to blink the moisture away.

Two customers were mumbling down the bar about the story, and Gloria stared at Ellie. "You knew the mother?" she asked.

"Not for a long time. But, yes. I knew her."

"Oh, honey, I'm so sorry."

Ellie nodded. Fu nodded.

"Hard to believe this kind of thing happened a couple miles from here," Gloria said. "These drug monsters are playing in our own backyard."

"Excuse me," Ellie said, then stepped out from under the tiki hut. She walked toward the pier as hot waves of anger pulsed through her. What kind of person does that to a kid? It was surreal. In the Middle East this kind of thing happened all the time. Terrorist groups gave no thought to whom they hurt or how they hurt them. They recruited children as soldiers and used them as shields. But here? The picture of the boy's legs flashed across her vision. She stopped at the wooden rail and looked down into the dark, stirring water. The wind whipped strands of hair across her face. If those bringing drugs into their coasts were willing for a twelve-year-old boy to be incidental collateral in their dark enterprise, then they would be willing to do anything. That young boy wouldn't be the last.

A couple large, cold raindrops hit her skin. Ellie pulled her phone back out and tapped the glass, set it to her ear. It rang twice.

"Garrett. Hey." She sighed and swallowed hard. "I'm in."

CHAPTER NINE

ELLIE PULLED HER SILVERADO NEXT TO THE GUARD house that commanded access to the parking lot of the Fort Myers DEA office. She plucked her temporary badge from a pocket in her backpack and rolled down her window. She handed it to the guard. "Good morning, Sam."

"Hey, Ellie." Sam Elton was on the heels of his twentieth year with the Administration. Two years ago he had transferred from forensics to security, a role he was fully overqualified for. He said he still needed the work but wanted life to move a little more slowly. He wore standard-issue cargo pants, and his thick arms and chest swelled underneath his white polo. His graying blond hair was trimmed tight to his skin, making it easy to confuse him with a Marine. He took her badge, scanned it with a handheld device, and looked at the reading. "Your temp badge expires today. Are you getting a permanent one?"

"Yes. They should have it ready for me inside."

He paused, looked at the picture printed on the plastic, and then smiled at her. "You're not all that photogenic, are you?"

She reached out the window and tried to playfully slap his arm. She missed. "Stop it, Sam."

He handed it to her. "You must be pretty special. Usually takes a good couple of months to get a permanent clearance."

"Well, there's a lot of work to get done," she deflected. "Thanks again."

"You bet." He went back in, and the gate slid open. The steel one-way spikes lowered under the weight of the truck as the tires moved over them and clicked back up once it passed. Ellie navigated the truck to an empty section on the far end of the lot. She liked parking farther away. It gave her time to think and process on the walk in. She turned off the engine and kept her hands on the steering wheel, staring out her windshield at the four-story building in front of her—beige-painted brick and lined with darkened windows. It was surreal being here, holding a badge that claimed her title as an independent contractor with the Drug Enforcement Administration. A badge that, for all intents and purposes, gave her as much clearance and authority as an actual agent. Seven months ago she had walked across the inlaid seal at Langley for the last time and moved here with the resolve to never work for any kind of GO again. But little Adam Stark's murder had immediately softened her resolve, and today would be her first day with her feet on the ground. After agreeing to Garrett's proposal to come work with him, Ellie had spent her first week here undergoing interviews, personality and cognitive testing, and mounds of onboarding paperwork. As Sam had noted, it was a process that usually happened over the course of a couple months, if not longer, but Garrett had massaged his influence to dramatically speed up the process. The last two weeks Ellie had spent eight to ten hours a day getting up to speed on agency policies and codes and steeping herself in the "Who's Who" of the local and wider world of drug trafficking. She had also worked out an agreement with Garrett's office. She would choose when she would work, a minimum of twenty hours a week and no more than thirty, with Garrett reserving the right to call her in if her absence was hindering specific progress or delaying results. Key people in the office would assist her where needed, but Garrett did not yet have the flexibility of pulling them completely off their own cases or workflows. Ellie would be getting Agent Mark Palfrey's help for up to twenty hours a week. Mark was young, just twenty-eight, and entering his third year with the DEA, coming on after getting a master's degree in special investigations and spending three years with the forensics division of the Atlanta PD. His current role with the DEA was an Intelligence Research Specialist which had him working closely with Special Agents as well as managing research into drug cultivation and production, trafficking routes, and analyzing the flow of money in and out of those trafficking organizations. As it was, the Miami office had co-opted him to focus so much into the workings of drug movements in the Fort Lauderdale area that he, as yet, did not have the freedom to cast his gaze and research onto Lee County. Bringing Ellie on and assigning her and Mark to a team was Garrett's way of subtly giving the finger to his superiors in Miami. He had taken the helm of the Fort Myers office to restrict the cartels' access to their coasts, and he had decided to make that happen with or without their consent.

Garrett was much different than the person Ellie remembered from their high school and college days. He was grounded and clear thinking, mature and confident. The choice he had made years ago to ensure that his life went a meaningful direction had clearly paid off. It was almost unheard of for someone in their mid-thirties to be in charge of a regional division, but it was easy to see why he was. In the short three weeks Ellie had been coming here, she noticed the high regard in which those in the office held their Special Agent in Charge. He had a reputation as a boss who wasn't timid about getting his hands dirty or performing routine, ordinary tasks. It was the reason he had bumped into Ellie and Major that day in the Sound. Carl Rickman, a Special Agent, had come down sick that morning, and Garrett took his place out on the water performing routine checks along the coastline. Garrett was also quick to acknowledge his lack of experience in certain areas and often deferred to the experience of older agents. The office loved him for this quality. Know-it-alls didn't get very far, and Garrett was an expert at creating teams that could function at a high level by drawing on the specialized talents and experiences of each member of the team.

Garrett had been spot on when he pitched his offer to Ellie at the coffeehouse last month. Ellie had met most everyone in the office over the last three weeks, and they were all tasked in some capacity with either finding drugs on the street or supporting the agents who did. Not a single team was dedicated to finding those at the top: the men or women connected to the Narcs, the ones actually bringing the drugs into local coastlines. Miami had a cargo ship full of agents designated for such anti-narcotic activity, but not one of them had a cubicle up here. Along the coast from Sarasota to Everglades City, there were hundreds of miles of coastline running along estuaries, coves, rivers, and the fringes of small islands, all providing sufficient opportunity to clandestinely import illicit drugs.

When Ellie had called Tyler and told him she'd accepted the offer, he'd been pleased and said that he would notify *The View* that she would be declining their offer. The news of the boy's death had spread quickly, raising tempers in every bar and fish house on the island. Tyler, like everyone else in the community, was angry at the apparent cause of, and connection to, young Adam's murder. It was Citrus who hadn't been so thrilled that she had taken the job. He was used to his owner being around all the time, coming and going throughout the day, often taking him with her to The Salty Mangrove or out on a run. She'd given him a good belly scratch this morning and promised him that, now that she was ready to get started, she wouldn't be stuck at the office as much. Citrus had run five full circles around the living room, yapping the entire time. He would have, of course, done so if she had only said "Good morning." Ellie had recruited Major to bring Citrus over to the bar on the days she wouldn't be around.

Ellie grabbed her backpack, stepped from the truck, and started walking across the dark asphalt of the newly paved parking lot. It was a perfect Florida morning. Warm, not chilly. Humid, not wet. A few clouds sliding lazily through the blue sky like stray wisps of cotton candy. A perfect day to be out on the water or lying on a beach.

Or for taking the first steps to track down a young boy's murderer.

The news of Adam Stark's murder had hit the wire nearly a month ago, and the county had, as yet, found nothing substantial in the way of clues. Tire treads were discovered in the soft soil from two different trucks, all of them ubiquitous. The cocaine found dusted on a saw palmetto was still at the lab, and results weren't due for another two weeks. A couple boot prints showing a size fourteen were discovered near the water. That was it. No hairs, no fingerprints, no fibers. Nothing that would lead them beyond the crime scene. No one had seen any trucks go or come out of the trees near the waterline, and there were no cameras within a three-mile radius. If the murderer was going to be found, it would only be through the result of digging into the undergrowth of the local drug industry.

Ellie walked up to the glass door at the front of the building, scanned her badge on the card reader, and opened the door once it beeped and the diode on top turned green. The ground floor lobby was everything one would expect from a government building. Gray marble floors, a couple leather couches in the corner that no one ever used. Three artificial trees on either side. She walked up to the guard desk and set her badge on the counter. The man behind it replaced it with three pieces of paper.

"Sign those for me." He handed Ellie a pen. She signed them and set the pen down.

"Thank you," he said. "I'll scan these in and email

them to your SAIC." He opened a drawer and pulled out her permanent badge. "Here you go. You're all set."

"Thank you," she said, then set her backpack on the conveyor belt and walked through the metal detector. Another guard watched a monitor as her bag went through and handed it to her when it came out the other side.

"Have a good one," he said.

Ellie walked toward the elevator. The building had been erected in the sixties and for thirty-odd years had been the offices for local businesses and a couple NGOs. As the decades moved on, tenants became attracted to newer office parks that had greater curb appeal, leaving half the spaces vacant save for the spiders and June bugs that squatted in them. The government finally purchased the building around the turn of the millennium, drove out the remaining tenants, and gave the exterior a facelift. Now, the first floor and half of the second were the local offices for the ATF: Alcohol, Tobacco, Firearms, and Explosives; the third floor was marked for the Department of Homeland but sat eerily vacant; and the fourth was the DEA. Ellie punched the elevator button and mentally massaged two words while she listened to the elevator click and rattle down the shaft.

Mateo Nunez. The name came with an image. Large round face with black hair slicked back into a ponytail. A square chin and a fat nose huddled under small but piercing eyes. He was one of two local men who were known as heads of their respective drug operations and believed to be operating somewhere in the general vicinity of Fort Myers. The other man was Sebastián Zamaco, and a clear picture of him had yet to be put in his file. A sketch from five years ago had been pulled off a surveillance camera at a gas station in Marathon, and it had only showed a third of his face in a grainy black and white. Some had doubted if it was really even him. No other likenesses of Zamaco had been seen. The dubious sketch showed a man with a high forehead and bushy eyebrows, full cheekbones, and thick lips. The image rendered by an artist had the artificial look that seemed inherent in composite sketches: obtuse eyes, unshadowed cheekbones, and overdrawn areas where the actual features were yet unknown or unclear. After spending the last week studying the files of both men, and what little was known of their organizations, Ellie had decided to start with Nunez's organization. Zamaco's file was cold, and Nunez's was warmer only because two drug houses busted in the last year had been his. He had not been on the scene during the raids, and a man in handcuffs had finally admitted the house was Nunez's. The man was killed in prison four months later, no one admitting to witnessing who had sliced his throat with a shank made from dozens of sharpened paper clips woven together.

The elevator gave a muffled ding, and its stainless steel doors slid open. Once inside the car, Ellie scanned her badge and rode to the top. The doors slid back to reveal an open floor plan. A pony wall enclosed two thirds of the floor space, interior windows rising off of it all the way up to the tiled ceiling. Behind the glass was a sea of cubicles, and behind them, along the exterior wall, were small offices. Garrett's was on the far end, was larger than the rest, and looked down on East Fort Myers. Ellie walked down a hallway and turned left into the main conference room where two people sat with their backs to the windows. They all exchanged greetings, and Ellie took a seat at the other side of the table.

"Ready to get at this?" The voice belonged to Special Agent Tim "Jet" Jahner. Jet was in charge of the office's Special Response Team and was approaching sixty, his gray hair trying to turn white. He had been a part of the Fort Myers DEA team for twenty of his thirty-one years with the agency, was as fit as a drill sergeant, and often acted like one. His strong, toned muscles pressed out on his blue polo. Jet's field experience was unsurpassed and envied across the entire floor. If it was illegal and was growing or being cooked in Lee County, Jet's team would lead the task force that would get it out of the wrong hands. Jet had been in Medellin the day Escobar was gunned down by the Search Bloc nearly three decades ago and had been a key figure in advocating for Garrett - young, talented, and motivated - to lead their office and to begin focusing their sights on the bigger fish. Part of the agency's agreement with Garrett in giving him the Fort Myers office came with a promise to give him the freedom and resources to dig deeper into the local underworld. Ultimately, they failed to live up to the promise. They gave him the office but kept him centered on street drugs instead of the high-level suppliers. Someone had noted it was like a parent giving their child permission to dig for gold in the backyard while keeping them busy with inside chores. Garrett wasn't against getting drugs off the streets, but he saw it as a Band-Aid solution instead of addressing the festering wound underneath.

Ellie pulled a notebook out of her backpack and looked at Jet. "You bet I am," she answered.

"Garrett should be here in a second," Jet said. "In

the meantime I think I'll grab a cup of coffee." He got up and walked to the Keurig at the other end of the room. It sat underneath a flat screen television on a small hutch that also held paper cups, coffee condiments, and a couple speakers that were connected to the television.

The DEA conference room was another testament to the distribution of taxpayer money gone awry. A twenty-foot conference table made of polished walnut sat in the center, surrounded by modern office chairs dressed in blue faux leather and set with chromed arms —pleasant to the eye but not to the backside. Two modern art statues sat in a corner. No one knew what they represented or whether they were supposed to mean anything at all. One was a twisted piece of metal that looked like it might be a giraffe reaching for food, and the other was a peculiar amalgam between a Rubik's cube and an apple tree. Framed pictures of beaches and sunsets hung on the cream-colored walls, and a regal chandelier hung over the conference table. Ellie thought the designer had too much money and advanced cataracts.

Mark Palfrey, Ellie's new partner, was positioned next to Jet's empty chair. Standing, he came in at five feet nine inches, and his short brown hair was thinning on top, giving him advance notice that he would be bald in the next four years. He was slender, had wide shoulders, sharp eyes. He smiled at Ellie and pointed at her with his pen. "First day on the job. I guess that makes you the newbie."

"Newbie!" Jet chimed in from across the room. "That says hazing to me."

Ellie's eyebrows shot up. "Try it, gentlemen, and see if you're not sorry for a very long time."

"I don't know, Jet...I hear she's like an ex-Navy SEAL or something."

"I heard she was Mossad and was single-handedly responsible for bringing down the KGB."

"You're both right," she said, grinning. Garrett had given the men, as well as a couple others in the office, a thirty-thousand-foot view of Ellie's past career. It was a hazy outline at best, with all details withheld. The secrecy only added to the enigma, and, over the last three weeks, the office had been taking guesses at what had occupied her past professional life. All things considered, her new co-workers had not the faintest clue about her previous employment.

Garrett walked in with a stack of folders under one arm and mug of coffee in the other. He shut the door with his foot and took a seat next to Ellie. "Morning, everyone."

"Morning," they chimed.

Jet returned from the coffee maker, took a seat. Garrett set the files down and pushed them out in front. "Everyone take one, please." He smiled. "This is a big morning. I want to formally welcome Ellie to our team. Mark and Jet, you know how passionate I've been about finding the cat instead of chasing the tail. I want to take a few minutes and make sure we all get started on the right foot and that we're clear on how things are moving forward from here. You all know that when I was given this office late last year, I did so with the promise that I would be given a team that would dig further down. A few weeks into my time here, my direct report in Miami was replaced, and I was never given that team." He leaned in, set his elbows on the table, and tossed his hands out. "This is where I grew up." He nodded at Ellie. "It's where Ellie grew up. Jet's called it home for a couple decades, and his grandkids live here. I want to clean up the rats that are invading the shadows. That's why I'm here, and that's why she's here. I'm not asking either one of you or anyone on your teams to stop what they're doing now. If anything, I'm asking you to add to it, so thank you for your willingness. Now, here's how we're going to do this." He opened up a folder, looked into it, and the three others followed suit.

"The three of you already know the two men we're trying to target, so I won't go into that now. It's in your folders, and you'll be getting an email today with further details. Mark, I want you to see what you can turn up with old leads. Suppliers, runners, dealers, you name it. Everyone knows someone, and that someone knows someone. If we can understand the network, the associations, we can start making progress. Ellie, if you need anything from another agency that would be helpful, I can get you in touch with the right person." Garrett's connections and associations with the other agencies ran deep. He was on a first-name basis with white collars in the Department of Homeland, Department of Justice, Coast Guard, Sheriff's Office, even some brass in the Navy. Every organization but the FBI. He had made some connections with the FBI soon after his arrival, but those didn't go very far. The FBI was exceptional at what they did, but interfacing and working smoothly with the DEA was not one of those things. The FBI was responsible for enforcing over two hundred categories of federal law. The DEA was a single-mission organization tasked solely with enforcing drug laws. When the two jurisdictions overlapped, some rooster was bound to spread his wings and show everyone that his agency was in charge. "Mark, you'll be Ellie's liaison with the agency. You're the only person in this building given a specific block of hours to help her. She needs more than that, you have to clear it with me first."

"Got it," Mark said.

Garrett looked at Ellie. "Wish I could give you more, but I'm already going to get questions I don't want for cutting his field hours in half."

"No worries," she said. "We'll make it work."

Garrett addressed Jet and Mark. "You need to know that I appreciate your commitment to this agency and what we stand for. You're some of the best at what you do. I don't want you stepping into something that detracts from your primary directive as given to us from Miami. If you can't do your daily job well and help me a little on the side, then don't. Track your bottom feeders, make your arrests, go on your raids, push your paperwork. That's what the top brass wants, that's what we're going to give them. If you can't continue doing that with excellence alongside what I'm asking of you in addition, then tell me, and I'll take you off. No harm done. We good with that?"

Two heads bobbed.

"Mark, I'll expect you to ensure Ellie has what she needs and that any requests get completed quickly. "

"So," Jet spoke up, smiling. "You mean Mark's getting a promotion to a glorified secretary?"

Everyone laughed, and Garrett said, "Find time this week to bring Ellie up on what you know. Logistically and organizationally, you know more than anyone here.

Ellie, for the time being direct your questions to Jet. He'll have answers I won't have."

"Got it."

"I don't have anyone else in here this morning because we're just getting started. If we start to see progress on your end, we'll loop in more to assist where needed. For now, there is a ton of paperwork to comb through and organize. You should be able to find something in there that launches you off."

When Garrett first joined the Fort Myers office just nine months ago, he'd discovered a storage room filled with stacks of file boxes rising so high some of them had pushed up the ceiling tiles. The agents that had worked those cases had, in the course of their careers, moved to other offices, some retiring. The thin film of dust over the room was a testimony to poor management and mishandled information. Garrett was intent at finding out what was in there. His experience had taught him that, in the drug world, where blood flowed easily and money was spent quickly, old cases and personal files were never irrelevant. Networks spread and moved dynamically, hardly the same today as they were six months ago. The low-level guys changed all the time. They got arrested, killed, deported. But it was rare that leadership changed. They were the feared ones, the leadership that everyone was too scared to touch. In Garrett's world, if you had even waved at anyone known to be connected with moving or dealing drugs, you were marked and noted. It was a good philosophy, even if it made his administrative staff try hard not to hate him. *Connections, connections, connections.* That was his motto. Everyone, he said, is connected. You sniff blow, you got it from someone. They got it from someone, and they got it from someone. You don't shoot up, but you know someone who does, you're connected.

Garrett continued. "Ellie is here to help us find the invisible hands. She'll have the flexibility to do things we may not be able to. Please do not ask her to do something directly. Run it through me first. You're to act as her support team where you can. She needs something, you give it to her. Good?"

Two heads bobbed again.

"If she finds some success, I'll have a better chance of convincing my own bosses to allocate more resources to what's she doing and hopefully build out a full team for that."

"We're looking forward to working with you, Ellie," Jet said.

"Yeah, we are." Mark agreed.

They spent the next fifteen minutes reviewing the documents in front of them and discussing strategies for moving forward. When they were done, Garrett grabbed his binder and stood. "All right, everyone have a bang-up day. Ellie, why don't you follow me to my office?"

Ellie grabbed her things and followed her old friend and new boss into his office. "Shut the door, will you?" The wall behind his desk was painted with whiteboard paint. He grabbed a large picture the size of a sheet of legal paper off his desk. He snagged a piece of tape from the tape roll, attached it to the picture, and stuck it on the wall.

Mateo Nunez.

Garrett grabbed another picture and repeated his movements.

Sebastián Zamaco.

"Okay…" he said. "There we are." He grabbed a

red dry erase marker that was peeking out from a stack of paperwork and drew a short line down from Nunez's picture and then traced a square. He wrote an address in the box and then repeated the action a second time with a new address in the next box. "These are the locations we raided last year. You have access to everything we've got on this and all the arrests involved. After that prison killing last year, I'm willing to bet that you'll have a hard time getting anything out of anyone remotely connected with Nunez. Everyone will probably be as quiet as a turkey on Thanksgiving Eve."

He took the marker and drew an empty box next to Zamaco's picture. I'm sure there's a third we need to be looking at, probably a fourth and fifth. The problem right now is that we don't know anything about them - or if they even exist." He jutted his chin toward Zamaco's likeness. "He's a big question mark right now, so again, the boxes of files may help.

"I've got time dedicated to going through all that," Ellie said. "But I think our best leads will come from interviewing the right people."

"Agreed." He tossed the marker on the desk and grabbed his keys. "Speaking of which. Come on. Let's go pay someone a visit."

CHAPTER TEN

Five minutes later Ellie and Garrett were in Garrett's agency-issue Ford Expedition, heading west into Cape Coral. He had the windows down and his cuffs rolled up. The radio was set to a low volume, the music welcoming someone to the Hotel California, which apparently was a lovely place and had plenty of room.

"Did IT get your remote access set up yet?"

"I haven't checked yet," she said.

"If it's not, it should be in the next couple days. That will give you access to certain files when you're out of the office. Not all of them, but it should keep you from having to come in as much."

"So who is it we're going to see?" she asked.

"Jimmy Joe Claude," He said slowly, like it was fun to say.

"Jimmy Joe Claude?"

"Yep. Three first names. He was destined for greatness, but his mother gave him three first names. He's been out of the can for a couple weeks now. I want to see if we can get something fresh out of him."

"So who is he?"

"Low level. I got him tossed in on minor possession charges right after I started here. The judge pinned seven months on him. Too stupid not to get caught doing something every couple years, but he's got more connections than Kevin Bacon."

"Where's he live?"

"A couple clicks north of St. James City."

Jimmy Joe Claude's house was a small, one-story box house that looked sad and neglected. An old gray Buick sat in front of a rotting wood garage door, had a flat tire, and the upholstery on the inside canopy was drooping down. The lap siding on the house was sagging, and most of its old paint had dried, peeled, and chipped off, leaving behind an unhappy exterior that was struggling under excessive rot and sun damage.

Ellie and Garrett stepped out of the car and walked up the cracked concrete steps and onto the porch. Garrett knocked on the aluminum screen door. The magnetic hum of a TV could be heard from the other side.

"Who is it?" a hoarse voice yelled from inside.

Garrett leaned in. "DEA, ma'am."

They heard nothing for half a minute. He raised his hand, about to knock again, when the lock clicked back on the door and it opened on a woman with shoulder-length, gray hair, curled tight like it had been over-permed. She wasn't fat, but she wasn't slim. Her breasts sagged into a ratty beige tank top that looked like it had been in the wash about the same time she had been in the shower. And that, apparently, had been quite some time ago.

The lady rolled her eyes. "What'd he do now?" she asked.

"Nothing, ma'am. We're just trying to find some answers and want to see if Jimmy might be able to help us."

"That damn boy," she said.

"Are you his mother?" he asked.

She sighed, shook her head, and started walking back into the house. "Come on," she said.

Ellie opened the screen door and stepped in first with Garrett following behind her. It was humid inside, like the air conditioner had rebelled, leaving it far warmer than even a pig's comfort level, creating an atmosphere that amplified pungent smells of cat urine, sour milk, and old newspaper. Ellie's throat cringed, and she took small, short breaths in an effort to delay the added smell of her stomach's contents to the mix.

The curtains were drawn, and sunlight streamed through the light blue fabric, giving the room a soft, eerie glow. An overfilled litter box was stuffed in a corner, and the dark green carpet was threadbare in places and littered with piles of dirty clothes, unopened envelopes, and empty cans of Bud Light. She returned to an upholstered easy chair that faced an old wood-paneled TV, blaring a midday talk show where someone was screaming about DNA and sperm and daddies and child support. The woman lifted a half-empty pack of Camels from a TV tray that functioned as an end table. She pulled out a stick, stuck it between her receding lips. She lit up and put the lighter down along with the pack. Keeping her eyes on the television, she asked reluctantly, "So, what do you want?"

Garrett's badge hung from a chain around his neck. He grabbed it and, in a show of display, held it up. "I'm Agent Garrett Cage, and this is Ellie O'Conner. You're Jimmy's mother...Loribelle?"

"Uh huh."

"Is Jimmy here?" Garrett asked.

"No."

"Do you know where he is?"

"Probably workin'. He don't tell me."

"Where is he working?"

"He don't tell me." She didn't bring her eyes away from the television.

Garrett released a curtailed sigh. "He hasn't told you where he's working?"

"That's what I said. He leaves 'round mid-mornin', comes home 'bout supper time. Brings me my TV dinners and mangoes, then goes back to his room. Don't know why he brings me the mangoes. He knows I hate the damn things."

"Then why do you think he brings you mangoes?" Ellie jumped in.

She shrugged. "Gets 'em from work probably. Or steals 'em. All of 'em are half bruised. Don't rightly care."

Garrett looked at Ellie and then back to Loribelle.

Ellie's lungs were screaming for an upgraded quality of air.

"What kind of hours does he keep?" Garrett pressed.

Loribelle sighed. "Don't pay no attention. I hear him

in the middle of the night sometimes, but I don't know if it's him leavin' or just gettin' up to use the head."

"Does he ever have any friends over or mention who he hangs out with?"

The older lady huffed, or choked, or sneezed; Ellie wasn't sure. "If he got friends that ain't locked up or dead, I don't know nothin' about them."

Garrett looked at Ellie again and nodded slightly toward the door.

"Thank you for your time," Ellie said. She laid her card on the TV tray between the half-eaten bag of Ruffles and the overflowing ashtray. Here's my number if you do come onto any answers. You might be hearing from me again if we need anything else."

Loribelle said nothing, immersed in her show.

Ellie and Garrett made their way to the door and walked out into fresh, salty air.

"Well, that was painful," Ellie said after they got back in the car.

"I think the agency needs to start issuing nose plugs. I'm pretty sure that's where plagues start," Garrett said as he put his hands on the steering wheel. "So, where to? Mangoes and nothing. That's all we got."

"We could try the Winn-Dixie or Mr. Jensen's fruit stand. Or we could visit a couple of the growers. Maybe he's working at one of them," Ellie said.

"Worth a shot. Let me try something first." Garrett pulled out his phone, searched his contacts, and dialed a number.

"Reece, hey, it's Garrett. Listen, I need you to find the number to Claude's parole officer and give him a call. Ask him if he has a job on file. It's probably bogus, but it's worth me checking out." A pause and Garrett replied, "No, he's not here. His angel of a mother doesn't know anything." Another pause. "No, I mean I really don't think she knows anything. She's...well, let's just say that Jimmy may have a good alibi for why he turned out the way he did." Ellie could hear more words coming through the earpiece but couldn't make them out. "I know," Garrett replied. "Just tell the parole officer we're working a lead on some product. Make it clear we don't currently suspect Jimmy. That's important. If he still won't give it to you, fill out a formal request and email it to his supervisor."

They hung up, and Garrett looked at Ellie. "I'll wait for him to call me back, see if that saves us from driving all over the island looking for him."

"If we're going to be tracking down mangoes, let's start at The Groovy Grove," Ellie said. "The Potters were over at The Salty Mangrove last week. They're good people and would help if they know anything. If nothing else, they may have heard another grower mention Jimmy."

"Fair enough," Garrett said.

Ellie spent the next several minutes reviewing a couple files she had retrieved from her backpack. Finally, Garrett's contact called him back. When he hung up, he said, "No dice. Parole officer didn't answer." He pulled down on the gear shift and started driving away from the small house, and Ellie stared at it as they left.

"Do me a favor, Garrett. Next time you want to take me into a place like that, at least have the courtesy to issue me a hazmat suit."

"Done," he said. "Speaking of which, let's stop somewhere and get something to drink first. I have to wash the scent of the pit of hell from my mouth."

CHAPTER ELEVEN

THE GROOVY GROVE WAS THE LARGEST AND OLDEST commercial mango grove on Pine Island, nestled in the center of Pineland. It boasted fifty-two acres of fully grown fruit trees, trees that shot upwards a hundred and twenty feet and extended their branches out fifteen feet from the center.

Garrett turned the Expedition west onto Pineland Road and crept along for a quarter mile before turning right into the dirt parking lot of the Grove. The parking arrangement consisted of two long rows separated by a thick steel cable threaded through short wooden posts. Ellie and Garrett stepped out and made their way to a small white building sitting at the edge of the grassline. The building had a quaint window that looked out to the street beyond and was surrounded by flower gardens full of petunias and sunflowers. Pots of yellow and orange marigolds were scattered around the perimeter. Wooden steps led up to the door.

"You ever been out here before?" Ellie asked him.

"Nope. You?"

"Sharla's an old friend. My father used to bring me out here to pick when I was little. It's been a long time."

As they approached the steps, an older lady appeared from around the corner. "Hello there," she said. "May I help you?" Strands of long gray hair hung out from beneath a wide straw gardening hat, and her eyes were hidden behind sunglasses. She was slender and wore an open, long-sleeved denim shirt over a muted pink T-shirt featuring the Groovy Grove logo. Her hands were enclosed in cotton gardening gloves. Ellie had always thought of Sharla as the embodiment of Southern hospitality and grace.

"Sharla, hi. It's Ellie."

"Ellie, sweetie. How are you? I didn't recognize you with those shades on." Sharla stepped in and gave her a hug from the side. "It's always so good to see you."

"How is business here at The Grove?"

"We're doing fine," Sharla said. "Still trying to hold out and remain traditional. Everything farming has moved into big time production, and sometimes it seems like we're back in the stone age trying to keep things the way we like them."

"Do you still have your own bees?"

"You bet your bell bottoms we do."

Ellie politely took a step back. "Sharla, this is Garrett. Garrett Cage."

"Ma'am." He nodded toward her and offered a hand. Sharla removed a glove and shook it.

"Hello, Garrett," she replied. "Nice to have you out here."

"Thank you."

Sharla turned her attention back to Ellie. "So what

can I do for you? Are you wanting to schedule a time to pick?"

"Unfortunately not." She looked over at Garrett. "Garrett is a special agent with the Drug Enforcement Administration, and I'm working with him now on a particular basis."

"DEA? Well, I'm afraid the strongest drug I have around here is a little bit of coffee." She smiled.

"Nothing like that, Mrs. Potter," Garrett said. "We're looking for someone specific and wanted to come by on a long shot and see if you might know anything."

"Of course, whatever I can do to help." She shook her head. "It's just terrible about that young boy a few weeks back. From what the news folks were saying, it sounded like he might have stumbled onto some drug deal or something."

Ellie pursed her lips. "It seems that way."

"It's hard to believe that things like that happen in our little private corner of the world," Sharla said. "Well, I don't know that I can be much help, but if I can offer anything that might put a dent in all this nonsense I'll be glad to."

"Thank you," Ellie and Garrett said in unison.

"Ellie, you're working with the DEA now? I thought you were working with Warren over at the bar?"

"I'm still helping down there. Garrett and I are old friends, and he asked me to help them out with a few things. It keeps me a little busier."

"Well, busy is good, especially at your young age." She smiled. "Do you remember when your father used to bring you and your sister up here to pick? You both were so little. Gary and I had just bought the place."

Ellie pushed off the wave of sadness that tried to wash over her and forced a smile. "I do. Those are good memories."

"If I remember correctly, your father thought he was tough enough not to need gloves and ended up with a rash that lasted over a week."

"He was stubborn sometimes. Well, most of the time."

Sharla waved a hand. "Anyway, you didn't come out here to walk down a lane called Memory with me. So how do you think I might help to stop this whole criminal underworld?"

"Well, ma'am," Garrett said, "we're looking for a man named Jimmy Joe Claude and thought he might be out this way. Any chance you've heard the name or know him?"

"Ah, of course," she said. "He came to us, oh, a couple weeks ago and asked for a job."

Garrett looked at Ellie and raised his eyebrows.

"Gary wasn't all that keen on the idea, but I believe everyone deserves a fresh start." She set her hands on her hips. "I sure hope that boy is serious about that."

"Is he here now?" Ellie asked.

"Sure is." She extended her arm and pointed beyond the office. "He'll be about halfway back through the grove, picking. Did he do something? I know he has a reputation around the island for trouble. I just hope he doesn't bring any here."

"No, ma'am," Garrett said. "He's not in any trouble. We only want to ask him some questions and see if he can help us find some answers. We don't suspect him directly of anything."

"Good." She nodded and relaxed the muscles in her

face. "Good. Well, he's back there if you want to have a talk with him. Just make sure he's not picking while he's talking. The new guys always forget the wash if they're talking or not keeping their minds on the simple things."

"Of course. Thank you, Sharla. It was good seeing you," Ellie said.

"You too, sweetheart. You let me know if you need anything else. Stop by the shop here on your way out, and I'll let you both go with a bottle of chutney."

"Certainly will. Thank you, Mrs. Potter," Garrett said.

Garrett and Ellie made their way through the rows of trees in the general direction pointed out by Sharla. The grass came in ankle high and looked to be about ready for a good mowing.

"So, your dad," Garrett said. "He was allergic to mangoes or something?"

"Allergic? No. Why?"

"Mrs. Potter said something about a rash."

"Have you ever picked a mango?"

"Nuh-uh."

"Mango sap is highly acidic, so when you pick off the stem it spits that stuff at you, and if it gets on your skin it can burn it. It doesn't show up for a day or two. Pickers have to wash or rinse whatever they pick within a few seconds or it will leave a mark on the fruit and make it hard to sell. I'll show you when we get out there."

"Who knew?" he said.

It was another five minutes of maneuvering between the trees before they heard snipping sounds a couple rows over. They followed the soft noise and came out onto a row where a man was standing on a small lift and reaching up into the higher branches of a tree with a picking stick. He snipped a branch, and the picking stick held onto the fruit. He lowered it down and released the mango onto a rubber tarp. Garrett came nearer and called out before getting too close.

"Hello, Jimmy," Garrett said, lifting his voice and crossing his arms.

The man swung around, and Ellie immediately concluded that he was the clear progeny of his mother. His face was sunken and narrow, the inevitable result of rampant drug use. His eyes sat too far back into his head, and the furrows on his face made him look ten years older than he probably was. His light brown hair was beginning to gray, slicked back so hard the lines left by the comb were still visible, so greasy it could have lubricated an entire diesel block and still have some left over.

He wore faded black jeans too big for his skinny legs and a thin Rolling Stones T-shirt that sat on shoulders the size of sticks. He eyed them suspiciously before recognizing Garrett, then sighed and shook his head. "Hey, I haven't done nothin', okay?" He looked around shiftily. "You gonna get me fired with them wondering why the DEA is out to see me."

"We're not going to get you fired, Jimmy," Garrett said firmly. "We already told Mrs. Potter that we wanted to talk with you and that everything is fine. We only have questions. Can you come down here please?"

"Well, talk with me later. I'm workin' right now."

"We already went to your house and spoke with your lovely mother," Garrett said. "I didn't waste my time tracking you down out here to talk with you another time."

"I'm not into anything. I've cleaned up and am going straight."

"Yeah, you and Boy George," Garrett replied. "You know things Jimmy, things that we would like to know too."

"So?"

"So I need your help. Can you come down here?"

Jimmy sighed again and pushed a button on the lift that lowered him down to the ground. He lifted the safety bar and stepped out into the grass. "I got nothin' to say." His eyes bored into Garrett's. "Especially to you."

Garrett smiled smugly. "I mentioned that we went by your mother's house. You know, it smelled like she was diffusing essential oils." He looked at Ellie and snapped his fingers. "I forget, Ellie, what was the name of that scent she had going?"

"I believe they're calling it Mighty Marijuana, Garrett."

Jimmy's eyes widened briefly. He rubbed the back of his neck, pockmarked by adolescent acne twenty years now gone.

"I'm sure I could go over there right now and find a dub bag or two," Garrett continued, "but I don't want to do that. If you say you're trying to go straight, I...well, I'm not sure I believe you, but I'll go with it. You're out here sweating for a few bucks an hour for whatever reason, so I'll buy it for now. Just help me out, and we can leave you alone."

Jimmy brought a hand up to his pointy, stubbled chin and rubbed it. "Well, get on with it," he finally muttered.

Garrett reached behind him and retrieved his wallet

from his back pocket. He slipped a couple fingers in between the leather folds and pulled out a small picture. He held it up. Jimmy squinted at it.

"You seen this boy in the news?"

"Nope. Don't watch the news." Jimmy turned his head - not enough - and spit into the grass, almost hitting Garrett's shoes.

"Well, he was murdered a few weeks ago by someone dealing."

"Who killed him?"

"We don't know who killed him."

"Then how do you know they was dealin'?"

Garrett sighed and put the picture back. "It doesn't matter, Jimmy. The facts are what they are, and we want to find the person who did it. What have you heard?"

"Look, man," Jimmy said. "I ain't into killing no kids. I ain't into killing nobody. Have I done drugs, moved drugs? Yeah, I done drugs and moved drugs. But that's it." He raised his thin eyebrows. "And not no more either."

"But you know people who deal who would be the kind to kill a child?" Ellie asked.

Jimmy rubbed a shirt sleeve across his forehead and looked indifferently at Ellie. "'Course I do. But that doesn't mean I know who done it. You got a couple hundred people in this county pushin' drugs on some level and ten thou or more using 'em. Who's willin' to kill a kid over it?" He shrugged. "Beats me. Coulda been high, coulda been for leverage, revenge. Who knows? Sounds like you got a snark on your hands. Besides, I ain't no snitch."

"I'm not asking you to rat anybody out, Jimmy," Garrett said. "I'm just looking for direction. Something -

anything - that can help us get these guys. Right now I'm walking in blind."

Jimmy sighed again, spit again. "There's a guy in the clink in Hardee Correctional. Works with Nunez on some level."

"Tommy?" Garrett asked.

"No, not Tommy. You gonna let me finish?"

"Go ahead, Jimmy," Ellie said.

"He's two through a dime for moving coke. Victor. Victor Calderón. But he's gettin' tired. Wants to get outta there. He was a tough guy going in but ended up getting a chitolean for a cellmate, and he's had to hold his pocket for two years now. You ask, he'll probably talk. If," he said with emphasis, "you cut him a deal. 'Cause if Nunez finds out he talked..." Jimmy ran his index finger around his throat.

"That all?" Garrett asked, jotting notes on a pocket-sized pad.

"Look, man. You come bug me at work, threaten about my mother. I give you some goods and you want more? Get the hell out of here. I ain't doin' your job for you."

"You were in the clink for what, six, seven months?" Garrett said. "I'll bet you held someone's pocket, didn't you?"

Ellie shot her eyes toward Garrett. "We appreciate the help, Jimmy," she said. "We really do." She shifted her focus behind him. "Do you mind if I borrow that picker from you for a minute?"

"Uh, sure." He shrugged but didn't remove his glare from Garrett.

Ellie walked behind him and grabbed up the eight-foot picker. She stood under the tree and looked up, trying to find a ripe mango near enough so she wouldn't have to use the lift. Finding one, she extended the pole and set the pinchers around the stem of the fruit. She pulled the handle, and it cut the stem and held onto it. She brought it down and released the mango into her hand. "Thanks, Jimmy," she said, handing the picker back to him. She motioned for Garrett to come closer. "Once you've got it in hand, you grab the top of the stem and pull it back." The stem snapped and what looked like spit flew out of the newly-formed navel. "That stuff is the sap." She stepped over to a large container filled with clear fluid and submerged it. "This is the mango wash." After leaving the mango under the clear liquid for a couple seconds, she pulled it out and held it up. "That's all there is to it. Just have to keep the acid off the fruit's skin."

"I never would have known." He smiled.

Ellie gently set the mango with the other picked ones, then wiped her hands on a rag hanging from the lift.

She turned and smiled at Jimmy. "Thank you again."

He nodded, put his gloves back on, grabbed the stick, and got back in the lift. She and Garrett turned and started the walk back to the car.

"Hey," Jimmy called out. They turned and looked at him. His face was softer but not soft. "Hope y'all find who killed that boy."

"Thanks, Jimmy," Ellie said.

They were both quiet on their exit from the grove. Ellie finally spoke up. "What do you think?" she asked.

"He gets under my skin, that guy. I haven't seen a turd like him clean up yet."

"I meant what he gave us."

"Yeah. I know. It's worth checking out."

"I'll do it," she offered. "If someone is going to try talking with Victor, we'll probably need a way to get him out of there so Nunez doesn't find out."

"For sure. Let's schedule a meeting tomorrow back at the office, and we can figure out a plan." They came out of the grove a few yards from the parking lot.

"Let's stop in and see Sharla," Ellie said. "I'm not leaving without cashing in on free mango chutney."

CHAPTER TWELVE

"He's late," Andrés said. "I don't like it when he's late."

Chewy looked at the dash clock. "We'll give him five more. After that we're wind and spirit."

They were positioned in a twelve-year-old Chevy Malibu behind the rundown visage of an old bank which had the good fortune many years ago of being home to Martin and Hooper's Savings and Loan until it was endowed with the bad fortune of being a casualty of the eighties' S&L crisis. It never recovered and would never be absorbed into a conglomerate in small part because Fenwick Martin thereafter perished of a stress-related heart attack and in large part because Clyde Hooper put a 12 gauge in his mouth one evening and pulled the trigger. His wife reported that Clyde had told her he was getting up to get a glass of milk. "He never drank milk," she said. The bank building was never repurposed and spent the last thirty years in a commercially abandoned area of town withering away under the hot Florida sun.

"I don't remember him ever being late. Do you?"

"Nope."

"Boss isn't going to like this," Andrés said.

"No, he's not. Now quiet. I can't hear when you're thinking out loud."

"*We spend our lives under the poison of other peoples' critical gaze, never allowing ourselves to be who we really are...*"

Chewy was prone to spend idle minutes listening to what he called "prophets of personal power." Self-help gurus: Zig Ziglar, Tony Robbins, Brian Tracy. Tonight it was Johnny Burkis, the big-haired, shiny-shoed, high-pitched sage out of Salt Lake City.

"*You. You are already what you want to be. You only need to actualize it.*"

Andrés huffed and pulled out a Marlboro from the half-empty pack sitting in the center console. He grabbed a lighter, flicked his thumb over it, and the tip of the stick glowed orange. He rolled down the window and breathed out. "Actualize this," he said to the stereo and lifted his middle finger. Chewy paid no heed. His head was laid back on the headrest of the driver's seat, and his eyes were closed.

Andrés shook his head. "You drive me nuts with this."

"You listen to it enough times, and you start believing it. It's affirmation."

"Well, I affirm that it's all a load of horse crap."

"*...these people who don't believe in you and won't follow through with anything they say. I'm telling you they are poison!*" Burkis's voice channeled through the speakers with the passion of a Southern Baptist preacher seeking to convert the wayward souls of the heathen.

A beam of headlights swung around, catching the

Malibu and momentarily blinding the two men. Chewy turned off Burkis and kept his eyes on the approaching car. "It's him," he said. As was customary, they remained in their vehicle until the other party stepped out of theirs.

The Town Car stopped directly in front of them. The door opened, and the headlights flicked off. A man with skin the color of the night around them stepped out of the car. Chewy and Andrés followed suit. Chewy shut his door and walked confidently and slowly to the front of the cars. "You're late," he said.

"Yeah. Sorry."

"You've never been late before, and it makes me nervous. I don't like being nervous, Simon."

Simon looked uncomfortable, shifty. He slicked a hand down a long goat patch hanging off his chin. His thick braids were covered by a Jamaican rasta beanie. "Yeah, well...look. I've got some news you're not gonna like."

Chewy exchanged a quick glance with Andrés. "And how's that?" he asked.

"The higher-ups. They don't like all the talk about killing this kid. Too much attention."

Chewy stared at Simon. Andrés looked away and took another draw of his cigarette, his head bobbing to a silent rhythm of fresh anger, his nostrils flaring like a fish's gills.

"They think you guys had something to do with it and—"

"And what?" Andrés asked, taking a step up to him. He got in the man's face and tilted his head. "And *what?*"

Simon took a step back, his calves now touching the Town Car's bumper. "Look, I'm just the messenger. I have to tell you that we're not taking possession of the rest of our order."

Andrés flicked his cigarette at a dead palm tree hugging the back of the building. "No. Simon. No." He shook his head vigorously. "We don't do half orders. You're in it for the whole."

"We've already returned the product to the drop off, so you won't be out anything."

"That isn't the point," Andrés fumed. "We are not in the inventory business. We are in the getting it out of our hands as quickly as possible business. We don't order what we don't sell in advance. You know that."

"Like I said, I'm just the—"

"Simon. When you wipe your tail, do you do it halfway?" Andrés asked him.

"What?"

"Just answer the question," Chewy shot back.

"When you wipe your tail, do you do it halfway?" Andrés asked again.

Simon, perturbed, shook his head. "No."

"And when you screw your girlfriend, do you do it halfway?"

"No."

"Uh-huh. And when you brush your teeth, do you only do the uppers?"

"What? No."

"Right...so why would I take half an order back from you when we have already made arrangements? See where I'm going with this?"

"Guys, look. We've done business together for a long time," Simon said. "This isn't my call. You know that."

Andrés took a step back. "I know," he said. He waved a finger at the dark man. "And I like you, Simon.

But that is not the point, is it? You've put me and Chewy here in a position where we now have to go back and explain why our product is now sitting back at the drop off point for anyone to just come along and stumble upon. I don't like having these conversations with my boss." He leaned against the hood of the Malibu, set a foot on the bumper. "So here is what's going to happen. We are going to get back in our car. You are going to get back in your car." He tossed out his hands. "And we are going to drive away. You are going to retrieve said product and sell it so it's never recovered by the feds. I'm going to have to talk with the bossman and see what the repercussions of this will be. You go get the product you're trying to return. I'm not touching it unless I get the go ahead."

"I can't go back and get it. Look, I've got some stuff in my trunk right now," Simon pleaded.

"So if I ask you to open up your trunk, I'm only going to see," Andrés lowered his brows, looked up, and tossed out a few fingers as he mumbled numbers to himself. "Twelve packages? I will only see twelve packages?"

"I think it's eleven," Simon said.

He jutted his chin toward the Town Car. "Why don't you just get out of here and tell your bosses no dice. You're an idiot to even come talk to us about this. You know how we work."

Simon sighed. "All right, guys. Look, I'm sorry." He walked back and disappeared into his ride. He drove across the potholed parking lot and pulled out into the road. His taillights disappeared behind a cluster of pines.

"You believe this?" Andrés said. He and Chewy got

back in the Malibu. Both took in a deep breath and exhaled simultaneously. Chewy started the car, turned on the stereo, and drove away from the carcass of the old bank.

Burkis resumed his sermon. *"...so now if people don't keep their commitment to you. Get rid of them! They are dead weight in letting you achieve your fullest. If they can't be trusted and won't follow through, just gggggget rid of them!"*

The corners of Andrés's mouth worked into a twisted smile. "You are not kidding," he said.

CHAPTER THIRTEEN

Ellie, Mark, Jet, and Garrett sat at the monstrous table. Four others had also been brought in to discuss what was known about Victor Calderón and whether or not what Jimmy Joe Claude had provided was worth pursuing. Discussions over the last thirty minutes had the room unified that Jimmy Joe Claude's lead on Victor Calderón was worth massaging. Victor was indeed a known lieutenant of Mateo Nunez, was two years through a ten-year stint, and as of a couple months ago had been sharing a cell with Boosie Maine, a large man whose sexual proclivities leaned heavily toward the male variety.

"We can't just walk right into the prison and talk to him," Garrett said. "That will make the wrong people think he's talking, or at the very least being questioned. I'm with Ellie. We need to find a way to get him out for a while."

Mark was staring at his laptop screen. "He doesn't have any kind of pass. Hasn't been out on garbage patrol, no laundry duty, isn't allowed conjugal visits, no temporary releases. So no getting close to him via his daily routine."

Garrett eyed those around the table. "Any suggestions?"

"What about talking to him in the library after hours?" someone suggested.

"No," Jet said. "We'll have to get him off site. Anything else is too risky. Someone even smells that he's being talked to, he'll have Xs over his eyelids before the week is out. Nunez doesn't mess around."

"What about a trip to the doctor?" Ellie offered. "You know, he gets sick and has to be rushed to the hospital."

"Go on," Garrett said.

"An officer or cook could slip him some ipecac—whatever they use these days—that would make him visibly sick. That might get him to the hospital for an overnight."

Heads nodded.

Jet picked up his phone and opened his maps app. "Hardee Correctional is an hour and a half from the nearest hospital." He continued thumbing the phone. "It's about an hour from anywhere, so we need to choose the destination hospital and plan for an overnight. We can engage him while he's there or on his way back. The latter would be preferable."

Garrett leaned back in his chair and tapped the top of his pen on his chin. "All right. Let's see about getting the ball rolling on that over at Hardee." He looked back at Jet. "Do you know if we have anyone on the inside we can trust over there?"

"I have a guy at the Sheriff's Office. He'll know how to help."

"Okay." Garrett made some notes on a pad. "Get me all the specifics on your contact by tomorrow. Some of these correctional officers are as crooked as a dog's hind leg. If nothing else I'll call the warden and see about getting one of us in there to make sure it's done right." He looked down the table. "Mark, get with Kevin. He'll know who to contact for the right cocktail and dosage to get Victor temporarily sick. I'm with Ellie. I don't have a clue what that might be.

"Will do, boss."

"Jet's right. We'll keep the lowest profile engaging him on his return. With him being higher up in Nunez's org chart, they're going to have their eyes on him while he's out. Ellie, we'll bring him back in a car. Why don't you pose as the escorting officer and do your thing. We'll get you set up so the handoff at the prison goes smoothly and everything looks normal."

"Sounds good."

"Let's be clear on the objective here, folks," Garrett said. "We need Victor to cough up names or leads that we do not currently possess. I know that boy's death hit many of you hard, but be reminded that we are not the Sheriff's Office or the FBI. Our job is to grab the bastards for dealing drugs. That's all. If we can stop them, we can make sure this kind of thing doesn't happen again." The room nodded in agreement. "I want a list of people we think we can trust on the inside on my desk by tomorrow. We pick the wrong guy at Hardee, this whole thing is a bust, and we're back to square one. Let's see if we can get this done by the end of the week. Everyone's dismissed." Garrett lifted his hand. "Ellie, hold on a second."

She sat back down, and the room cleared. Garrett waited for the glass door to shut before speaking.

"You good with my suggestion? Posing as an officer?"

"Sure. It's a good idea."

"Okay. Then we'll leave him overnight at the hospital and not touch him. If I remember correctly, Hardee doesn't employ female correctional officers over there, so you'll pose as a transport officer. We'll have an unmarked cruiser behind you."

"Perfect," she said. "I'll see what I can get out of him. I already have a good angle."

Garrett closed his folder and jammed his pen into his shirt pocket. "Couple of us are grabbing lunch at Rosa's. You want to come?"

~~~~~

It was Friday. Victor Calderón had been in room 309 at Blake Medical Center in Bradenton since early last night, ever since he fell ill in the prison mess hall. He had taken his meal tray of mashed potatoes, fried chicken, and steamed carrots to his usual table in the center of the room and begun eating. Three minutes later and all at once, his face broke into a hot sweat, his skin flushed red, and projectile vomit the distance of three tables flew across the room. Inmates had scattered and cursed at him. Victor landed on the floor, lurching and dry heaving and wishing for someone to shank him to end whatever ailment had come upon him. It didn't stop once he was carried to the infirmary. He'd spiked a hundred-and-five degree fever a half hour in, and the decision was made to send him off site for advanced medical care. Once in the ambulance, they stuck an IV in him. The dry heaving eased, and the nausea waned. He slept the whole hour to the hospital and was handcuffed to his bed on the third floor with a guard posted outside his door.

He had been cleared to leave at nine this morning with all paperwork resolved in the system by ten. He would be brought out a side entrance used for staff. The hospital was privately funded, and a single officer standing down a hallway was one thing. Having a man in a blue jumpsuit and handcuffs walking out the front door didn't exactly protect their brand. People would talk, and some would think of the hospital crawling with prisoners every time they would visit.

Ellie stood outside the metal door in the khaki shirt and dark brown pants of a correctional transport officer. A .40 caliber Glock 23 was strapped to her side, and her ponytail was pulled through a dark brown ball cap ensigned with the county's correctional transport logo. Other than the driver, Ben Richter, a real transport officer, Ellie would be the only one in the car with Victor. She would sit in the back seat directly behind Ben. He and his superiors had been informed as to the nature of Ellie's presence.

The side door opened, and Victor stepped through with two armed officers flanking him, each with a hand clasping the upper part of his arm. She put her hand on the top of Victor's head, and he lowered himself clumsily onto the seat of the Crown Victoria. She shut his door, walked to the other side, and got in behind the driver's seat. Ben's responsibility was no different today than any other day: drive the car safely to the prison. A blacked out Chevy Tahoe belonging to the Sheriff's

Office was behind them, providing additional, standard protection. Because of his position in Nunez's network, Calderón was considered a high-value prisoner, raising the possibilities that his associates might try to intercept him on the way back. People with Nunez's influence had eyes and ears everywhere. Calderón probably hadn't even arrived at the hospital yesterday before his associates knew he was there.

Ben started the cruiser, eased out of the parking lot. The one-hour drive back to Hardee Correctional would consist of taking Highway 41 north until it merged into 683 which would carry them east, finally connecting to Highway 62, the longest and final leg of the trip.

Ellie said nothing for a while. Waiting would give Victor time to think through the events of the last eighteen hours and for his thoughts to start drifting toward what waited for him when he got back. Ellie felt right at home. This is what she had been trained to do and did it well for many years. Working herself into people's circle of trust was a skill as much as it was a talent. If she couldn't gain his trust, she would make it clear who among them had the upper hand.

"How are you feeling?" Ellie finally asked.

Victor dipped his head in her direction. Transport officers didn't strike up conversations with prisoners. "Fine." His guts were sore, but he wasn't going to tell her that. He looked back out his window at passing trees and scattered farms. He looked tired and uninterested in talking.

"I hear you might not like your cellmate," she finally said.

His brows lowered. "What?"

"I've been told you would be up for a transfer to

another cell block. Maybe with a more 'accommodating' cellmate."

"You don't know nothing about me." He gave her uniform a once over. "You're transport," he said. "What do you know about who's on the inside?" He asked in a way that made it hard to tell if he was actually curious or just thinking out loud. He looked in her eyes. "You got something to say, say it."

Direct. Just what Ellie preferred. She smiled. "Victor, I'm with the Drug Enforcement Agency and wanted to use this as an opportunity to speak with you."

Victor scoffed. "DEA? Man, I ain't talking with you." He looked back out the window. "Whatever you want to say to me can be said in front of my lawyer."

"Sure. I can arrange that. But I'm not willing to say what I came to say in front of your lawyer."

"Then I guess it don't need to be said." He shook his head. "*Estúpida*," he mumbled.

"Why would you call me stupid when you don't even know what I want to talk about?" Ellie asked.

"Man, I'm in here because of you shanks. One of your people stood me up and got me stitched. Gonzales. Mario Gonzales."

"I don't know him," she said.

"Doesn't matter. All you the same. Up on your white-collar high horse thinking you own the world. I got news for you. We"—he jammed the finger of a restrained hand into his stomach—"own the world. You can't figure us out. You never will."

A satisfied smile rested on his lips.

"Fair enough," Ellie said. She waited a full minute, let Victor breathe the fresh air of his moral high ground, then spoke. "The word on the street is that

Boosie Maine likes to get friendly with you on a whim."

"What?" Victor's tone was laced with a mild panic.

"You heard me. We know, Victor." Ellie shook her head. "And we're always the last to know something. So you must be aware that everyone else knows of Boosie's proclivities too." She shrugged. "I mean, some have even suggested you don't really mind the arrangement."

Victor's hands were chained to those coming up from his ankles, and he couldn't raise his hands more than a few inches off his waist. But he tried. He lurched against them and swung them in Ellie's direction, his face now red like he'd been holding his breath a minute too long.

Ellie didn't flinch. "And if I know that, everyone knows it. One might get the idea that if you're not willing to go the distance to change your immediate living arrangements then, well, maybe you like them."

He cursed at her. His smile vanished. His lip curled.

"So Victor, this is where I talk. Where I make a proposal. You go ahead and sit there acting like you're not interested, but you think about it. Then we dialogue. Got it?"

He didn't answer. This lady was tough.

"I'll cut right to it. I can change your living arrangements. Simple as that. Not just living quarters—cell blocks, yard time. You'll never have to see your overly-friendly cellmate again. But then, of course, this is where I ask you for something that can help me. You see, Victor, we're starting to get serious about getting what you and your people like to put on my streets. We're also serious about getting the people that put them there. What did Dylan say, 'The times they are a changin'?"

"Who?"

Ellie almost rolled her eyes but didn't. "Victor, I need you to give me a lead on drugs coming into the area. A where, a who, a what."

He let out a low whistle. "I guess today is the day, isn't it?"

"For what?"

"The day hell freezes over. Lady, you're nuts. You got a pretty head on those shoulders, but I don't think there's a lot filling the space between your ears. I'm not giving you nothin'."

"You know, I'm sorry, Victor. I really am sorry for all this. Someone on my end got the wrong information about you, and we acted on it. You got a free night outside the concrete hotel for your troubles. I should have made sure we did more research." She shook her head in frustration and sighed. "For some reason they thought you were a heterosexual. It appears they were wrong."

Victor's faced bloomed red, and he spit toward Ellie. The thick glob missed her face by an inch and hit the glass. It stuck and didn't move. She smiled. "You have to agree that I have a point. Give me something. Anything. Anything that I can use that will get me up one more step. I'm not looking for you to get me up the whole staircase."

Victor got the metaphor. He remained silent for a long two minutes, staring at the seatback in front of him. A rookie might assume the conversation was over. Ellie knew it was not.

"There's a place between Pine Island and Cayo Costa. Mondongo. You familiar with it?"

"Of course." Mondongo Key Island was a few acres in size and privately owned.

"It's not the island. It's out on Mondongo Rocks - one of the little islands. There's an old commercial fishing boat." Victor stopped and sighed. He was unused to betraying his cause, and it was clearly not something he was enjoying. Ellie waited patiently for him to continue. She was familiar with the boat. "It's beached up on a sandbar. Been there forever from what I know about it. The crews make their stash there every few weeks."

"Stash of what?" she asked. "Drugs?"

"No. We didn't get this far by being stupid. We don't leave kilos hidden out in the open like that. Gasoline. They hide gasoline in there. For the boats."

"For the return trip," she said.

"Yes. They offload, go grab the fuel, and head back."

Victor's admission confirmed Ellie's fears. Massive amounts of drugs were being swapped in her backyard, right under their noses. "Where do they unload the product?" she pressed.

He smiled and shook his head. "No. Nice try." He shrugged. "Anyway, I've been in the Greybar Hotel two years now. They change routes all the time. Who knows where they channel in now? They don't tell me. I don't need to know."

"So how can you be sure the boat is still in use for such a purpose? That boat gets visited by tourists and passersby every now and then. It's hard to believe no one has ever noticed gallons of gas in its guts."

"I just do, okay? It's only there for a few hours - half a day at most. All happens at night."

"All right, fine," Ellie consented. "Let's say that's all correct. How do I know you won't be on the phone within the hour telling your boys the DEA has been snooping around and you tell them what you just told me? No one will drop gas within thirty miles of that boat."

Victor bent his chin down and rubbed it on his left shoulder, relieving an itch. "In a normal case you would be right," he said. "But I have a - how do you say - a beef? I have a beef with one of the usual runners."

"What beef?"

His grin was crooked. "Once again, no."

She smiled. "Okay." If Victor was telling the truth about the boat, then she had a solid lead on something tangible. If he was lying, she would go back with nothing. Ellie didn't do all this just to go back with nothing. "Victor, if you're lying to me, I'll have you back in your old cell with Boosie bending you over like a palm frond before you can say, 'Blessed Mary, help me.' We clear?"

Victor swallowed hard. "Clear as my mother's eyes."

"One more question," she said. "You ever heard the name Pete Wellington?"

He frowned, thinking, shook his head. "No. Never heard of him. Who is he?"

"Doesn't matter. Nevermind."

The ride was quiet for the next two miles until Victor spoke up again. "You're moving me today, right?" His urgency was apparent.

"No. I'm not."

"What? Why?"

"Think about it. You go offsite for a day, walk right

back into a new cell block...people will figure it out. Once I do we'll have a chat with Warden Nickels and have him structure a good reason for moving you so it doesn't look like you pulled any strings."

Victor nodded. He didn't seem happy about having to wait it out. "Okay. Okay. But don't leave me hanging." He leaned in and stared at the brass nameplate that sat above the chest pocket of her uniform. "Jones," he said. "You screw me, and I'll have my people find you."

She smiled. "You think Jones is my real name, Victor? Come on. You're smarter than that."

"A hot blonde DEA agent. Wouldn't be hard to track down. We'll find you."

"Appreciate the compliment."

In the driver's seat, Ben put a couple fingers up to his ear, listening to what was coming through his mic. He adjusted the rearview mirror and said to Ellie, "We've got company."

Ellie turned and looked out the rear window. The Tahoe was following behind them the standard twenty-yard distance. Behind it, Ellie could see a portion of a yellow Dodge Charger hovering just off the Tahoe's tail lights. A black Expedition followed behind it. Ellie sighed and turned back toward Victor. "These your people?"

He shrugged. "How would I know?"

"Do you have anyone who wants to hurt you?"

"Sure, but not bad enough to do this, I don't think."

Ellie spoke through the cage. "Ben, what's the play?"

"We continue on. We have a no slow, no stop policy. The Sheriff's vehicle behind us has already radioed it in. Backup should be here in fifteen minutes."

"We won't have five minutes."

"The Tahoe will try and keep them off of us." Ben punched the accelerator, and the Crown Vic quickly added another fifteen miles an hour to its speed.

Ellie swiveled so she could keep an eye on what was transpiring behind them. Victor tried to follow suit but was constrained by his chains. The Charger was moving back and forth behind the Tahoe, trying to gauge the right time to move ahead of it.

"Ben, I know transport officers typically don't ride in the back. If we do end up coming to a stop for any reason, I'm going to need you to make it a priority to get out and open my door." The rear doors could not be opened from the inside.

"I will," he said, flicking his eyes back to the rear view.

Tires squealed behind them, and Ellie watched as the Charger lurched forward into the other lane, empty of oncoming traffic, and pulled up next to the Tahoe. A darkened window came down, and a meaty hand clutching a handgun came out, pointed at the Sheriff's vehicle. It discharged; they heard the chatter. The front tire of the Tahoe took the impact of the second round and slapped around on the pavement.

Three more clacks. The rear tire exploded, and their escort swiveled hard to its left and ran off into a field before coming to a stop inches from a barbed wire fence.

"Oh, crap," Ben said.

"Ben, we're going to have to stop," Ellie said.

"I'm not going to—"

"Ben, I don't know what they taught you in training, but I'll tell you this." She raised her voice. "If you stay at this speed and play cat and mouse with them, it's not going to end well for any of us." She stared into his eyes through the rearview mirror. He was young. Probably no more than twenty-five. "Ben," she said, "this isn't the movies. You get us flipped at this speed, and it's lights out for all of us. You married?"

"No."

"Do you want to be?"

"I...well, I'm engaged." His knuckles were white as they gripped the wheel with everything he had. The Charger pulled up behind them, the Expedition following.

"If you don't do exactly as I say, your fiancée will have to find someone else to marry. Do you understand?"

At that moment a burst of semi-automatic fire erupted from the Charger. Bullets pierced the trunk lid behind Ellie and Victor and sounded like soda cans being popped open. Ben screamed, "What do I do?"

"If we stop I can have more control. They're going to shoot our tires out too. I'd rather not be approached by Victor's friends hanging upside down by my seatbelt and no way to get out."

"How do I do it?"

Ellie scanned the road ahead, looking for any structures lining the road. "Hold on," she said. Without taking her eyes off the road, she spoke to Victor. "You've got some super nice friends, Victor."

"Hey, this wasn't my idea! I didn't know anything about it."

"Keep them behind us," Ellie told Ben. "Don't let them up on our side." The Charger slid to the right, and Ben moved the cruiser in front of it. It moved left. He moved left. Ellie looked at Victor. "Who am I dealing with back there?"

"How am I supposed to know?"

"Victor, take a wild guess." She quickly glanced at him. She wasn't convinced that he was properly motivated to help her, so she said, "If I don't know who I'm dealing with, then I will only make more mistakes. You end up in my crossfire, and you'll only make it out on a medical examiner's gurney. I need to know who might be in those vehicles."

The Charger slammed into their rear bumper, and all three passengers lurched forward in their seats.

Victor shook his head. "I don't know. Maybe José and Juan—"

"I don't need names, I need skills. Weapons."

"Uhh, no big skills, I guess. Couple shotguns probably. Other than the SMGs they just opened up. Can't be sure."

Ellie spotted a large red barn ahead on their left, sitting in the corner of a vacant field. "Up there, Ben. That's as good as it's going to get. Turn off behind that. Do it quickly so they don't anticipate it."

"All right."

"I need your shotgun as soon as we get out." Ellie unbuckled. Two vehicles, one of them an SUV. Ellie figured that there would be as few as four men coming to get Victor, as many as eight. Probably no more than eight. "Ben, are you any good with your sidearm?"

"Yes." His voice trembled.

"We'll get out of this," she reassured him. "Just follow my lead. Stay calm. Remember your training."

Ben reached over and unhinged the security latch on

the shotgun rack and returned both hands to the wheel. "Hang on," he said. He slowed just as the cruiser's tires turned hard off the asphalt. The rear tires spun out as they struggled for purchase on the dry, loose dirt. The tires hitched in, and the axles jiggled hard as he drove off into the grass, brought the vehicle around the old barn, and slammed on the brakes. He threw the transmission into park and opened his door, got out, and opened Ellie's. She jolted out, and he slammed it shut and locked it. They could hear Victor yelling something unintelligible from within. He handed her the shotgun. It was a 12 gauge Benelli M4, a rough and ready battle weapon, a Marine-issue standard. It was a gas-operated, low-recoil weapon, its two pistons located just in front of the chamber, driving the action.

The Charger wasn't prepared to stop so suddenly. It overshot the dirt road and spun on the blacktop, finally coming to rest facing away from the barn. The driver shoved down the accelerator, and a black cloud of smoke plumed up, and the car shot forward. The Expedition, being farther back, had more time to accommodate the turn and came in only thirty yards behind them, barreling in fast.

Ellie ran into the barn through its open double-wide doors. Ben followed close behind, his sidearm drawn, his eyes wide with fear. The inside smelled of a combination of new lumber, old dirt, and fusty hay. A pile of fresh two-by-fours sat off to the left along with a couple hammers and a box of nails tipped over, half its contents strewn across the surface. Other than some old hay in the back, the barn was empty and looked like it hadn't been put to use in a long time. The naked field beyond sat fallow. At the rear of the barn was a high open loft with a wide exterior opening that looked out onto the road. Ellie could see old bales of hay up there, strewn about like discarded building blocks. A ramp led up the right side, a pattern of old wood and bright pine where recent repairs had been made. There were no other doors or windows, no other means of access beyond the wide mouth they had just entered through.

Car doors being slammed could be heard from behind the back of the barn. Ellie pointed to the stack of lumber. It was about four feet high. "Get behind this and watch my six. Cover the door. I'm going up. If they're smart they're going to move in from both sides. Be ready."

"Okay." Ben maneuvered behind the lumber and squatted down.

Ellie moved swiftly and cautiously up the ramp, a firm grip on the shotgun. There would be seven rounds in the pipe; another seven were in the shell carrier on the side of the gun. She had fourteen shots. After that, if she needed to, she would have to turn to her Glock. She didn't anticipate the need to use her handgun.

Just before her feet hit the top landing, she heard voices barking orders in Spanish. She put one knee down and peeked out the wide opening that looked over the vehicles and the road beyond. Three men were jogging away from the Charger and moving quickly toward three others who had presumably exited the Expedition. They grouped up and spoke in hushed tones as they quickly made a plan. They were all armed, one clutching a shotgun, four holding handguns, and another gripping a submachine gun; Ellie couldn't tell which make. She moved behind the wall, looked back toward the inside of the barn, and clicked her tongue on the roof of her mouth twice. Ben turned and looked. She held up five fingers, made a fist, held up one more. Ben nodded nervously. Ellie didn't know anything about Ben and had to assume that he was not qualified to get them out of this. Instead, she felt the added burden of keeping him safe, helping him get out of this alive, making sure he kept his wedding date. By the terrified look he was trying to suppress, he would probably be more of a liability over the next few minutes than an asset. For now, though, she needed that doorway behind her covered.

The men started to break up and spread out, three toward one side of the barn and three toward the other. Ellie would have to make the first move. And she already had her target selected. It was the man with the submachine gun. She had to take that gun out of the equation. She peered through a crack in one of the exterior boards, found him, and noted his pace of movement. He was bringing up the rear on the group in front of her and was only feet from disappearing around the corner. So like a snake that sinks his teeth in and quickly pulls back, Ellie shouldered the shotgun, brought the barrel out through the opening, and put the man into the ghost-ring sights. She pressed the trigger. The gun bucked against her, and a one-ounce slug tore into the man's leg. He dropped like a sack of flour, forgot his weapon, and lay on the ground screaming, holding his leg. Ellie couldn't see his friends; they were already down the side of the barn. He lay there in agony, stunned by the pain and the sheer trauma. The submachine gun was now lying six feet from him and no longer presented a threat.

One down.

Five to go.

Suddenly, gunfire erupted from outside the barn, piercing the old wood and the corrugated tin roof above. They didn't know the layout of the inside and were firing randomly into the top area, hoping to hit whoever had shot their friend. Ellie ran to the far side of the loft and ducked in behind the woeful coverage of a couple bales of hay.

The firing ceased, and Ellie turned and clicked her tongue again. Ben turned, looked. She extended three fingers and swept them toward her right and then swept two toward her left. He nodded, turned back to the door, his weapon ready.

She couldn't go back down the ramp. That was the wall they had fired into. They might do it again. As she had come into the loft, Ellie had noted her exit point. The loft provided a higher perspective that gave her the upper hand. But things could quickly change, as they just had, and being able to relocate, to stay mobile, was essential.

Unfortunately, from here, there was only one way down. Ellie quickly slung the shotgun, moved to the edge of the loft, and slithered feet first over the side. As her body swung into the open air, she gripped the edge of the loft floor. She looked down. The floor was clear beneath her. From the soles of her feet to the dirt, there was still another ten feet. She let go.

Her feet touched the bottom, and in one fluid motion Ellie swept her arm back, clearing the butt of the shotgun away from the floor, and allowed herself to land into a crouch and disseminating much of the impact of the fall. She landed cleanly and darted over to Ben. She motioned for him to cover the left side of the wide doorway. Ellie would cover the right. She watched, waiting for what she knew was inevitable.

And there it was. The light streaming through a tiny slit in the boards turned dark, covered by shadow. All the men would be huddled together. There was no reason for them to spread out. She put a knee in the dirt and brought the gun up, sending off three slugs in succession, placing each one eighteen inches from the other. A painful yell and grunt came from the other side. The shadow disappeared.

Ellie heard Ben's handgun discharge from behind her. She looked and saw a fat man fall into the left side of the doorway, holding his stomach, his shotgun now lying at his feet. Then, at the same moment, a black shotgun barrel appeared from around the opening, and Ellie called for Ben to duck. The shotgun erupted in a volley of fire, buckshot chewing into the lumber, sending a couple top boards flying onto Ellie and Ben. Seven shots later the man had an empty gun. Ellie peeked out and saw the man stepping into the barn, and, as he dropped his empty shotgun and reached around his back for a handgun, Ben rose up, fired twice, and missed. The man jerked back in fear, stopped reaching for his weapon. "Freeze!" Ellie yelled. He stopped and put his hands up. "Cover him, Ben!" Ben swung around and trained his weapon on him, still staying low.

Ellie saw the man's eyes lock onto something on the outside, and a shadow retracted from the dirt and disappeared. They were fleeing. She came out from behind the lumber and peered out. To her left it was empty. Just to her right, where she had fired the three slugs, two men lay on the ground in pools of blood, one of them shot in the thigh, another above his waistline. They were both breathing but incapacitated. Ellie scrambled over and kicked their weapons out of reach.

"On the ground!" she heard Ben yelling from inside.

Ellie ran to the corner and cautiously turned. A man was running furiously back toward the Charger with every intention of getting away.

Ellie wasn't about to let that happen. She ran the length of the barn and quickened her pace as she watched him get to the car, open the door, and get inside. As he cleared the barn, Ellie glanced to her right to make sure the man she had shot first was still clear of his submachine gun. He was, and as the Charger roared to life Ellie put a slug in the rear driver's side tire.

That didn't stop him. The man, desperate for an escape, put it in gear and started to pull away. Ellie fired two more slugs, one right after the other, the first one missing the front tire, but the second plowing through the driver's side window and out through the windshield.

The car stopped. Ellie ran up to it and, keeping her gun trained on the driver, yelled at him to get his hands up. He did. She opened the door and ordered him out. His hands were shaking. "On the ground!" she said.

Sirens drifted through the open fields from police coming in for backup.

Five minutes later the area around the barn was filled with Sheriff's cruisers and county ambulances. More ambulances had been called in. All told, there were four injured and two clean arrests.

Garrett had received the news and called Ellie, telling her that he and Mark were on their way. Following procedure, she turned her handgun and the shotgun over to the Sheriff's deputy. She saw Ben leaning against his cruiser and walked over to him. He looked stunned. "Hey," she said. "Are you all right?"

"I think so. I just can't believe it."

She knew that all Ben had probably expected from this job was to be nothing more than a glorified taxi driver. He had been trained for times like this, but they occurred so infrequently most transport officers never saw more action than a bad attitude. "You did really great," she said.

He looked at her. "Where did you learn to fight like that?"

She smiled. "It's a long story. Open the doors for me?"

Ben unlocked the cruiser, and Ellie opened the rear door. She returned to her seat. "Hello, Victor."

"Hey," he mumbled.

"I assume you knew some of those men. They were friends?"

He nodded.

"I'm sorry for how that went down."

His voice was flat, quiet. "I didn't know about it."

Her ears were still ringing from a firefight with no ear protection. "I believe you. Last night, when you went to dinner in the mess hall I know you didn't expect it to end with a night off premises. Look Victor, I'm going to honor my agreement. If this Mondongo angle amounts to anything, I'll make sure that Boosie Maine is out of your life."

He looked out the window at one of his friends being loaded into an ambulance. He nodded.

Ellie got out and shut the door.

CHAPTER FOURTEEN

The agency-issue laptop was slow. It froze up intermittently, and the internet connection came and went, making the simple task of logging a report through the secured intranet an education in patience. Ellie tapped her pen on the desk and waited for the hourglass to disappear.

All four men who had been shot trying to break out Victor Calderón were still in the hospital, and all were expected to make a full recovery. The other two still had ink wearing off their fingertips and were being held without bail. The first man she had shot had his left leg amputated below the knee after the slug shattered his femur. One of the men had just been moved from ICU into a regular recovery room. Another remained in ICU having lost five feet of his intestines. None of the men were talking. Mateo Nunez ran a tight ship. The men knew that if they gave up anything they would be killed, even if they were inside a hospital or a prison. Nunez had a history of eliminating problematic persons regardless of where they were.

"You daydreaming again?"

Ellie swiveled her chair around and found Garrett leaning over her cubicle. "We can spend billions fighting the war on drugs, but I can't get a computer that can outrun a turtle?"

"I'll have Glitch look at it. Leave it here when you're done, and I'll see if we can't get it working a little faster for you." Glitch was the office's IT gopher. "Everything set for tonight?"

"Yes," she said. Mark, Ellie, and Major would be going out into the Sound later this evening to take a look at the drop spot Victor had given to her. Her team wasn't overjoyed that she was taking a civilian, but she had convinced them that no one knew the waters of the Sound better than her uncle, and there was no sense in bringing the Coast Guard in on this yet. All they needed to do was get in quickly, survey the boat, and get out of there. Ellie needed that first assessment before she could request a wireless camera that would notify them when someone was present on the tiny key.

Garrett reached over the cubicle and set a folder on her desk. "I want you to take a look at this today."

Ellie set her pen down and picked up the paperwork. She opened it and scanned the contents. "Jorge Changa?"

"Miami just sent it up. Their intel thinks he's working out of our area now. They've tracked a series of credit card transactions to an alias. Process mandates that we have this and know what's in it, but they aren't expecting us to do anything unless it can lead to our agents smiling for the camera over a pile of drugs. Look it over. See if you can make anything of it. He's not top shelf, but he's not small beans either. If he's here I want to at least know where he is and what he's up to."

"I'll see what I can make of it," she replied.

"Call me as soon as you're back at dock tonight," Garrett said. "I'll be up."

"I honestly don't expect to find anything more than a half-rotten boat, but, yeah, I'll call you."

"Good luck," he said. "I'm glad you're a part of my team."

Ellie looked up from the paperwork. "Me too." She smiled. Garrett walked back to his office, and Ellie checked her screen. The hourglass was still performing half turns, taunting her with its very presence. She sighed and started familiarizing herself with Mr. Changa. She quickly learned that he had five arrests and two prison stints that kept him behind bars for a combined six years. He'd been out for three years and maintained associations with known criminal networks in places as far away as New Orleans, Houston, and Jacksonville.

Her laptop gave off a muted beep, and Ellie noticed the hourglass had been replaced by the mouse's cursor. "Finally," she muttered. She logged in and searched the database for any additional information relating to Changa, comparing it against what Miami had just sent up. Then a name crossed her field of vision and gave her pause.

Jimmy Joe Claude. He and Changa had been arrested together six years ago for possession, but any intent to distribute was absent from the record. Whatever his business up here, Jimmy might know of his usual haunts. It looked like Ellie would have to return to the home of the man with three first names.

But not before she secured a set of hazmat-grade nose plugs.

~~~~~

Later that evening, a couple hours after dark, Ellie, Major, and Mark were on the water, slowly making their way out to the Mondongos. Instead of putting out from Major's marina in St. James City, they had opted to start out from Pineland Marina, which was ten miles farther up the western side of the island and would save them time not having to cross as much water. It also meant they had only a few miles to their destination. Once they arrived, the plan was for Ellie to quickly check things out herself. In and out. If this drop-off was legitimate, then the less they disturbed the area the better.

The old wooden fishing boat in question sat on a tiny key that was more like a glorified sandbar just to the west of Patrico Island. They dipped south around East Part Island and made their way north to the Mondongos. Half a mile from their destination, Major switched off all the lights: courtesy, cockpit, docking lights, and the few ambients. Ellie turned off the chart plotter, and the bright screen went gray and slowly faded to black. Major was on his own now and had the challenge of keeping the twenty-four-foot Stingray in deep enough water. In this area of the Sound, the bottom was only a few feet below the waterline, but the tide was slack, and that meant he had a little more water to work with. A small skiff would have been ideal to take out, but Mark had thought it prudent to bring something with a little more horsepower in the event that they ran into anything suspicious. The odds were against it. These drug runners were like ghosts: they came and went, and no one ever seemed to notice. At some point, somewhere, they would leave a footprint behind, and Ellie and her team would be there to track it to its source. Then she would find the people responsible for killing Adam Stark. Then she would make them pay.

Major cautiously and slowly drew the boat near their destination, and Ellie walked to the bow and removed a small LED flashlight from her pocket. She had fitted it with a red lens earlier in the day to minimize the effect and carry of the light. Their goal was to assess the spot and try to remain as inconspicuous as possible. Ellie was hopeful they might at least find something that would clue them into the location being what Victor said it was. If the boat was truly utilized for storing gas used to get back to Mexico, then they had a strong lead. They would have the evidence they needed for the cartels squatting in their pristine backyard.

Major idled the Stingray closer to the sandbar and then turned off the engine. The boat swayed gently in the calm waters. "I'm not going to drop the hook," he said. "Just be quick." Their position left Ellie about forty feet from the boat once she got onto the sand. "I would have gotten you closer, but the sandbar extends further out on the lower western side. I'd rather you not have to push us off."

"That's fine," she said. Ellie slipped her backside onto the gunwale and sat down. Mark put a reassuring hand on her shoulder. "Be quick," he said. "We'll keep an eye out." She nodded and, letting her feet dangle, eased her body into the warm water. Her sneakers hit the bottom, and the water stopped just below her breasts. She waded through, and water eased off her the closer she got to the key. Ten yards in, when the water was at her ankles, she stopped moving toward the key and kept wading through the water. She didn't want to walk on the dry sand if she didn't have to. Tourists sometimes visited the key and took pictures with the boat, but Major had said that such occasions were rare. Minimizing human footmarks through the sand would keep any suspicions low. If, that is, she wasn't being duped. There was no moon to speak of, and only the stars speckled a tiny fraction of light into the darkness around her.

The little key was no more than three acres and protruded up from the water in the shape of a slightly curved finger: long, not wide, moving east to west. The old boat sat alone, stranded and forgotten, the bottom edge of its stern partially submerged in the tide. It was one of the few boats that hadn't been burned out when the commercial fishermen set fire to their boats as a result of the law banning gill nets. That was over twenty-five years ago now, and, not long after, a tropical storm had torn it from its loose moorings and landed it here. The eternal slap and rhythm of the tide had forced its hull deeper into the sand until the small key became a permanent resting place of sorts. In the daylight, it was both intriguing and ominous and hinted at a corpse still waiting for its funeral. In the pure darkness of the night, it looked more like the sun-bleached carcass of a whale's skeleton, with a few extra bones tacked on.

Ellie approached the boat's broken stern and set her sneakered foot into a rotten space where a thick plank used to reside. She tested her weight, then reached up and, using her hands, pulled her head over the edge. She could see that the back half of the old deck was rotted out, leaving a large, dark cavity beneath her. She leaned in and dipped her hand down, then mashed her thumb into the end of the flashlight. Red light flooded the cavity, and her heart thumped in relief at what she saw. Five-gallon gas cans - all spray painted black - were stacked two deep and trickled back into the dark space. There had to be fifteen or twenty of them. Flecks of black paint had been struck or rubbed off in some places showing the original red plastic beneath. Ellie smiled.

Victor Calderón was about to get a new cellmate.

She shined the light deeper into the boat, beaming it toward the bow, but the meek red light wasn't powerful enough to reveal anything else. She brought the light back to the cans and inspected them again. She couldn't believe it. For who knew how long, this had been a little storage unit for the Mexican cartels. And it was literally right under their noses. It also meant that whoever placed them here would return for them soon. She remembered Victor's words: half a day at the most. Always done at night. They needed to get surveillance out here quickly. Whoever would come to retrieve the gas would be small minnows. But they could lead them to bigger fish.

Ellie clicked the light off, and her feet splashed back into the water as she climbed back down. She sloshed through and walked around to the port side, shining the light across the hull. No other cavities on this side. They could place cameras and infrared in the sand. They could position one of Jet's teams in wait on the key just east of here to intercept them when they returned for their fuel. She took a couple steps away from the boat and froze. She heard something. It was a drone. The deep drone of large, powerful engines. Ellie's adrenaline kicked in, and she quickly moved west and around a small cluster of mangroves. She craned her neck and saw what she expected, not what she wanted: a silvery glint of light bouncing off a stainless steel window frame. She squinted and could make out the faint outline of a speedboat moving slowly toward her. "Oh, no," she muttered. Her heart thudded in her chest and, ducking low, Ellie retraced some of her steps. She stopped with the mangroves at her back and pointed her light toward Major's boat. She mashed the button: two dashes and a dot, then three dashes. Morse code for "go." She repeated this three times. "Go..." she said under her breath. "Go." She tried again and heard the Stingray's engine come to life. As it backed away from the sandbar, Ellie caught herself holding her breath. She hoped they understood not to come to her and added the longer code for "away." She relaxed only slightly when she watched them moved east and out of sight behind the high fringe vegetation on the other side of the key.

The muffled drone of the speedboat's engines grew louder, and Ellie turned and dashed into the cover of the coastal shrubs. She slipped in between their branches and moved into them until she was satisfied that they provided enough cover. She could see only a slight trace of the small wake from Major's exit, and she prayed the incoming boat wouldn't notice where the water had clearly been disturbed.

She waited another minute, and the boat eased around her hiding place and up to the broken stern of the old fishing boat. She could make out the profile of a man standing behind the wheel. He killed the engines, and Ellie heard whispers in Spanish, a language she knew almost as well as her own.

"Go!" someone whispered, as the boat's hull slid into the sand and came to a stop. "Two minutes, no more." Three figures jumped off and headed toward the old boat.

Ellie remained where she was. If they saw her, this whole expedition was for naught. The cartels wouldn't use the boat for fuel storage again if they knew it was being watched. The whole ordeal with Victor Calderón and the trip out here tonight would be in vain. She would also have to find a way to make a hasty retreat to save her life.

The figures worked quickly, silently, with one inside the rotting cavity of the old boat retrieving the gas cans and two taking them and securing them in the speedboat. They repeated this several times, receiving a can of gas from over the wooden gunwale and wading into the water with it before handing it off to the man in their boat. They didn't know Ellie was here, that they had company. She could sneak out from her cover and slip up the thirty yards to the north side of the key and walk aft. Then, when the burden-bearers were walking back to the boat with their load, she could jump up into the cavity and take out the man inside. After that, she could take out each man as he came back. By then they would know something was amiss. Taking four men under the cover of darkness wasn't anything she hadn't done before. Part of her ached to do it. Even now, her adrenaline was primed, ready to shoot a cocaine-like rush of energy and clarity into her blood. But she couldn't, she knew. As long as they left unaware that they were under watch, the odds were strong that at some point they would be back. Ellie could get surveillance on the island to find out when they came back and how often.

The men were done in a couple minutes, and all but one figure got back into the boat they came in on. He said something to his driver that Ellie couldn't hear. He stopped at the waterline and slowly looked toward the mangroves. He leaned in and looked like he was straining his eyes. Then he started walking across the sand toward Ellie. She froze. Surely he hadn't seen her. There was no way they could have seen her. She wore dark clothes and her hair was fastened up underneath a black ball cap. Still, he maintained a course in her direction. He grabbed something from his front waistband. It glinted in the starlight. A long knife, just shorter than a Bowie. She shrank back as far as she could without moving her feet off the slippery roots or her hands from the branches. The man came to a stop and placed the back side of the knife's blade in his teeth. She heard the metallic sound of a zipper followed by the stream of his urine hitting the sand just a few feet from her position. He hummed, and his head bobbed to the rhythm. Ellie's muscles relaxed, and she almost laughed out loud as she waited for him to finish. He zipped back up. He removed the knife from his teeth and stuck it back in his waistband before retracing his steps back to his ride. The engine started, and Ellie could hear Mr. Pee-body being chastened for not holding it until they were clear of the coast. Within two minutes the drug dealers had disappeared around the west side of the key, and Ellie came out of hiding. She walked twenty feet farther up and watched the boat head northwest toward Boca Grande Pass, most likely on its way back to Mexico's cocaine-dusted shores to pick up a new load of drugs. Its drone finally disappeared completely into the night, and Ellie retraced her path past the groves and back out into the shallow water. She jammed her fingers into her teeth and whistled hard. A shrill note pierced the air and carried across the water. After waiting patiently, the low muffle of an outboard caught her ears just before she saw the outline of her ride. Major brought the Stingray in as close as he could, and Mark helped her back on board.

"Did you see?" she asked.

Mark handed her a towel. "We saw the boat leave out of the north but never saw it coming in. We'd have been SOL if it wasn't for your little light show."

"What are they teaching you kids these days if you don't know Morse code?" Major said. He rolled his eyes. "He thought your flashlight was shorting out."

Ellie pulled off her hat and took out her hairband. She ruffled her hair and then gathered it and threaded it through the band again. Major eased away from the key and back toward the marina. Once they were well enough away, he turned the lights back on. He looked over at Ellie and put a hand on her shoulder. "You all right?" His tone was fatherly, protective. "I'm fine. There was gas in that boat all right. I counted seventeen cans they carried out. Five gallons each."

Mark shook his head in frustration. "I can't believe they were right there and we didn't come prepared for an intercept."

"We didn't know," Ellie said. "Besides, they didn't see us. We'll be ready for them when they come back." She asked Major, "Who owns the private island? I want to talk with them." Mondongo Key Island was a half mile west of the little key the fishing boat was beached on. It was privately owned.

"It's an older couple that only comes down for a few weeks a year. I can't remember their names. They keep to themselves as far I know."

"Someone must be maintaining the place," Ellie said. From what she remembered, there was a large house on the island and several small buildings. "Mark, why don't you and I get out there tomorrow and see if anyone is home? Maybe they've seen something and just need us to help connect the dots."

"Sounds good."

Major set a hand on Ellie's shoulder, kept one hand on the wheel. "Good job, kiddo. You go get those bastards. I can't believe they've been here the whole time."

"Garrett is going to be thrilled," Mark added. He looked at his new partner. "Good job tonight. Real good job."

"Thanks, gentlemen." Then she smiled and added, "Mark, we need to get you a book on Morse code."

CHAPTER FIFTEEN

"I'LL GO TALK WITH HIM. JUST WAIT HERE." CHEWY'S voice boomed like a Calusa war drum.

Andrés lit up a cigarette and rolled his window down. "Hurry up. I'm not missing my show because of this."

Chewy sighed and got out of the car. Andrés lived in an apartment on the other side of town. And not a penthouse or flat kind of apartment. Just your standard apartment with cheap linoleum in the kitchen, too much old caulk in the bathroom, and cheap poor-boy carpet. And yet, Andrés wouldn't miss new episodes of Fixer Upper. He claimed he was educating himself for when he bought his own place one day. He had a thing for surfing, which he had never done, and home renovation, also something he had never done. If Andrés had picked up a hammer once in his life, it was probably to bash someone's head in with. In fact, Chewy thought, he probably had.

The bell to the pawn shop jingled a merry hello, and Chewy made his way to the glass encasing that made up the front counter. He pulled his wool trench coat across his body and tried to ignore the cold he felt deep inside.

The man at the counter - a thin, short man wearing a sleeveless Gas Monkey T-shirt and an orange Florida Marlins hat - got off his barstool and smiled at his visitor. "If you would have told me you were coming, I would have turned the A/C off."

"It's all right. I'm not staying."

"What's the word, my friend?"

"I'm looking for Scotch. You seen him?"

"Scotch? Man, you lose an employee?" He clicked his tongue, shook his head. "You know, the kind of business you're in, that kind of thing happens sometimes, I guess."

"You heard from him?"

"Yeah. Couple days ago as a matter of fact."

"And?"

"And he came in looking to sell a .45. I told him I already had more than I wanted and I wasn't in the market right now."

"Anything else?"

The man scratched at his thin mustache. "Come to think of it, I would say he was acting kinda strange—shifty, you know? But I guess Scotch always acts shifty."

"He say anything about where he was going? Where he might be?"

"Nope. No, he was in and out pretty quick. Was aggravated that I wouldn't buy the gun. I've been doing this long enough to know the difference between people who just want to offload something and those who are cash lean. As you might imagine, most fall into the second category. That's where Scotch was. Had the cloudy disposition of someone who realized they were missing out on the payday I could give them. I know your boss pays him well, so it beats me why he needed the money so badly." The man in the bowling shirt laughed. "Maybe he was planning on getting that lazy eye of his fixed and was cash-strapped. That eye gives me the creeps. It's like it has a mind all its own. Like that all-seeing eye on the back of the dollar bill, you know?"

"You'll call me if you hear from him again?"

"Yeah. Sure, Chewy."

"Thanks." Chewy turned and walked back outside. The sun was trending downward, just below the tops of the palms, casting growing shadows along the pavement. He got back in the car.

"Well?"

Chewy shook his head.

"I figured." Andrés flicked his cigarette out the window. "He'll turn up. He's too stupid to not make a mistake. And you know what day it will be when he finally turns up?"

Chewy, uninterested, asked, "What?"

Andrés smiled. "Demo Day."

CHAPTER SIXTEEN

The outboard hummed loudly in the water as Ellie and Mark worked their way back through Pine Island Sound for a return trip to Mondongo. They had met at The Salty Mangrove for a quick breakfast of fried eggs and toast that Ralphie had whipped up. Ellie's coffee was still hot in her YETI, and the morning air was cool against her skin. They had chosen to take out a runabout from Major's marina instead of one of the official DEA boats docked at the federal marina on the Caloosahatchee River. Ellie wanted to keep their official presence as low as possible. She and Mark were wearing shorts, ball caps, and flip flops. Just a regular pleasure ride on a beautiful Thursday morning.

It took them thirty-five minutes to arrive at the private island. Mark reduced their speed at the channel marker and approached the private island slowly. The tiny key Ellie had traversed last night lay a half mile to the east. Mondongo Key Island was much larger, twenty acres by Ellie's estimation, and was fringed with thick mangroves and sea shrubs, making it difficult to see anything on the island but a couple rooftops and the large upstairs balcony of the main house. On their approach, pilings stuck out of the water every fifty yards with signs tacked on, reminding passersby that the island was private property and was not to be approached unless you had been invited to do so. Mark guided the boat to the west side of the island where its only dock resided, a large boat house sitting just to its north. Ellie tossed a couple fenders off the starboard and then tied off. Mark cut the engine, and they stepped onto the long dock. A green and white sign greeted them, warning once again of trespassing. A white security camera hung above it, staring down at them. The dock ended thirty yards later onto a pebble road that quickly forked. They had just begun the walk toward it when a golf cart whisked out of the left turn and made its way toward them. They paused and waited.

A middle-aged man pulled up and jumped out. His tone was clipped. "I'm sorry, but you're on private property." He had a distinct appearance. His hair was a platinum white, and his skin was pale, creamy white, as if he had escaped an underground bunker and just arrived in sunny Florida. His accent sounded European. Ellie pegged it for one of the Scandinavian countries. High, flat cheekbones and a hard set jaw also spoke to a genetic makeup sourced across the Atlantic. He was tall, fit, and wore a navy blue windbreaker over white shorts.

Ellie removed her badge from her pocket. "I'm Ellie O'Conner, and this is Mark Palfrey. We're with the Drug Enforcement Administration. We have a few questions if you don't mind."

The man's eyes shifted. "DEA? I don't believe you have an appointment with anyone."

"No, sir," Ellie smiled, trying to be polite. "But we're hoping someone might be able to help us with a couple questions. Who might we speak with?"

"You can speak with me," the man said. "I am Arnold. Arnold Niebuhr. I am the director of security for the island. The owners are not here at present. Is there a problem?"

"No," Ellie said. "Would there be a place we can talk?"

Arnold considered the request for a brief moment. "Yes. Yes, of course." He motioned back to the golf cart. "Please. We can speak at the staff house." Ellie opted for the front passenger seat, and Mark took one on the back. Arnold tugged a radio off his belt and let whoever was on the other end know that he was bringing the guests up. It took less than sixty seconds for them to arrive at a stucco building that could have easily passed for a suburban home fit for a large family. Fifty yards beyond, the pebble path turned to concrete and swung out in front of what could only be called a mansion. It was built in a Mediterranean style with a pastel finish and a stacked stone apron that went all the way around. It boasted a red tile roof, high arches, balconies wrapped in wrought iron, and large windows intended to let in generous amounts of light.

Arnold stopped the cart and pushed the brake down to lock it. He got out. "Please follow me." He opened a glass door that led into a marble-tiled foyer with a high, arched ceiling. A younger Hispanic man was sitting behind a receptionist desk staring at several monitors. He wore a black hat with a red stitched logo that read *Hawkwing*. A prominent scar ran up the right side of his face from the side of his chin and mercifully stopped a half inch below his eye. He stared at the visitors as they passed but did not greet them.

"This way," Arnold said. He led them down a broad hallway and through a door that opened into an expansive room with two couches, a flat screen TV, and regal bookcases. Exposed beams ran the length of the ceiling. The bright white room was decorated in pastels, which gave a fresh, breezy feel to the room. Spacious windows hung on the southern wall and looked out to the main house beyond. Broad pictures of sea life graced the walls, placed with precision. Wooden employee lockers lined the wall behind the door they had entered. "Please have a seat." Ellie and Mark planted on the end of a twill-shrouded couch, and Arnold sat in an accent chair across from them. He removed his sunglasses and looked at his guests. His eyes were a pale blue - almost grey - making his gaze feel more like an x-ray. "So," he said, "what is it I can help you with?"

Ellie said, "We're investigating possible illegal activity in the area and wanted to see if you have seen anything suspicious in the waters around the island?" Ellie was intentionally vague.

"What do you mean by 'suspicious activity'?" he prompted.

"Boats running with low or no lights. Maybe late at night or in the very early hours of the morning."

He shook his head. "No. Not that I am personally aware of."

"Have you caught anyone trying to get onto the island?" she pushed.

He chuckled, sounded like a father responding to a child's foolish question. "Of course. That is why we are here. Tourists think it's funny or harmless and are curious about a private island. We get them all. Drunks, college students, dreamy retirees. Some try and get in through the fringes and some, like yourself, come right up to the dock. You may have noticed all the signs on your way in. That is why they are there."

"Would you mind telling us how long you've worked here?" Mark asked.

He smiled and leaned back. "Is this where you begin to move from general questions to personal ones?"

Ellie didn't like his haughtiness. "Mr. Niebuhr, we're simply trying to make sense of some information we have. Would you mind answering his question?"

His smile faded. "I have been the head of security for the Michaelsons for almost three years now."

"And how many employees work on the island?" she asked.

"Full time? Five. Two at the main house, two are groundskeepers, and myself. My security team has two on the island besides myself at all times, but they all live off island and come in on shifts."

Ellie looked around the room. "This is where the staff live?"

"Yes. It has seven bedrooms and as many bathrooms." Arnold's eyes narrowed. He looked at Ellie. "How is this relevant?"

"Again, we are only trying to unravel the comings and goings around the area," she said.

"Mrs. O'Conner—"

"Miss," she corrected.

He nodded politely. "Miss O'Conner. I can assure you that no one here would present a problem for you. You do not work with someone such as the Michaelsons and not go through the highest level of vetting. Those of us that live here work directly for the Michaelsons. All the others are brought in with an outside agency that handles the vetting and staffing on every level."

Ellie moved on. "The cameras you have around the island. Would we be able to access any footage you have if needed?"

Arnold frowned. "These are private cameras. That is not a question I am free to answer."

"Of course. May I ask how many you have facing the water, looking away from the island?"

He looked reluctant to answer. "Eight." He paused, then shook his head. "No. Nine. We had an additional one installed at the north end two months ago."

"Any specific reason why?" Mark asked.

"Not particularly. The joined angles of two cameras facing away from each other left a blind spot that we were not comfortable with. "We now have a three-hundred-and-sixty-degree view of the waterline."

"And you have someone watching them at all times?" Mark asked.

"Again, I am not at liberty to discuss our security protocols. You will want to go through more formal channels for such things."

Ellie thanked Arnold and stood up. She produced a card and handed it to him. "If you think of or see anything, please give me a call."

"Of course."

They followed him back down the hall and into the foyer. The man at the front desk was staring at the screens. He lifted his eyes and made eye contact with Ellie as she passed. "Ma'am. Sir," he said. "Have a good day."

"Thank you," she said.

Two minutes later Ellie and Mark were in their boat headed back to St. James City. A mile out Mark slowed the boat so they could talk without yelling over the sound of the wind or the engine. "What did you make of that?" he asked her. "That guy gave me the creeps."

"I didn't like him either."

"He wasn't telling us everything. I can tell you that much," Mark said.

"I'm not sure," Ellie said. "Assuming someone that works there is in on the gas can situation, it doesn't make a lot of sense to store them on a glorified sandbar a half a mile from the island if they could just do it there."

"Well, Jet's already getting surveillance in place to get set up out there. We need to have a team on hand to intercept when they come back out." He brought the throttle up, and the boat strengthened its push through the water. "You going into the office today?" he shouted over the noise.

"No. I'm taking a couple days off," she said.

"Well, enjoy them. You deserve it."

CHAPTER SEVENTEEN

Ellie slid the dishcloth across the bar top and tossed it to the side. Grabbing a couple clean glasses, she slid them into the hanging glass rack above her head. After coming back from the Mondongos yesterday, she had put the investigation out of her head the rest of her day off. She had gone home, changed, gotten Citrus, and went for a ten-mile run around the island. After coming back and washing the El Camino in her driveway, she had grabbed a shower and spent the rest of the day relaxing around the house. She woke this morning itching to make herself productive and came down to The Salty Mangrove just before lunch where there were always a hundred things that needed to be done to keep things running smoothly. Major and Ralphie did just fine without her, but she enjoyed being around the people and the knowledge that she was contributing in some way.

Gloria, perched on her usual stool, fanned herself with last week's copy of *The Pine Island Eagle*. "Ellie, it's good to see you down here, honey. Haven't seen you a lot since you took that new job. Everything going all right?"

Ellie wove another glass into the rack. "It's a little early to tell, but I think we're heading in the right direction."

"Fu was watching this documentary about the narcotics industry, and they were talking about what they called the 'balloon effect.' That when you squeeze hard in one area it bulges out somewhere else. Do you think since the feds at the south end of the state are working so hard against drugs down there that the balloon is expanding up here?"

Ellie paused and set her palms into the counter. "Could be. Honestly, Gloria, it's all convoluted. It's not so much that consumption is so rampant around here as much as we just have a lot of coastline to bring the merchandise into. Most of what comes in here is probably headed into well-populated states—Georgia, Virginia, probably even as far as New York and Chicago."

Gloria leaned in, eyes wide, voice low. "You don't think the drug lords come here, do you? Do you think someone like El Toto comes *here*?"

"No, Gloria. Men like him don't do the runs. They just enjoy the benefits."

Gloria nodded, the answer successful in dissolving any encroaching fear. She took another sip of her Long Island Iced Tea, the first of many she would have that day. Fu leaned in and spent the next minute whispering something in Chinese to his wife. Her eyes widened again, revelation entering into them, like a small child who just found out that Santa isn't real. "Oh," she nodded. "Oh Fu, you're so smart."

He smiled and nodded. "Yes."

Ellie, looking curiously at the both of them, asked, "What did he say?"

"He said that the cartels are like the big box stores. They don't make anything. They just buy it all up and distribute it. He said that if you're a really big buyer, like say a Walmart might be in the world of household goods, then you have enough leverage to buy a lot and so you can control the price. The Mexican cartels are so big now they can control what they'll pay the growers in South America."

"Impressive, Fu," Ellie said. He was right. Over the last few weeks, Ellie had been further enlightened to the changes that had taken place in the global drug trade - cocaine especially - over the last few decades. The farmers who grew the coca leaves were lucky if they made any more than two dollars a day. The difference in the farm gate price and what it could sell on the street in a destination country could be an increase of more than thirty thousand percent. One gram of cocaine in Florida would typically sell for around two hundred dollars, with everyone along the transport chain making greater a yield than the one who came before. The money involved was staggering and only emboldened those selling it to make greater profits.

Fu said something else.

"Follow the money," Gloria said.

"That's right, Fu." Most everyone they had busted over the last couple years had yielded no money to follow. They had worked mostly in cash. The few thin money trails they had left behind ended up dissolving into a dead-end of fake accounts and front businesses that provided no additional direction. Ellie smiled at Fu. "Maybe you should join my team."

He shook his head and ran a hand slowly up Gloria's thick arm, looking at her lustfully. "He doesn't want to be without me," Gloria said. He winked at Ellie.

"You two are like a couple teenagers on prom night," she said. "Fu, you want another beer?"

"Yes."

She grabbed a Landshark from the fridge, popped the top, and set it on the bar.

"You know," Gloria said. "I think we're going to buy a drone."

"A drone? What for?"

"I was thinking about creating a YouTube channel with videos from different areas of the island. The side roads around here can't always get you to what you want to see, and I wouldn't have to take a boat out to get a good shot of the perimeter."

"What made you think of doing that?"

"Jim Upton put a video up of his drone flying around Bokeelia. It has over five thousand views already, and he only put it up four or five months ago. Given, that's not Chris Singleton numbers, but it's a lot for a place like this. I think people would want to see more." She looked to her left. "Right, honey?"

"Yes. Yes." Fu was beaming with excitement the way a man might if someone had just told him he and his wife had won the Powerball.

"There are so many options to choose from," Gloria continued. "I get confused. We want to make sure and get one with a long range and good battery life. Did you know a lot of those drones only have twenty minutes of battery before they have to get charged again? That's no better than a remote control car!"

"Technology has come a long way the last few years," Ellie said. She thought of the military grade UVAs she had seen enter the skies from a tarmac at Camp Phoenix and the ten-foot ScanEagles used by the Coast Guard. The DEA had a fleet of small drones as well. "Drones are a lot like houses. You can get decent manufactured home or spend fifty million. Keep digging. You might have to spend a little more, but a short- to mid-range drone might be what you're looking for. There are a lot of good recreational ones these days. You might even ask Jon Upton what kind he has."

"Good idea." Gloria stopped fanning herself with the paper and set it down. We'll keep looking. I'm going to lie down for a bit and see if I can get a nap in." She looked at her husband. "You coming, Fu?"

"Yes." They got off their seats, and he winked at Ellie.

She laughed and shook her head. "See you guys later," she said, then watched Gloria walk off with her husband, Fu's head and shoulders rocking back forth beside her.

The business of the lunch hour had passed, and the early afternoon saw no one else at the bar. Ellie busied herself with inventory, taking Major's yellow legal pad and jotting down what items were on their way to becoming scarce.

"Excuse me, miss. Can I get a tall Kubuli, please? Draft if you have it."

Ellie smiled and turned around. "What are you doing down here?"

"I come here sometimes, remember?" Tyler nodded

to the marina behind him. "I see I just missed him, but Fu and I wanted to finish a robust conversation we started last week."

Ellie laughed. "Coming right up." She filled a glass from the tap and set it in front of him. "All the classes finished up last week, didn't they? How'd they turn out?"

"Not bad, I guess. Lee County now has half a dozen eighteen- and nineteen-year-olds who can shoot an apple off your head at two hundred yards. And every time I teach the women's class, I get a little better at deflecting the world's worst pick-up lines." Tyler lifted his voice, trying to mock that of one of his lady students. "*Tyler, my target is available if you want to shoot at it.*"

"Someone said that?"

"I kid you not. Seriously, though. You need to teach that one for me next time. I can't do it again. Ted and Harry won't go near it."

Ellie leaned back and silently counted the empty kegs underneath the bar then scratched some numbers on the pad. "You want me to teach at Reticle?"

"Sure. Why not? I mean, you know, when you're not busy trying to track down those crawling around on Florida's most sinister underbelly or tapping a mean keg...yeah."

"I'll think about it. Seems like my plan for a laid back life is slowly slipping away from me."

"You do that." He took another draw from his glass and wiped a line of foam from his lip. "So how's all your investigating stuff going?"

Ellie set down the legal pad and the pen. "You wanna go for a walk?"

"Sure." He shrugged. "Should I leave this here?"

"No. Bring it."

"But I thought there was a no glass policy on the pier."

"Just bring it. I'll pay your legal fees if Major sues you."

"Fair enough." Tyler grabbed his beer and exited the barstool.

Ellie stuck her head into the small kitchen. "Ralphie, I'm going to step out for a few. Keep an eye on the bar for me, will you?" She looked back at Tyler. "Let's go."

They put the tiki hut to their backs and slowly made their way down the long pier. Light gray clouds blanketed the sky, but the water below them was calm, and a light breeze gently stirred the air. A few people had their lines in the water, hoping to bring something up.

"I like it," she said, answering his previous question. "I think I'm starting to realize how much I might need it."

"Need what? Something to keep your butt busy?"

"Yeah, I guess so."

"So I was right?"

"I wouldn't go that far."

"Oh, come on. It wouldn't hurt to say it. 'Tyler, you were right.' Come on, try it. Just a few syllables."

"Tyler, you were…really good at teaching that ladies class."

He rolled his eyes. "Fine. Don't say it. But we both know it's true."

Since Ellie had spent the last few weeks holed up at the Fort Myers DEA office, she hadn't seen much of Tyler. She hadn't even stepped onto Reticle's property since Adam Stark was killed, even though picturing his killer at the end of her scope might be good for her. Now that she was in the field, her part-time hours had kicked in, and they would be able to get back to their standing meeting to shoot together each week. Being here with him now, walking casually down the pier, she realized how much she liked being near him. "I'm glad you came today," she said. "Everything has just been so…" Her voice trailed off. Images of Assam Murad's family, of young Adam Stark, her father, even her sister and little niece drifted across her vision. "So hard," she finished.

Tyler stopped, looked down on her. "Come here." He set his glass on the top of the railing and pulled her in close. "You've been through a lot. Just take things in stride. I'm not going anywhere, okay?"

His strong arms felt good around her. "Yeah."

They were quiet for a while, both of them standing in the middle of the Norma Jean pier, holding each other, both feeling the satisfaction of each other's presence and a mild awkwardness at the intimacy of the moment. Up until now their physical contact had gone no further than exchanging the occasional quick goodbye hug. Tyler squeezed a little tighter and locked Ellie in. "I could throw you over."

She smiled at his naïveté, or maybe it was his ignorance. "Tyler. I was in the CIA," she reminded him.

He relaxed his hold, brought his arms down, and took a small step back. "That doesn't mean you could take me."

"Oh no? Then why did you move away?"

"I don't want to hurt you. My mama said to never hurt a girl."

"Right…" She laughed.

"Besides, you still haven't told me what you did for

the CIA. For all I know you took out the trash. Someone has to take out the trash, right?"

"Yes, Tyler. I'm sure someone has to take out the trash, but I think they're probably contracted from the outside."

"Oh. Yeah." Tyler grabbed up his beer, glad that Warren Hall wasn't around to see him with the glass out on the pier. "Well, come on," he said. "I'm hungry. Let's see if I can get Ralphie to whip me up a burger. Maybe you can help him with the trash."

CHAPTER EIGHTEEN

Ellie pulled the El Camino into the cracked driveway belonging to Loribelle Claude and got out. An old beat-up and beat-down single-cab F-150 sat between her truck and the dead Buick nestled up to the garage door. She walked across the dirt walkway that was covered in weeds, tabs belonging to aluminum cans, and bite-size candy bar wrappers. Old lead paint flecked off the wooden door when she knocked on it. She heard nothing inside, and nobody came to the door, so she tried again, louder this time. More paint jumped off the door. Finally, the door creaked on its rusted hinges, and Loribelle appeared, looking less lovely than the first time Ellie had seen her.

"Yeah?" the older lady said. She didn't recognize Ellie.

"Hi, ma'am. I was here last week with an associate. I'm with the DEA. Ellie O'Conner."

The woman's shoulders slumped. "Oh hell. What now? Can't y'all just leave us alone?"

"I'd like to, ma'am." Ellie meant every syllable. "But

I have a couple more questions I'd like to ask Jimmy. Is he here?"

Loribelle tossed her hands out. "I don't know," she said. "You think I keep track of him?"

"I—"

Before Ellie could answer, Loribelle turned and yelled: "Jiiiimmy! You here? Jiiiimmy, get out here!" As they stood there awkwardly, the scent of moldy food and rancid garbage drifted into Ellie's face. She stopped breathing and waited.

A door clicked open in the back of the house, and she saw Jimmy come out of the hallway. He walked up behind his mother, then realized who was at his front door. He rolled his eyes. "What do you want?" He was wearing cut-off jean shorts, a sleeveless plaid shirt, and looked like he hadn't showered since the last time Ellie had seen him.

"Can we step into the yard and talk?" A billion red blood cells were pleading with her for fresh air.

He lifted his chin and looked over Ellie's shoulder, scanning the yard and the driveway. "You alone?"

"I am."

"I ain't talkin' with you out there. Meet me out back."

"Okay." Jimmy and his mother disappeared back into the house, and the door closed behind Ellie as she walked down the steps. She turned toward the end of the house opposite the garage and quickly realized that it provided no access to the rear. Aged red tip photinias grew away from the house, and a rusty chain-link fence was hiding deep within their branches. Ellie walked back to the driveway and slid her legs through the narrow space between the Buick and

Jimmy's truck. She came out onto a pile of old wood littered with cigarette butts and empty beer cans. A depressed chain-link gate hung on one hinge, and an old tire was propped against it. Ellie leaned down and moved the tire. She pushed the gate open. Walking down the side of the house, she navigated around crushed beer cans and passed the air conditioning unit. It clanked like the fan was off center or possibly a protest from the quality of the air it was forced to draw out of the house. Ellie walked into the back yard and waited. Everyone had different means; there was no shame in that. Pine Island had its share of millionaires and plenty of those with lesser means. But this place was in a class all by itself. More tires littered the yard, and old lawn chairs were stacked with a rusted-out coffee can sitting on top. Bags of garbage never taken to the curb sat piled in a corner, creating an ecosystem of their own.

She stood waiting in the yard for three minutes before the back door clacked open and Jimmy stepped out. A freshly lit cigarette dangled between his thin lips. He walked up to her shaking his head.

"Listen, lady—"

"It's Ellie," she corrected.

"Look, lady," he said. "You can't keep coming around like this." He slowed his speech for emphasis. "You are going to get me messed up."

"Victor Calderón helped us out."

He looked satisfied and terrified at the same time. "He did, huh?"

"Yes, he did. We are thankful for your help with that."

"Now what you think is gonna happen if someone

finds out I told you Victor might squirm? Man, I'm gonna end up fish food, that's what."

Ellie was pretty sure that, by nature, fish did not tend to consume food that they detected was poisonous. She set her eyes to his. "Jorge Changa," she said, watching his expression.

His eyes shifted, barely noticeable. He took another drag, closed his eyes, and blew out. "What about him?"

"You seen him?"

"So what if I have?"

"If you have, I would like to know."

He shrugged. "Don't matter if I have or not. I'm out of the game. I already told you and Agent Dumbass that."

"Jimmy, here's the deal. I like to play nice unless I'm given a reason not to. You helped me have a chat with Victor, and I would consider that playing nice. Now, I need to know about Jorge. So you can give me something on him right here in the privacy of your backyard, or I can leave, do a little digging, then come back with a crew of my own and bring you in for formal questioning. How might certain people feel about that?" She smiled. "Your choice, your pick, better make it quick." She'd heard the last line in a movie - couldn't remember which one - and had always wanted to use it.

Jimmy flicked his half-smoked cigarette across the yard. It landed in an open ice chest filled with old rain water and algae. "He was here last night," he said. His jaw was set hard. He was obviously angry with himself for saying anything. "For about an hour."

"What did he want?"

"What do you think, man? He wants me back shuffling the deck...rolling the dice as it were."

Out of pure curiosity, Ellie asked, "What made you quit, Jimmy? Assuming that you are telling the truth. Why get out now and go pick mangoes for Sharla Potter?"

Jimmy got a look in his eyes that made Ellie unable to distinguish between relief and regret. "My old man passed." There was a darkened coal mine of details behind that statement, and Ellie felt somehow that pressing forward would be insensitive, as if she would be trying to press the sole of her foot onto sacred, or possibly even unholy, ground.

"Do you know who Jorge's working with?"

"Jorge works alone. He don't work for no one but himself."

"Let me ask this another way. He's up here for a reason. Obviously, he sees a chance to make more money here than he was in Miami or to make the same money with less risk. Either way, he's not doing it alone. So who is he connecting with. Zamaco? Nunez?"

Jimmy cleared his throat, scratched a shoulder with the back of a thumbnail, then muttered something.

"What's that?" she asked.

"Nunez," he mumbled louder. "As far as I know. That's who he was working with last time we did some work together. I would suspect he's tied in with him again. But he didn't say. And don't ask me where to find Nunez. I don't know where he is. Nobody knows that."

"Where might I find Jorge?"

He shook his head. "No. See, that's where I draw the line. I'm fine tellin' you to talk with Victor. But I ain't a snitch. I don't give people up."

"Fair enough," Ellie said, nodding like she was in agreement. She was prepared for this. She reached into her pocket and produced five crisp hundred-dollar bills. She opened and splayed them out for his viewing pleasure. In the CIA Jimmy would have been what they called an "access agent." He was not a large cog in the wheel, but he knew those who were. It was men like Jimmy and Victor who collapsed empires. Men who did not like to hold the pockets of other men and those who enjoyed spending a little time with several images of Benjamin Franklin. Jimmy had already talked, but he could also be bought. Offering a bribe of any kind was without question against DEA agent policy. Ellie was pretty certain there had been a paragraph about it in the contractor paperwork she had signed a few weeks ago. But someone was going to find those responsible for the death of Adam Stark, and that someone was going to be her.

"What is this?" he asked.

"This, Jimmy Joe Claude, is five hundred dollars. It would be a 'thank-you' from me to you."

"I already told you I'm not—"

"This would buy a lot of Milwaukee's Best or Pall Malls...or Lysol," she added.

"Huh?"

"I'm sure this could help you and your mother. How many hours would you have to pick for Sharla to get this? Sixty? Seventy? Just tell me where I might happen to get lucky enough to bump into Jorge, and it's yours."

"I ain't stupid enough to think you're not breaking some rules with this," he said.

"When have you ever cared about the rules, Jimmy?"

Jimmy looked back down, hungrily eyed the money, then shifted his eyes away like a guilty boy with an old issue of *Playboy* in his lap. Then he looked at the money again like a boy who had just put his guilt to rest underneath the closed layer of a seared conscience. He reached out for it. Ellie pulled it back. "Jorge, then money. That's the logic I'm working with."

Jimmy took a long breath, cleared his throat. "He didn't tell me where he's holing up, but it's probably one of two places."

"Which would be where?" she asked.

"There's a space at Coralwood Village and another at Ridgeside."

Ellie pulled up the memo app on her phone and handed it to him. "I need the addresses."

Jimmy ran his cracked, nicotine-stained fingers across the screen and gave it back to Ellie. She checked it, then handed him the money.

"You tell anyone, and I'm a dead man. Do me a favor. Don't come 'round here no more." He walked to the back door and opened it. "You comin'?"

Ellie thought she would have to get on the list for a nostril transplant if she did that. "Thanks. I don't want to bother your mother again. I'll go back out from the side."

"Suit yourself."

She navigated back to the front of the house and got back in her father's old car. She looked up the addresses Jimmy gave her on her phone. One was in a trailer park in Cape Coral, the other just across the river in Fort Myers in what appeared to be a run-down area of town. She dialed Mark and waited for him to answer. "Hey, I've got a couple places I need us to check out. You good for a stakeout tomorrow night?"

There was a pause. Ellie knew that no one, whether

they were agency or law enforcement, enjoyed sitting in a car looking over their shoulder for hours on end. "Who are we looking for?" he asked.

"I'd rather not say over the phone. Let's circle up tomorrow, and I'll fill you in." They disconnected, and Ellie shifted the El Camino into reverse. A sheer curtain moved in the front window of Jimmy's house. Ellie kept her foot on the brake and looked. Loribelle was staring at her through the dingy glass, her eyes squinting, looking like a disheveled witch. Jimmy must have shown her the money. Loribelle wouldn't forget Ellie the next time she knocked on her door.

And hopefully, by the grace of heaven, Ellie would never have to again.

CHAPTER NINETEEN

Fridays are for grilling. And not just any kind of grilling. Backyard grilling. Such was Major's life philosophy and one that he invited everyone to espouse. Ellie pulled the El Camino into his driveway and parked behind his black Jeep Wrangler. She turned off her car, or truck, whatever it was, and grabbed the sweating six-pack of Coronas off the long bench seat. She paused and stared at the dark spot the beer brought out of hiding. It was a fuzzy circle the size of a half dollar made of black ink, written by a seven-year-old girl daydreaming with a pen. It was one of the few times her father had ever snapped at her. She'd cried, and he had tried to clean the spot, but the smeared stain remained like a burn mark on a perfect patch of skin. He had come to her later, apologized, hugged her, and told her he was leaving it there, said it would remind him that his car wasn't as important as his little girl. Ellie ran the tips of her fingers across the blot and smiled sadly. Then she shook her head and allowed the memories to fall away as she stepped onto the driveway.

Major's house was a modest two-story a couple miles north of hers and sat right on Dobbs Preserve on the far east edge of Pine Island. A second floor balcony came off the master bedroom and looked over a perfectly manicured front yard filled with palms, a large sapodilla tree, and gardenias that cast a sweet aroma around the yard. Major had owned the place for nearly thirty years, and though he could now afford a home three times the value of this one, he was comfortable right where he was.

Ellie walked in and shut the door behind her. "Hey!" she called out.

"In here!"

She walked down the hall and turned left into the kitchen. Major was leaned over a cutting board, chopping bell peppers and onions. "Hey, kiddo."

"Hey, Major." She pulled out a couple beers and put the other four on the top shelf of the refrigerator. "You making shish kebabs again?" She popped the cap off a bottle and set it in front of him. She did the same for own bottle and took a long pull.

"Yep. Steaks are marinating now." The kitchen was an open design, spilling into the living room and looking out on the back yard. Ellie walked to the sofa and sat down.

"Gloria was telling me that her mother used to put cauliflower on her kabobs. You believe that?" he said.

"Guh. Really?"

"Yeah. I mean why ruin a perfectly good meal with cauliflower?"

"Might as well stick a few radishes on there while you're at it," Ellie said.

Major looked up and pointed the knife at her.

"Exactly." He looked back down and kept chopping. "How was work today? Catch any drug lords?"

"Hah." Ellie took another pull off her beer. "You know, I didn't think I would end up saying this, but I think I might be enjoying it. I mean, all of one week in the field. We'll have to see how it goes."

"You mean, Tyler and I were right about the whole 'you need to be doing something else with your life' bit?"

"Yeah, I guess so. You were." She grinned. "Tyler wasn't. I still can't believe Garrett Cage is heading up an entire DEA office. I would have put my odds on Dennis Rodman being the next pope over that."

"You'll have to bring him over to The Mangrove for lunch one day. Right now, all I know is that he ruined my fishing spot that day you and I were out on the water. Probably need a do-over with him."

"You need any help?" she asked.

"Nah, just about done." He jabbed some shrimp and vegetables onto a skewer. "I'm telling you, Ellie. This whole thing about Pete not showing up is getting to me. It's been almost two months now. A plank on my pier would go missing before he did."

"Yeah. I've got the heebee jeebees about it too."

"This whole island searched the coast for three days. His body would have shown up somewhere. Pete wasn't rich, but he wasn't poor either. Not kidnap-for-ransom material if you ask me. Not that anyone tried that angle. Maybe you'll get lucky and find some answers."

"I hope so." Ellie looked above the fireplace and saw a framed painting of two pelicans flying low over the water. "Is that new?"

Major looked up, nodded. "Yep. Had Jean Oglesby paint that for me. It turned out really nice."

"Jean did that? You're kidding?" Jean was a local exhibitionist painter who had a gallery on Matlacha. She was known and loved for the bright colors she used in her flamboyant representation of local wildlife and scenery. The painting in Major's living room was much more sober and reflected the muted colors of a graying dusk over the water.

"Jean can do about anything. You just have to ask. Which reminds me. I have a thank-you card here on the counter for her. I'm leaving for Marco tomorrow and would rather not mail it. Can you take it by in the next few days?"

"You bet. Remind me before I leave tonight. One of these days I'll go down to Marco with you. You still have that Grady-White I can stay on, right?"

"Of course. I would like that. Just let me know when."

Ellie's gaze fell onto the end table, and she reached over and picked up an old picture. It was set into a dark and unassuming wooden frame. The image was old, overcome with sepia that was representative of shots taken with an old SLR camera. Two young men in their late twenties or early thirties were sitting against the gunwale of a Lund fiberglass boat, both clutching a beer and their eyes squinting in laughter. One had an old trucker hat sporting the Baltimore Orioles logo, and the other wore scraggly blond hair that grazed his shoulders. Both were shirtless and wore short cutoff jean shorts typical of the era.

"I haven't seen this before," Ellie said. "Did you just set it out?"

"I was going through a box of pictures I had in the guest room closet. Found that little gem in there."

Ellie looked at Major's swelling midsection and then back at the picture. "Which one is you?"

"That bad, huh? I'm on the right, not wearing the hat."

"The blond one? No kidding."

"Yeah," he huffed. "Age has a way of growing your gut and shrinking your hairline."

"So who's the Orioles guy?"

"Gunny. He didn't even like the Orioles as far as I know. But he wore that hat all the time. No idea where he got it. Maybe winning beer pong at a carnival."

"He was best friends with you and Dad, right?"

"Yeah. That was the last image we got of him. Norma Jean's the one who took the picture. Probably the last one she ever snapped."

Ellie returned the frame to its place and curled her feet underneath her. "I remember Dad vaguely saying something about them when I was little. What happened?"

Major stopped and set his hands on the counter. He leaned in on them. "The four of us - me, your father, Gunny, Norma Jean - we started our own charter company on Boca Grande."

"No kidding."

"Was Norma Jean dating one of you?"

He smiled and kept looking into the past. "No. Not really. I think she and I were going somewhere, but it's hard to say where it would've ended up. She flirted with Gunny too, so who knows? Your dad had just met your mother and was taking night classes at the college. He would come out on weekends and take a couple charters out."

Ellie knew there had been some kind of tragedy but didn't want to ask. She waited.

Major grabbed his beer and took a long, patient swig. "Gunny and Norma Jean booked this gig with four guests to head out and bring up some king mackerel. They had this spot, and it hooked every time they went out. Every single time. But...they never came back in." He stared down at the polished black granite. "I knew their spot and finally went out to find them. It wasn't like them to move spots without radioing it in. They weren't out there, of course. Besides, by then it was early evening; sun was almost gone. No way they would be gone that long. I was coming back in when I saw something orange at port. I pulled up and it was..." Major paused, winced, and widened his eyes to keep the tears back. "It was her. Floating upside down. She was completely naked except for the life vest. I pulled alongside her and got her in the boat." He shook his head. "She was already gone."

Ellie waited a few breaths for him to gather himself. "What do you think happened?"

"I know what happened." Major closed his eyes and pinched the bridge of his nose. "They were murdered. Norma Jean was shot twice."

"Oh my God."

"Whoever booked the charter had malintent from the beginning. Gunny, we never found him. Your father wanted me to take over the charter business after that. He was focused on school and already had his sights set on working for the DOJ. They weren't married yet, but your mother got fearful with him staying in the charter business after that."

"Dad never talked about them. Not to me anyway."

"I never told him."

"Told him what?"

"That they were murdered. All he knew was that they vanished."

A hollow spot inside Ellie's chest was growing increasingly heavy with sadness. "Why not?"

"It wouldn't have helped anything. Around here the local news would have nitpicked every bit of flesh off that story. I couldn't have people thinking about her like that, that being the last mental image they had of her. I'm not sure, but with her having no clothes on I'd say she'd been raped. The bullet holes were in her back. I don't know if she was trying to escape or not."

"Don't you think it would have helped to catch whoever did it?"

"They weren't going to find them, Ellie. Because of the missing person report, the cops looked for the men she and Gunny took out there. Turns out the names and identification they gave for the charter were bogus. That boat and those men were gone. Major blinked again and started back at filling the skewers. "I went a few miles further out, removed her life vest, wrapped some old anchor chain around her and slipped her over the edge." He sighed deeply. "Geez, Ellie. I feel like I just turned on a rusty spigot that goes a mile down." He wiped the moisture out of his eyes with the back of his wrist.

Ellie stared at the picture. "Yeah," she said, silently relating. She hadn't talked about Kabul since her return home. For one, she wasn't allowed to. But she hadn't mentioned it even in generalities, not even to those closest to her to let them know that ever since she had felt undone. Like an unbuttoned blouse flapping in the wind.

"While we're talking about losses, have you been to the cemetery yet?" Major asked.

Ellie finished her beer in three chugs. "No."

"Feel guilty about it?" he asked.

"Yep. It's been half a year. I should be able to go by now."

"You'll get there eventually. You'll know when the timing is right. He would have wanted you to heal in your own way."

"There isn't much that scares me, Major, but visiting my father's grave almost makes me dizzy." She sighed. They just didn't make men like Frank O'Conner anymore. "I miss him so much sometimes my bones ache."

"Me too, kiddo. Me too."

Major ran his hands under the water, wiped them on a dish towel, and grabbed the plate of raw food. He smiled at her. "Enough of all that. Come on. Let's go fire up the grill."

CHAPTER TWENTY

Ellie brought her truck into a parking space near the motel entrance. Mark exited his Honda Accord and got into her passenger seat. Ellie said, "I'd ask you if you were ready to do this, but I think I know the answer."

"I'm ready," he said. "Just not excited."

"You looked at the address I gave you? The one at Ridgeside? I'll take the one at Town View Village."

"I did. We made a bust in that area late last year. A meth lab two streets over if I'm remembering correctly." He nodded. "Yeah, it was a Puerto Rican family. Even had the kids involved. Parents got taken off, and I had to wait back for Child Protective Services to show up. Crazy, isn't it? Here we are poking around for those driving the coke wagon, but then you've got all this other crap going on too. If it's not meth, it coke; if it's not coke, it's heroin, or that new zombie drug, flakka. Always something new and old."

Ellie exited the map app on her phone. She looked out her windshield at the evening traffic passing by. Moms, dads, kids, grandparents, going to soccer practice, PTA, and coming home from jobs meant to stock their cupboards and fill their 401(k)s. Ellie jutted her chin toward the street. "That's who we're working for, Mark. The Gina Starks of the world. The moms in Tahoes and minivans and the young kids who want to grow up and be teachers and firemen and astronauts. We can't get all the creeps and find all the stuff. But we're going to get a few of them and find some of it. A few of them are going to feel the hurt. If we can do that, I can sleep well at night."

Mark looked over at her, genuine surprise written across his face. "Well said. You might have a little politician in you with that speech."

"Get out of my truck." She smiled. "Keep in touch while you're over there."

"Will do," he said, then opened the door. "Good luck."

~~~~~

Town View Village was the oldest mobile home community in Lee County, came in at twenty-three acres with almost two hundred homes. The carved and painted wooden sign displaying the name of the neighborhood sat over an untended flower bed filled with milk thistle, nutsedge, and velvetleaf that threatened to continue rising and cover every letter of the sign. Jimmy had given Ellie an address on Rickshaw Avenue. She drove past a couple side streets before seeing Rickshaw on her left. She looked down the street and scanned it as she rolled by. The yards were square and small, like dirt postage stamps. Chipped concrete driveways took up most of the space. Plastic tricycles, tipped-over garbage cans left by the trash collector, and newspapers never retrieved from the curb lined the length of the street. The neighborhood had almost no vegetation to speak of. Trees and large bushes were absent. Saplings, with the dirt around their root balls still freshly turned, were half dead and lined the splotchy grass near the sidewalk, no doubt planted there by a property manager who cared more about sprucing up the area than did its residents. Ellie turned left down Hixson and moved the air conditioning knob from high to low to minimize the noise inside the cab.

The sun was an hour into its evening descent, and the shadows of the saplings and trash cans stretched down the street beyond their forms like blackened putty. At the end of Hixson, Ellie turned left, then swung left again onto Rickshaw. She quickly located a lot number and compared it with the address she was looking for. The place would be on her left-hand side, the opposite side of the street from where she was now. Exactly what she wanted. Her Silverado's windows were tinted to the maximum allowed by Florida law and afforded her a little anonymity as she grabbed her field glasses and set them to her face. Some of the lots had the address number next to the front door and some only on the tattered mailboxes lining the street. Ellie found the number she was looking for three lots down, which meant that, for now, she was parked perfectly.

Stakeout was one of those words that struck a chord of intrigue through the average person's mind, along with words like *asset*, *mole*, or *spy*. Over the course of her past career, Ellie had been involved in many stakeouts in various cities across Europe. This would be only her third sitting in a vehicle. In Stuttgart she had positioned herself on a church roof top; Prague, atop a pallet rack in a canning warehouse; Antwerp, and her least favorite, the limb of a chestnut tree. Each time, she was looking through the scope of a long-range rifle, waiting for her target to appear. Working for the DEA was keeping her busy, but it wouldn't compare to the adrenaline, the sense of imminence and danger, that came in the role she played with Langley. Stakeouts behind the wheel of a car or truck simply for the purpose of gathering information could be among the most boring and mind-numbing experiences available to man. Pushed too late into the evening and yawns had to be stifled, bladders held, and stiff legs stretched.

Ellie played with the switch that controlled her side mirrors. In a stakeout you were always checking your mirrors, making sure no one came up on you unnoticed. She grabbed a metal clipboard from her backpack and set it on her lap. A white construction hard hat sat in the seat next to her. Clipboards and hard hats were a stakeout's best friend. If someone noticed you at any point, you could look down at your paper, pull up the first page and make notes on the second. This gave the appearance of being busy with some kind of official work. If someone approached your vehicle, the hat would provide substance to a quick alias.

Ellie punched the stereo knob and pressed the CD button. Jack Johnson's soft and humble voice hummed through the speakers, singing a chorus about banana pancakes. She turned the volume knob to low and kept her eyes on the mobile home in question. Farther down the street, four small children were riding their bikes and kicking a worn soccer ball around a cardboard box that had been repurposed for a goal.

An hour elapsed before Ellie received her first dose of external stimulation. An older lady wearing a pink robe and slippers emerged from the mobile home Ellie was parked in front of. She walked down the steps and approached Ellie's truck. Ellie grabbed a pen, raised the clipboard higher so the top half rested on the steering wheel and the bottom half rested on the top of her thighs. She rolled down the window.

The lady's face was old and seamed with deep furrows created by thin and aged skin. The jowls on either side sagged liked they were about to drip off her face. Her shoulders hunched, and her eyes were set deep underneath thick and scowling brows. She maneuvered up to the open window, her voice hoarse from years of cigarette tar coating her lungs. "Are you looking for something?" she asked.

Ellie's smile was that of a professional arborist. "No, ma'am. I'm surveying the neighborhood for these saplings we put in a little while back. As you can see they're all dying out. I had to go around and count which ones aren't making it. I'm filling out my notes before I leave."

The lady snorted. "They didn't put in any damn soaker hoses. That was the problem. You need to put in soaker hoses. No one around here is going to water them."

"Yes, ma'am. We're trying to get the city to pick up the tab on the irrigation. That seems to have been an oversight that we're trying to correct."

The lady knitted her brow then stepped back and took another look down the length of Ellie's truck. "Okay. As long as everything is all right."

"Yes, ma'am. Sure is."

"All right then. Have a good evening."

"Thank you. You too." Ellie rolled her window back up as the lady walked away, still mumbling to herself about soaker hoses.

Ellie fixed her eyes back on the mobile home: 2797 Rickshaw. A powder blue double-wide with wooden steps that led up to a tiny porch holding a plastic chair. A ceramic ashtray straddled the railing. A Chevy Cobalt and a Lincoln Town Car were parked bumper-to-bumper in the driveway. The door opened, and a man stepped out wearing black jeans and a pink polo shirt two sizes too large that hung down to his knees. Whatever hair he had was buzzed close to the scalp. A gold chain hung around his neck. Ellie lifted the field glasses to her eyes and focused in on him. The hue of his skin hinted of Spanish descent. He set a cigarette to his mouth and lit it up, then leaned against the wood railing and stared down at the yard below. The door opened again, and another man came out. His skin was dark, and he wore a Jamaican rasta beanie and sported a long goat patch on his chin. Neither of the men resembled the image in Jorge's file. The second man borrowed a cigarette from the first and lit up. Neither spoke; both stared at the large patch of dirt below them.

Ellie's passenger seat buzzed, and she reached over and picked up her phone. The call was from Mark. She answered. "Hey, how's it going out there?" she asked.

"Ellie." Mark's tone was a mixture of excitement and concern. "You need to come over here."

"Are you okay?"

"Yeah. Yeah, I'm fine. But you need to see what I'm seeing."

"What is it?"

"Just come over. I think it's someone of interest."

"Jorge?" she asked.

"No. There's this guy and...well, I feel like an idiot because I've seen him before, but I can't place where. I don't have a surveillance camera, and my phone can't get a good picture from that far away."

Ellie looked back at the two men on the small deck. She studied their faces and memorized their features. "There's a parking lot across from the subdivision entrance," Mark said. "I'll meet you there and ride back in with you."

Ellie slipped the clipboard into the side pocket on her door. "I'll leave now." She put the truck in gear and drove up the street past the blue mobile home, keeping her eyes on the road as if she was as indifferent to the men on the deck as a Lee County arborist might be.

CHAPTER TWENTY-ONE

Seven minutes later, Ellie pulled into a newly paved parking lot and navigated her truck into the space next to Mark's Accord. Mark got in and shut the door. Sliding the seatbelt across his chest, he said, "Sorry, Ellie. It's driving me nuts. I can't place the guy. I swear I've seen him before."

"No worries. Just show me where to go."

Two minutes later, they were parked on the curb of a corner lot where they could get a good view of the house in question. It was across the street, on their right. The neighborhood was lower-middle class, not as run down as the mobile home park from which Ellie had just come. The houses appeared no older than twenty years, were small with some of the porches featuring a porch swing or room for a set of chairs. The house in question was a one-story, brown-painted brick with a framed awning over the porch. The yard was perfectly cut and, from what Ellie could see through the growing haze of dusk, was a deep green only made possible by fertilizer and regular watering. "Someone is taking care of the place," she said. "The yard is nicer than mine."

"Nicer than mine too," Mark said.

"Don't you live in an apartment?"

"Yep. That's why this one is nicer."

"So who are we looking for?"

Mark kept his eyes on the front of the house. "A guy wearing cargo shorts and a white T-shirt comes out every few minutes, paces, then goes back inside. He'll look at his phone like he's waiting for a call."

"Does he look nervous?" she asked.

"No. I wouldn't say nervous. More...anxious. Expectant."

"Have the curtains been drawn the whole time?"

"Yes," he said. "I was parked down that part of the street earlier. I couldn't see in when the door opened."

The porch light flicked on, and the door opened. Someone stepped out and shut the door. "There." Mark tensed. "That's him."

He looked young - maybe mid-twenties - had short dark hair, and a cell phone planted on his ear. He walked down the concrete walkway leading from the house and out to the sidewalk. He kept his head down as he spoke and paced back and forth every few yards.

"Can you tell?" Mark asked.

"Not yet. He hasn't looked up." She grabbed the field glasses and set them to her eyes. He completed a few more circuits and started shaking his head, keeping his eyes on his feet.

"Looks like he's having the call he was expecting," Mark noticed out loud.

The man walked back, stopped, and looked up. Forgetting a face was outside Ellie's repertoire. Her years of experience meant she recognized and remembered things most people didn't. Mark was a good agent, but the man he had seen for just a few seconds a few days prior had escaped him. It had probably slipped Mark's attention that the front door swung open toward the street. That it had been reframed and the hinges switched, making it difficult for the door to be kicked or rammed in during a raid. He may not have picked up on the fact that the large, dark peephole on the front door was a camera lens. Thankfully, they were out of its line of sight.

Ellie brought the field glasses down. "Smith," she said.

"What? You know him?"

"Mondongo. He was the guy sitting behind the security desk when we walked into the staff quarters. The Hispanic man with the long scar on his face."

"Oh yeah…" Mark snapped his fingers. "I knew I'd seen him before. How do you know his name? He had a name badge?"

"No. Do you remember seeing the lockers in the corner next to the little counter and coffee pot? In that living room where we spoke with Arnold? There were five of them."

"I must've missed that."

"The front of each locker door had a small placard holder with a name and thick lines embossed in it. Thick lines like a rank of sorts. One card was blank, two of them had three tick marks, and the other had two."

"And the guy at front desk only had two dashes on his shirt or something?

"Yeah, on his shoulder. That locker card said 'Smith.'"

"Geez," Mark huffed, impressed. "What were the names of the other two?"

"Ingles and Vargas. Arnold wasn't wearing a uniform so I assumed the blank one belonged to him, or he doesn't have a locker or rank for whatever reason. From what he said, some of the security don't live in staff house. Hence the lockers."

Mark kept his gaze out the window and shook his head. "Unbelievable. Did you count all the floor tiles too?"

"No, just the boards on the dock," she joked. They watched, and the man outside kept pacing, clearly growing more agitated. His free hand was animated, waving wildly beyond his body.

"How do you want to play this?" Mark asked.

Ellie slowly rubbed her hands together and stared at the dash, thinking. "We need to keep a tail on this guy. I'll bet you a salt-rimmed margarita that his connections run into places we weren't prepared for."

"How do you mean? You think all those guards on the island are in on it?"

"No, no. *Think*. Who does he work for?"

Mark pondered the question. "Uh, Hawkwing."

"Right. And their employees are vetted up to the eyeballs. Even Arnold Niebuhr said as much. Companies like Hawkwing are leaders in an industry composed of billion-dollar corporations and deep geopolitical connections."

"Okay..."

"So they aren't going to just hire some street pusher by accident. That wouldn't just slip through the cracks. All of Hawkwing's clients are big money. You saw the setup at Mondongo Key Island. Their clients have their own jets and buy islands for crying out loud."

"So, what's your point?"

"That if they hire a bad apple and that bad apple negatively steals from or negatively affects their clients, then Hawkwing's brand suffers. Image is everything in that industry. Especially on the domestic side. On the international front you can get away with just about anything. Over there it's basically murder for hire. Contract armies."

"This guy could have gotten in wrong after he started working with them," Mark offered.

"Doubtful. They'll keep an eye on everyone on their payroll. Anything less would be incompetent." Ellie looked over at her co-worker. "In my past life I rubbed elbows with international security firms. A lot. Even Hawkwing has a division that extends to global clients. Anybody working for the company will be highly trained, deeply scrutinized, and well paid."

"You're suggesting this goes higher up in the company?"

"Mark. I knew you'd come around."

"Quit it." He grinned. "I'm with you now."

"I want us to go dig around and see if anything surfaces. Let's start by finding out this guy's real name. I'm starting to think 'Smith' isn't the name he got from his father."

"If he's out there to keep an eye on the comings and goings of that little key that they stash the gas at, don't you think he would have seen us that night we went out there?"

"He could have. It's unlikely, but he could have been

off that night or may not have been able to inform the crew in time that someone was out there. Who knows?"

The door to the house opened again and a bald white man of average height wearing jeans and a white V-neck T-shirt walked out toward Smith. Smith held a finger up to him and leaned in like he was struggling to hear the voice on the other end of the line. Then his back straightened, and, even from their distance of twenty yards, Mark and Ellie could hear him yelling into the phone. He hung up and started talking to the other man who had just come out, arms flailing while he screamed. The bald man put a calm hand on Smith's shoulder and nodded across the street. Smith nodded and followed.

They crossed the road and started walking toward the truck. Mark tensed. "If they come over here knocking on the glass, Smith is going to recognize us when he sees us," he whispered.

"It's too dark outside for them to see through the tint," Ellie said. "If he knocks we bail. They'll get creeped out that they're being watched, but we won't have given our faces away. Look."

The two men stopped at the corner of the driveway and resumed their conversation, still oblivious to the two DEA agents sitting a few yards from them. Ellie slipped a hand onto her door and tapped down on the button that controlled her passenger window. It came down an inch. She repeated the motion, faster this time, and it came down another inch.

"What are you doing?" Mark whispered frantically.

She whispered through clenched teeth. "Do you want to hear what they're saying or not?"

The bald guy was talking quietly, trying to calm his

partner. Smith interrupted, spoke quietly, but just loud enough for Mark and Ellie to pick it up. "I don't know what to tell them. We're screwed."

"Did he know who it was?"

Smith's voice carried higher in his anger. "It's that Ringo guy....whoever he is. He snuck in somehow, and they gave the order to him...again."

"Ringo?" The white man's voice was louder now, charged with panic. "You're kidding?"

"I'm telling you, he's eating up everything now," Smith said. He looked out toward the truck, but his thoughts were elsewhere.

"What are we gonna do?" the other guy asked.

Smith shrugged. "For me, for you, business as usual. This is above our pay grade. We just won't be getting paid if this keeps up." Silence ensued as they both stared at their feet. As they imagined the money flowing a little less freely. Smith closed his eyes, made two fists, and cursed. "I can't believe this!" he yelled. "You're killing me, Ringo!" The men stood there silently for another half minute, then walked back across the street, into the house, and shut the door behind them. Then the porch light blinked off.

Mark sighed, relieved they were gone. He turned and looked quizzically at Ellie. "Ringo?" he said. "Who's Ringo?"

CHAPTER TWENTY-TWO

Of the very few who personally knew Ringo, all but two were scared of him. And not a generic fear of spiders kind of scared. More like a shark swimming past your kneecaps scared.

Ringo sat on a long white couch with an arm resting across the back, a leg crossed over another, puffing on a cigar, thick gray smoke enveloping him like a steam shower. White cotton pants covered his thick legs, and a burgundy, short-sleeved button-down blotted with prints of cream-colored seashells covered his wide midsection. A white fedora sporting a black band sat on his head. He looked across his living room, out the floor-to-ceiling windows and onto his magnificent green lawn, gardens, and pool, which was surrounded by a flagstone path and Cuban palms.

Chewy stood stationary against a sidewall, his large hands crossed in front of his waist, statuesque and looking past his boss as he stared far ahead into the opulent kitchen beyond. A single white earbud hung from his right ear, ascending from an iPod resting in the outer pocket of his wool trench coat. He was listening to Burkis's most recent rally, recorded at the Rex Theater in Pittsburgh and downloaded from the guru's website just last night for the exclusive member price of $149.49. Chewy stood there listening, pondering, actualizing; his face calm and indifferent, almost droopy but not. Chewy never smiled. It wasn't that he was unhappy. He was very happy. He just never smiled.

The doorbell rang across the front portion of the house. Footsteps traversed the tile and stopped at the door. It opened, and Andrés greeted Ringo's guest with a nod. "Come in," he said. "He's expecting you."

"*Gracias.*" The visitor - Hector Lomas - wore black ostrich skin boots that created an echo as their heels struck the Spanish terracotta floor. His dress slacks were a couple inches too long at the ankle, gathering at his feet, and his pudgy stomach pushed at the lower buttons of his light blue dress shirt. His long black hair was pulled back into a ponytail that swayed on his back as he made his way into the living room. Ringo stood to greet him.

"Ringo," Hector said. "How are you, my friend?"

Ringo pulled the cigar from his lips and tossed his hands away from his body in a showing of hospitality. "Hector. My faithful engineer. Good to see you." He stepped in and gave the man a kiss on the cheek. "Come have a seat, please. I hope we're making progress."

"Yes." Hector settled into a white couch cushion. "Much progress." He took a handkerchief from his pants pocket and dabbed at his forehead. He knew he had done well. It had been two months since Ringo commissioned the new items, and he would be pleased.

But there was always the lingering question of just how pleased he would be. Hector was a technology gopher that, given enough time and resources, could make almost anything, do almost anything. He set a small suitcase on the hickory coffee table, unsnapped it, and brought out a laptop. He opened it, typed in a password, and performed a few clicks on the trackpad. He turned the laptop toward his boss.

"Okay. Here are the pictures taken at the lab. I will explain them as I go."

The first picture showed the inside of a speedboat, fit with a metal contraption. A metal cylinder half the size of an oil drum. A lid opened on hinges showing a cavern within the container.

"This is where the product goes if necessary," Hector began. "As you requested, the machine is small enough not to take up much room. It is also made from high-strength aluminum alloys to lighten it without sacrificing utility."

He glanced quickly at Ringo to gauge a reaction, got none, then continued. "In the event that the shipment is being pursued by authorities, three kilos can be inserted at a time."

"Three?" Ringo said.

"Yes." Hector couldn't tell if he was impressed or disappointed, so he quickly said, "As you know, go-fast shipments carry one to one-and-a-half tons, so they have nine hundred packages to deal with, give or take. This can handle three kilos at a time and receive new ones almost every thirty seconds. With two of these on a boat the crew can be rid of it all very quickly, relatively speaking."

Ringo asked, "How does it work?"

"The machine - I'm calling it The Growler - it—"

Ringo put a hand up. "Let's...forgo a pet name and continue with the explanation."

Hector dabbed his forehead with the handkerchief again and nodded. "Of course." He put his hand back on the keyboard and moved to the next image. This one showed a framed metal skeleton atop a hollow cylinder. "Here is what the inside looks like," Hector said, "once the outer cover is removed." He touched the screen where it showed a rectangular mouth. "The product is fed into here and sent into the cylinder where these tubes feed in the solution. It mixes, and then ten seconds later it is pumped out of the boat through a customized exit port in the hull. The mixture is a solution of dythanerum and ammonia that dissolves the cocaine and allows it to sink beneath the surface of the water leaving no traces at all. As you can see from this image, the system is built directly into the modified transom. So now if one of your boats is apprehended, there will be many questions as to why the boat is outfitted in such a way, and I am sure they will quickly come to the correct conclusion. However, there will be no trace of any illegal product. Now,"—he smiled broadly—"this is the best part. On a molecular level—"

"I don't need to know the science. Just the mechanics."

"Of course." He switched pictures and zoomed in. "The dythanerum surrounds the material - the cocaine - and does two separate things over the course of several seconds. It fully encapsulates it and then begins to eat away at it. Once it's blown into the ocean, it sinks." He flicked his fingers away from his hand. "It's gone. Just like that. No residue in the waters, no samples for the feds to recover."

"If this is such an easy solution, why hasn't it been done before by someone else?" Ringo asked.

"Because it's not just the dythanerum. It's a cocktail, more or less, that my chemist has spent months trying to perfect." Hector beamed, pleased with himself. "He finally has. Once all the product has been pushed through, a mild bleach is pumped through the system and flushes out any trace of the drugs. It's a closed system with each package being dissolved before you can push in another. This prevents the product from blowing out while the boat is moving at sixty or eighty knots. The worst that can happen upon engagement is the feds see the boat has been modified. But no traces of specific cargo." He changed images again. "Here is a metal frame that can be erected within a minute and canvas sheets drawn over it. This will keep all eyes off what is transpiring at the back of the boat. And video footage made by a pursuing authority will not see what is being done."

"You say it will take three kilos at a time. How long does it take to dispose of them and be ready for more?"

"Right now we have it at thirty-four seconds per every three kilos," Hector answered. "What I call a batch."

Ringo stared at the computer screen, took a long draw off his cigar, and blew out. "I don't like it," he said.

Hector thought his boss was joking, laughed too early, stopped when he realized he was serious, and swallowed hard. "Ringo, we have worked very long on this. What is it you do not like?"

"Hector. You have done well. Exactly what I asked."

Hector's shoulders relaxed.

"I need it to happen faster. You said we can fit two of these contraptions on the boat. That mean six kilos spit out every thirty-four seconds. If there are nine hundred packages on board that translates into..." Ringo paused, stared toward the computer but looked through it, and five seconds later said, "Eighty-five minutes. Almost an hour-and-a-half."

Hector lifted his brows and raised a finger. "Yes, but remember that when a boat is found and pursued - which is becoming more rare - it can take up to a couple hours for them to be caught or stopped."

Ringo smiled patiently. "My friend. Think with me. If my crew spends an hour discharging almost a thousand kilos of cocaine into the Gulf of Mexico, only to be caught with two hundred kilos, how does this help anyone? They still end up incarcerated."

Hector nodded. His boss was right. He would need to find a way to speed things up. He wanted to sigh but didn't. This whole endeavor was a mystery to him. Here Ringo was spending hundreds of thousands of dollars on R&D for the sole purpose of disposing of millions of dollars' worth of product. All to save the necks of a couple runners should they even get caught. He had never seen or heard of anything like this. No one cared for runners. They were the dust on the warehouse floor, the cockroaches that could be introduced to the sole of a boot and be replaced before the boot retreated. As if divining his thoughts, Ringo spoke up.

"Hector, what if those running my boats know that if they get caught by the U.S. Coast Guard or Border Patrol - with no drugs - they will get extradited back to

Mexico instead of tied up in the defunct American prison and legal system? Do you think they will want to run my boats over another?"

"Yes. But they will then serve time in a Mexican prison." Which is far worse, he wanted to say.

"César gets them out," Ringo corrected. "Either by greasing palms or breaking through concrete. You see, my men are like family. You know this. I'm willing to risk millions of dollars being lost to the waters of the Gulf in just one run for the sake of loyalty. In this business you don't earn loyalty as much as you invest in it."

Hector nodded. Ringo was right. To the last, everyone who worked for Ringo respected him. They knew he would take care of them. It was only when someone broke one of his few rules that things went very bad. And his rules were clear and easy to follow. And yet there was an underlying violence within him. A pool of darkness that you couldn't even see in his eyes but could feel radiating from him like an icy breeze that chilled every vertebra down your spinal column. There was an evil unrest embodied behind his physical exterior, and it teetered on the edge between loving others and ripping out their Adam's apple if they stepped outside the lines.

Ringo continued, "You have not been on the Mexican side of things for a long time. If you were running boats across the Gulf and you knew that you would be taken care of no matter what...who would you want to work for?" He didn't wait for an answer. "I have their trust, I have their heart, and I can assume a certain level of loyalty that most people in my position leave to chance. So find a way to cut forty-five minutes off without adding a third machine, and we'll be good."

"Yes, Ringo. We will get it right." A faint buzz pulsed in Hector's bag. He reached in and took out his phone. He looked at the number glaring off the screen. "It's César."

Ringo nodded his approval. Hector answered it, spoke in Spanish for the next two minutes. He hung up. "He would like to meet with you in person, Ringo."

El Toto was Mexico's most successful and notorious drug lord, at the helm of the country's most ruthless and arguably, most successful cartel, Ángeles Negros. César Solorzano was one of only four associates in his inner circle and headed up the cartel's U.S. maritime operations. Ringo took a long draw off his shortening cigar, blew out, and shook his head. "That man has too many meetings. I guess you have lots of meetings to look busy when you don't know what you're doing."

Hector's brows rose in surprise and did not go unnoticed. Hector worked for Ringo because César suggested that Hector do so. Hector didn't have much of a say so in the matter. In the decade he had known César, Hector had never heard someone speak of him in the way Ringo just had. At least, not above a whisper.

Ringo continued. "César is full of fear. And when you're full of fear, you make decisions based on the premise of maintaining control. But that is no way to live. How can you gain more control when you are only trying to keep from losing that which you have?" Hector struggled with his question, coughed. Ringo set a reassuring hand on Hector's knee. "You tell César that I will meet with him."

"Yes, Ringo."

Ringo stood up. Hector shut the laptop, zipped up the bag, and came to his feet. "Hector, you're a good man." Ringo looked at Chewy who was still standing against the wall, motionless. He jutted his thumb toward Hector. "This guy. He puts the 'can' in Mex-i-can."

Hector smiled. Ringo smiled. Chewy did not. Because Chewy never smiled.

CHAPTER TWENTY-THREE

Ellie flipped open the top of the Keurig. She grabbed the edge of the used coffee pod and tossed it in the trash. "You sure you don't want one?" she asked Mark.

He kept his eyes on his laptop screen. "I'm good."

She peeled the foil lid back on two Mini Moos and poured the contents into her cup before walking back to the conference table and sitting down. "Okay, listen to this," Mark said. "Hawkwing's regional office is based out of Tampa and oversees all private security for clients in Florida, Georgia, Alabama, and South Carolina. Their regional vice president has been in his position for two years now. Paul Greenberg. Looks like he moved over from Johnson & Johnson and had been on the Board of Directors over at Brinks. Twenty years ago...get this..." He raised a finger. "Twenty years ago he spent thirty months as an economic liaison in República de Colombia."

"No kidding," Ellie said.

"Yeah." Continuing his summary, he said, "Greenberg worked with their Ministry of the Public Service on creating more efficient logistics to get vaccinations into the countryside. Once he left there, he ended up at Yale for a stint as an adjunct professor in applied economics." He slid a small stack of paperwork in her direction. "This is everything Sandra pulled on their Tampa office, leadership, and their area managers like Arnold Niebuhr."

The name struck Ellie's curiosity. "What's his story?" she asked.

Mark leaned back in and shuffled a few pages around. "Let's see...came stateside from Norway three years ago. Looks like he worked for the Norwegian Army for seven years, spending all his time with the Bardufoss Battalion. Apparently, that group is equivalent to our Signal Corps."

"What's he doing over here?"

"Not a clue. Haven't dug that far. Don't know that we have that much on him."

"And how long has he been at Hawkwing?"

"Three years, which matches what he told us. I don't see anything domestic before that."

Ellie sipped her coffee and said, "So this Greenberg guy. He spent some time in Colombia. That's something but could be nothing. Greenberg's a VP. These billion-dollar security companies have stockholders and politicians to answer to and to make happy. Hard to believe they would have a shady VP caught up in drugs or letting it happen under his watch. Guys in his position typically go south, when they do, in other directions. Like I said before, these people are vetted and audited up to their hairlines. But either way, if that Smith guy is part of what's happening over at the old boat on that tiny key at the Mondongos, then someone higher up has to be in on this. A guy this low wouldn't just slip through the cracks by accident."

The glass door to the conference room opened, and a dark-skinned lady wearing a gray skirt suit and her hair clipped up neatly behind her head walked over to Ellie and handed her a folder. "This is what I've found on your Mr. Smith," she said. "His real name is Eric Cardoza."

"Thanks, Sandra," Ellie and Mark said in unison.

"Sure." Sandra turned to leave. "I'll keep looking and see what else I can pull."

Ellie thumbed through the folder's contents. "Eric Cardoza...just who are you?" She scanned the contents, quickly and skillfully noting what was pertinent to the immediate. "He grew up in Iowa, got his bachelor's degree at Michigan State, and entered the Air Force. After finishing basic at Lackland in San Antonio, his first station was at Buckley in Colorado and then he was shipped off to Germany with the 86th Airlift Wing. He was honorably discharged and moved out here."

"Discharged? Why?"

"Doesn't say. His record is clean though."

"I wonder why he chose Florida," she wondered out loud. "Any family associations here?" She kept scanning.

Mark flipped through a few more papers. "None that I can see. Father is deceased. Mother lives in Colorado. No siblings or cousins according to this."

She looked up. Her mind was whirling, seeking associations and connections. "We need to be aggressive on how we handle this. Let's see where this Hawkwing angle goes. Maybe it will lead us to whoever this Ringo guy is."

"How do you want to play this?" Mark asked.

"I'll go up there and talk with Greenberg."

"What? You mean, 'Hello, Mr. Greenberg. I'm with the DEA and would like to know if you or anyone in your company is currently co-opting your clients' properties for the movement of illegal drugs'?"

Ellie looked at him flatly. "Yes, Mark. That's exactly why Garrett brought me in. To do smart things like that."

He laughed. "Well, shoot. I could have figured that out on my own."

Ellie stood up and walked to the window. She looked out. "I am rich, Mark. Did I ever tell you that?" Her voice curved into a southern drawl. "I...am from a little ol' town in...North Gaw-jah, and I inherited a large sum of wealth from my aristocratic father. Bless the old man's heart."

"What..." Mark stopped and smiled as it registered. "Yes. You did, didn't you? I had forgotten about that."

"I'll work on my name," Ellie said, bringing her voice back to normal. "But I'll need to look the part when I go up there."

"I'll get all that set up. You can work with Sandra on it. She's worked with plenty of agents on undercover operations." He picked up a pen and jotted a note. "When?"

"Next week. I'll come in as a potential client in need of what they offer. Create a narrative for me and get the minimal loaded onto the internet and backdated where you can. Whoever I come to them as, they'll do their research on me."

Mark's eyes sparkled. He nodded. He grinned. "Now we're talking."

Ellie stood up. "You coming?"

"Where?"

"Garrett's office. We need to update him on what we've found."

CHAPTER TWENTY-FOUR

Ellie parked the El Camino under the shade of the awning. She turned it off and stepped outside before she changed her mind and tore away from the building. It was time, she knew, but that didn't mean she had to want to. She reluctantly walked to the large, heavy wooden door, pulled it open, and walked inside. The smell of too much potpourri hit her nostrils, so strong she knew it would embed itself into the fibers of her clothing and stick to her skin the rest of the day. She made her way to the open receptionist's window on her left and tapped the tip of the silver bell.

Ten seconds later, a tiny lady came into view, looking three hundred years old and as many millimeters tall. She wore a long burgundy dress complete with shoulder pads and a white lace pattern around her neck. Her small feet shuffled toward the receptionist's window.

"Hello. May I help you?" Her voice was as frail as her bones.

"Yes, ma'am. I'm looking for a name."

"Of course." The lady slowly - like she was racing

molasses and losing - nestled into a large black chair that rose up behind her. She placed her glasses on the bridge of her nose, raised her chin, and squinted into the computer screen. "What would the name be?"

Ellie bit down on the inside of her cheek. "Frank O'Conner."

"All right, let's see..." The mouse clicked, and she squinted through her glasses. "Ah, yes. It's going to be..." She looked up at Ellie. "Would you like me to write it down for you?"

"No, ma'am. Thank you."

"Okay." She turned her eyes back to the screen. "It's going to be section thirty-six, row nine."

"Thirty-six. Nine," Ellie repeated.

"That's the one."

"Thank you for your help."

"Of course, young lady."

Three minutes later, Ellie was sitting at the back end of the cemetery, underneath the extended branches of a mighty white oak. On the right, standing in the grass, a short concrete column displayed row number nine. Her heart ached behind her ribs, making it hard to move, hard to breathe, and her legs felt stitched to the seat, and she just wanted to turn the car around and leave.

She took in a deep breath and exited the El Camino. Walking around the car she stepped onto the hallowed grass. The row was formed entirely of raised headstones:

Lester Johnson, 1934-2013; "I Know That My Redeemer Lives."

Renée Woodruff, 1950-2018; "The Best Wife A Man Could Have."

Bobby Lyons, 2011-2017; "God Bless our Little

Slugger." A baseball glove and bat etched into the stone, a small and sun-faded leather glove lying at the base.

Justin Hetfield, May 5th, 2012-May 8th, 2015.

Ellie's heart sank even further, and she pulled her eyes away, scanning only the surnames: Dungey, Richards, Chesterton, Wrigley, Koch...

O'Conner.

Her feet and breathing stopped simultaneously. She stared, blinked. Frank O'Conner, October 3rd, 1956-September 9th, 2016; "On Earth You Toiled. In Heaven You Rest." The gravestone, light gray marble with black engraving, sat on a polished marble base. Live sunflowers, only slightly wilted, sat in a bronzed metal vase on the edge of the base. She frowned, unsure who placed them there.

Her mother was absent from this sacred place. She'd requested that her ashes be scattered across North Carolina's Blue Ridge Mountains where she and her husband had honeymooned. Ellie bent down, set her knees into the grass, and stared blankly at the name. She set her hand over the letters and slid her fingertips across each one. A tear glistened on a lower eyelid.

"I miss you," she whispered. "I miss you so much." Words were trivial, impotent to reveal the deep ache that losing a parent brought. Half of her was mad at God for taking him so early; the other half was thankful for such a decent man to miss. "I'm back home now. You should be here. It's not really home without you, you know."

An emotional tornado hurled memories at her: Frank O'Conner tickling her before bedtime; fishing in the Sound; holding her after she broke her arm in a soccer game; teaching her to drive the El Camino down Highway 78, white-knuckled and pale as she nearly hit an ice cream truck. She longed to set her face on his chest and wrap her arms around him just one last time. A good father was like an old college sweatshirt: something you would come back to on the hard days. Death was malicious to disavow a proper goodbye.

"Katie still won't talk to me. I'm so sorry I didn't make the funeral. I think, in some way, it's taken me so long to come here because it reminds me all the more that I missed that day, that I couldn't be here. I should have been."

A fleck of red caught her attention a couple rows down, and she lifted her swollen eyes. A tall man with white hair and hunched at the shoulders slowly made his way to a headstone and laid his hand on top of it. His body sagged, and Ellie could only imagine that he was visiting his wife.

She stood on her knees, slid her fingers into her shorts pocket, fished out the picture, and looked at the image for the thousandth time. "I made a copy of this for you. It was a good day, remember?" With a trembling hand she set it on the cool marble, not yet warmed by the sun.

It was her favorite picture of him. He was younger. He was sitting in the El Camino. One hand was on the steering wheel, one arm hanging lazily off the outside of the door. He was looking into the camera - not smiling - just cool and calm like all was right with his world. He exuded a cool confidence typical of James Dean. Ellie must have been about ten years old. They had made sandcastles on Sanibel all afternoon. His face held the anxiety brought about by the sudden loss of her mother, but it remained fresh and vibrant. To this day she didn't know who snapped the picture. It didn't matter.

She shook her head angrily. Who drives a gas tanker with a portable DVD player on the dash? At eleven o'clock at night? Apparently some man named Ottie Huntington. She should have been home. It would have changed things. A thousand questions intent on increasing her guilt pulsed through Ellie's mind. She pushed them back, remembering healing words Major had spoken to her a few months ago. "Guilt is a hot sun that robs us of the fresh breezes given today."

"I love you, Dad," she whispered. She pressed her hands into the grass and stood back up. She wiped her face with the backs of her hands. And then Ellie O'Conner walked back to the car and a life without her father in it.

CHAPTER TWENTY-FIVE

Cuba was an anomaly to him. Rich in culture but forever marred by the restrictive policies and human rights abuses of Castro's regime. Ringo had arrived in Havana by boat early in the morning before being escorted another forty miles east to a private cove at Cárdenas. Years ago, when his shadowy career was just beginning, this large island nation had been the perfect launching pad for moving product into South Florida. And it still was for much of his competition. But the last couple years the choice to bring boats directly in from Mexico had proved most satisfactory. Ever since Hector had built him a few boats out of a radio-reflective fiberglass and had fitted custom covers over the engines, it had become much easier to avoid radar and thus capture. Cuba was still a favorite meeting place for César Solorzano, and, unlike Ringo, César preferred meeting face-to-face to discuss business. Coming to Cuba from Mexico posed a lesser risk for César than it did for Ringo. It was Ringo's belief that the less he went out of the waters of Florida the better his operation stayed in the dark. On a personal level Ringo simply did not like the man. In Ringo's estimation César had gotten as far as he had by sheer luck, not by ability. César had been childhood friends with El Toto. As four- and five-year-olds, they had played with sticks and mud and rocks in the small town of El Jícaro, located in the Mexican state of Veracruz. From ages six to twelve, they worked odd jobs together around town—feeding goats, digging trenches, trimming trees, patching roofs—in order to provide for their younger siblings and single mothers. When they were twelve, they were walking along a dusty road to make it back home for dinner when they were kidnapped by a crew who worked for a local drug lord known as "El Martillo." The Hammer was the most feared man within two hundred miles, and in six months he had poisoned the boys' minds against all that was good. Within a year they were hardened criminals, carrying out local executions for the feudal lord. César may have grown up with the most-wanted drug criminal in the world, but he had failed to inherit his sense of leadership. Somehow, César had been appointed as the cartel's director of eastern maritime operations nine years ago, and Ringo had been stuck working with him. César, or rather Ángeles Negros, had, hands down, the cheapest and purest product to be had. They were the largest purchaser of what the Colombians grew and thus commanded the price.

Both men stood on the aft deck of César's Viking 92 Convertible sport fishing yacht, both of them staring into the clear turquoise water of the ocean beyond, each holding a glass filled with ice and amber liquid. Tall ladies in bikinis holding mixed drinks mingled with them in conversation and laughter. A few of them, already buzzed at one in the afternoon, swayed loosely to the Mexican ska that shot out of the boat's speakers.

César stepped up to his American associate. He tossed out an open hand and swung it around him. "So, what do you think?" he asked. César enjoyed flaunting his wealth and the ten-million-dollar, ninety-two-foot yacht was his most recent toy. The luxury craft boasted an opulent interior design and was top in its small class of brands that poured everything into attaining seagoing excellence.

"It's a nice boat, César," Ringo said. "Very nice."

"Thank you, Ringo. It is important that we take time to enjoy what we work so hard for."

Ringo took a long puff off his Opus X cigar and let the smoke swirl around his mouth before releasing it. "Please tell me you did not bring me to Cuba simply for a private party."

César's smile slowly faded. "Come," he said. "Let's talk."

Ringo followed him inside the opulent salon and closed the door behind him. The salon was spacious and boasted a seating area with built-in couches, coffee tables, and chairs; a full dining area that seated eight guests; and a unique L-shaped galley, featuring five bar stools in front of a custom granite countertop. Wide windows were strung around the perimeter to give passengers a sense of the ocean's nearness. César sat into a couch on the sidewall, and Ringo chose a chair opposite him.

César was a man of average height. His legs were short but his torso long, so when he sat down it looked like he was taller than he was. His face was chiseled hard, his skin a rustic orange that hinted at his Mayan roots. Grey hairs peppered into his temples, and thick bushy eyebrows sat over his eyes, giving him a grave appearance that did not communicate with his personality. He, like his guest, wore tan shorts, leather sandals, and a button-down nylon shirt. Ringo wore a white fedora.

"You are not having a good time," César noted.

Ringo smiled, playing the part. "I am. This is a wonderful ship you have here. You're right; it is important to enjoy life. But you know how I feel about not being stateside. Meeting you here comes at a greater risk to me than it does to you. We have an understanding that we will not meet in person more than once a year. We did this back in March if you remember."

"Relax, Ringo. You are too uptight. It might help matters if you would ever choose to speak over the phone."

"I didn't come this far in the business by making myself accessible to surveillance. No one even knows I exist. That's the key to my success and my efficiency. The more often we have to meet means greater chances that my anonymity will evaporate. If the feds start looking for me, then you know this will mean that I end up moving less of your product, not more."

César shook a finger at him. "They know your shadow. Eventually, they will find its substance."

Ringo offered no reply. César was a fool. Who went into business like this with the expectation of being caught one day? Only those who ended up getting caught.

"You have done very well," César continued. "El Toto is pleased with your routes through Florida and up into the rest of your country. Your volume has been most impressive. I am pleased too."

Again, Ringo said nothing. He didn't care what César thought.

"I have asked you here for a specific reason. I want to ask you to begin to diversify your offerings. To put new products on your shelves as it were."

"An old conversation for a new day. Is that it?" Ringo asked. "You already know my stance on that."

"Of course, but I need you. Cocaine...is like a good beach to which people keep returning over the years. It is a reliable resort that we know will always have vacationers. We don't even have to advertise it. It is purely a pleasure vacation. But heroin...heroin is like the prison that tourists get thrown into and never get out of. It's not recreational. It's a taskmaster that rules over them. A taskmaster that sometimes allows his prisoners to feel like he loves them. This means demand is always rising. The world we inhabit is hard; more and more people are seeking relief from their meager existence. Ringo, you know that I control Ángeles Negros' maritime routes into Miami, New Orleans, New York, Rotterdam, and Genoa." César extended a hand, palm up. "But you. You are my most reliant, my most trusted. And your volume exceeds what most of our associates get through Miami and at almost no risk of loss."

Ringo leaned back and crossed his arms. "Why do you think I'm your most reliable distributor?" He continued before César could answer. "It's because, as I said earlier, no one knows I exist. I have moved your dust for over a decade, bringing in only yours. I don't play both sides. I don't buy from your competitors." He nodded at him. "You're my guy. I work with no other cartels or suppliers."

"And I thank you deeply for this."

"I know nothing about heroin. Can I bring it in? Sure. But I have no terminus for distribution. I have no one to trust on the backend. You know as well as I do that it's a different market than cocaine. Different people moving it. We're not talking street dealers who open up their proverbial trench coats and offer any product that could be desired. I don't have a network in place I can trust. To do so would take a few years. I would rather stick to what has worked and what will continue to work for the both of us. You want to talk about moving more dust, I'm all ears. I'm all ears."

César leaned in and placed his elbows on his knees. He clasped his hands. "I will be honest with you." His relaxed confidence had diminished. His eyes were darker now, like they were pooling liquid anxiety. "El Toto has commissioned me to move more heroin into the southern U.S. He is getting impatient with the pace at which this is occurring. My European routes are strong…"

That's because they are not dependent on your acumen, Ringo thought.

"…and between Miami, New Orleans, and you in Southwest Florida, cocaine distribution is as good as it has ever been. I have much pressure on me to push more than just what the coca leaf gives us. We go a long way back, you and I. I was hoping I could count on you."

You're one of the most powerful men in the world and yet you sit here whining to me about the consequences of your inability.

"I was hoping you could do me a favor as it were. I am in a hard spot," César finished.

It's because you are weak. You've been lucky to get where you are because of El Toto's nepotism toward you. A Guerrero pack mule could run this side of the business better than you. You flaunt your women and your boat and your influence as if it were your genius that secured it. It's your ineptitude that will lose it. Maybe you'll lose it to me.

"I can't, César. I won't. I don't see why I should be the one to solve your problems. I have enough problems of my own."

César's face tightened. "My problems trickle down to you. You are the fingers on my hand - the most faithful man I have in your country. That, as you know, is saying much. Very much," he emphasized. "Finding people to get this product off my hands will not be a problem. Finding the right people is. If I don't solidify the proper channels soon, I will be in hot water."

"It sounds like you already are."

The tension in the salon began to thicken.

Ringo said, "I didn't get where I am by playing around or catering to the whims and incompetencies of others."

"You are suggesting that I am incompetent?"

He knew César couldn't do anything to him. He was too valuable to him. "César, it is not my intent to offend you. We have been doing business together for a decade now, so you must know that I do things on my side of water my way. I consider it a compliment that you want me to help you build another side of your business." *But you disrespect me by asking me yet again to do something I have a clear position on.* "Let me ask you this. When your runners get assigned the routes across the Gulf, which ones do they want? Mine, or Cuba, or the Dom Republic, or Haiti? Honestly now. What routes do they prefer?"

"Yours, of course."

"Why do you think that is? It's the longest route. It's the most vulnerable to radar."

César shrugged.

He doesn't even know. The Guerrero pack mule doesn't even know.

"Because they know I have my ear to the ground and know when the routes will be the safest. It's because they know I have their back. I will never commission or sanction a run when there is a high chance of being intercepted, regardless of how urgent a shipment is. If they need safe housing when they're stateside, I provide it for them. Not a roach motel. A nice spread with a stocked kitchen, pool, game room, and women. Who treats bottom-of-the-barrel runners like that? No one. That's who. And I have spent much of my own money testing technology that will further insulate them from detection or being intercepted with product on board. That benefits them as well as myself. That is why Andrés wanted to leave Mexico and come work for me. He knows I'll treat him right. You might try that yourself."

César nodded but seemed either uninterested or unimpressed. "You are direct," he finally answered. "You might be cautious with such an approach."

Ringo ignored him. "Direct is the only way to get things done. You surround yourself with yes men. They are scared of you. They tell you what you like to hear."

César narrowed his eyes, slowly lifted a brow. He wasn't used to being talked to like this.

"Your leadership is based off fear," Ringo continued, "and that doesn't win their affections. It doesn't make them loyal." Silence ensued while Ringo lifted the cigar to his lips, took a long puff, held the smoke in his mouth, and let it slowly curl out like charmed snake. "Do you read the Bible, César?"

"What do you think?"

"Well, I am not a presumptuous man. There is a book called the Proverbs. It is a... collection of sayings. Sayings that some would suggest are wise. In these proverbs, a man writes to his firstborn and says, 'My son, give me your heart.' He asked his son to trust him, to love him. This is leadership. So, I only ask those under my care to give me their trust and their confidence. I see no reason to lead from fear."

"Strange coming from a man who has relieved many people of their lives."

"I only take the lives of those who are not my sons. Those not loyal to me, those who have intent to harm my family name."

"You mean those who would seek to expose you, your business."

Ringo dipped his chin, grinned sinister, maybe evil. "Like I said, my family."

"Like that young boy? What was he, eleven?"

Ringo's eyes narrowed.

"I heard about it. I also keep my ear to the ground."

"Twelve. He was twelve. And no, not like him. That was different. That boy was…"

"A problem?" César finished.

"Of course. But I wouldn't have handled it that way. The man who killed him did so under his own authority, not mine. I will bring him to repentance and after that the judgment. In Mexico, children are murdered in your drug war every day in every province. But in my stretch of water, murdering a child is like a pimple on the chin of a Kardashian. Everyone notices. That was a mistake that will be rectified. It was not me leading by fear."

César stood and looked out the salon window to the water beyond. "We have a philosophical difference between us, Ringo. You and I do things differently. Much of this is defined by our cultures. In Mexico, the drug war is a part of our lives. Innocents die because they must. It keeps us ahead of our impotent government and keeps the people in line. Our *modus operandi* is fear. It is how we keep control and how we recruit."

"I disagree."

"Of course."

"Let me tell you a story about something that happened to me as a child," Ringo said. "When I was eight, almost nine, we lived in the hills north of San Francisco. A little town of Willits to be precise, not ten miles from where Seabiscuit used to train."

"Seabiscuit?"

"Nevermind. Anyway, my mother had five children to raise. As I said, I was eight, almost nine - the oldest by a year - my mother had a boyfriend who lived with us. Fenwick Parsons. It would be too gracious to say that he was purer than the bottom of a toilet brush or nicer than a badger. He would beat my mother, my siblings, and myself. My father, you see, split years earlier. He ended up dying in a motorcycle accident running from the cops in Nebraska after holding up a five-and-dime for twenty-three dollars. They said he hit the side of a police cruiser going sixty-eight, and they found him in a fallow corn field fifty yards over. In time, Fenwick Parsons was happy to take his place. Ol' Fenwick was the most mild-mannered man you'd ever meet. I never did hear him raise his voice or lose his temper. But he controlled us through fear. Sometimes - with a serene smile on his lips - he would grab one of my sisters by the hair and wail on her in the other room. Same with my two brothers. He did it to me twice. When he was done he'd lean down and pat me on the head and softly tell me it was going to be all right. Then he'd walk away. I figured I couldn't kill him. I wanted to, but I knew my mother needed me around. So I decided - I don't know where I got the idea - to be nice. I asked Fenwick what his family was like, what he liked to do when he was a kid, and did he want to throw the baseball with me? I kept it up, and I would imagine that he started to see us as friends. He kept beating on my mother and siblings but never touched me again. Turns out I didn't have to kill him. My mother did that a year later and made it look like he fell down the well at the bottom of the property." Ringo sighed impatiently. "César, Fenwick Parsons taught me something my mother didn't. He taught me that weak people can be bought with your love, with your respect."

"It is a good lesson to learn, my friend. Respect is a value worth possessing. Come, let us go back outside."

Ringo doused the nub of his cigar into the marble ashtray sitting on the coffee table and followed his host out the door to the deck lounge. He shut the door behind him, walked over to the rail, and leaned against it. Two women came near and flanked him. One offered him what was left of her piña colada. He took it and drank it down. He hated this. The flaunting of power, the prestige, the cheap women.

César had one of these women on each arm. He gave the blonde on his right a long, deep kiss, then pulled back and looked out over the blue waters. "You ever going to retire, Ringo?

"Are you?"

"I might. But I asked you first."

"Why would I? I'm just getting started."

"You've been at this for a while now. One would think you would take that thick pile of money I'm sure you are sitting on and see the world."

"Nah, I've seen enough of the world. I watch the Discovery Channel. Or what's left of it after all their reality shows. I have a long way to go in this business."

"So you have ambition? Dangerous, my friend."

"Not ambition," he corrected. "Ambition wants to be the king, thus must kill the king. I am not the king. I only want to be a prince. I want to help the king - the Caesar - get richer," he lied.

César eyed him—almost suspiciously—and smiled. "Then you are wise."

"And you? You're not a young chump anymore either."

César ignored the question. "I can get you as much cocaine as you like. You just tell me when. One day I will get you to help me with the other product," he said confidently.

One day, you will be out of the picture.

César smiled, showing his perfect teeth paid for with no less than a kilo of snow. He clapped a hand on Ringo's shoulder. "Come. Let's get these beautiful ladies and this beautiful boat into the open water."

CHAPTER TWENTY-SIX

Ellie slid the rag down the barrel and set the weapon down on the stainless steel table top. "There," she said with a note of satisfaction. Her gun lay before her, perfectly cleaned, oiled, and reassembled. For the last half hour, she and Tyler had been sitting at the back of the gunsmithing shop in Reticle's main building, cleaning their rifles while listening to a Spotify mix of Jack Johnson, Jimmy Buffett, and Bob Dylan. Ellie had run thirty rounds through her .338 Lapua, and Tyler had fired as many through his Barrett MRAD, chambered in a .300 Win Mag. She generally would stop to clean her gun at twenty rounds, but her groupings had been tight all morning, and so she kept on.

"Speedy Gonzales over there," Tyler said.

"I'm not fast," she said. "You're just slow."

"I'm not slow; I'm detail oriented. My mama always told me that was a good thing."

"I think your mama just didn't want to tell you that you were slow."

Tyler loosened the retention screw on the barrel and

broke the action open. "I think I'll swap out the barrel for an eighteen inch," he said. "I've had the twenty-four on for a few weeks. I need a new kind of a challenge."

"Are you bringing your targets in?" Ellie asked. "You're going to lose velocity if you shorten the barrel."

"Haven't decided yet."

The telecom speaker in the corner came to life, and one of Tyler's employees called him to the front counter. He rubbed his hands on a cloth. "Be right back. I'm important around here and need to go do important stuff."

"I'll be here." Ellie grabbed her rifle case and set it on the cleaning table. She opened it and placed her gun into the molded foam. She closed the lid and snapped it shut.

As she waited for Tyler to return, she thought of the progress they had made with the investigation these last few weeks. How they had started with only a couple names taken from dusty files and finally had a lead that looked as if it could guide them to those bending the rules. She and Mark had a meeting scheduled with Garrett two days from now to review the case in detail and get quick approval for how they wished to proceed. Ellie had pushed to make the meeting happen tomorrow, but Garrett had left last night for a meeting at DEA headquarters in Springfield, Virginia, and wouldn't return until the morning after next. Ellie was finally on the cusp of something big, and it rattled her nerves to have to wait, even for a couple extra days. In the meantime, she and Mark had plenty of work to do. She had already conceived the perfect name for her undercover persona.

Ellie noticed Tyler's range bag sitting at the other

end of the table, the zipper open. She walked over to it and peeked in. Inside, a handgun grip poked out from behind a cloth. She was curious, so she dug around and pulled out the weapon. The overall weight and its distribution told her what it was before it even came out. A Desert Eagle 50 AE, painted in two-tone military green. She turned it over, admiring the size, enjoying the feeling of it in her hand. As handguns went, her personal favorite had always been the Beretta M9—the feel of the weapon in her hand, its reliability and accuracy. She preferred it over the SIG she was issued in Afghanistan and the many others she had used over the years. Even now, with a host of more modern handguns available, Ellie had selected an M9 as the gun to keep on the nightstand in her bedroom. The Desert Eagle had been Voltaire's favorite; he had even saved her life with it once on a backstreet in Libya. Its three-hundred-grain bullet discharged from the triangular barrel at 1,500 feet-per-second. The weapon chambered the largest centerfire cartridge of any magazine-fed, self-loading pistol. Voltaire had referred to it as a skull splitter—a hand cannon. He didn't always take it on missions. The gun wasn't the most practical, especially in situations when anonymity was in order. But when it made sense, Voltaire would bring it along.

Voltaire. It had been a long time since Ellie had allowed herself to think of him. She hadn't seen him in nearly four years now, six months before the team had disbanded. He had been sent to Croatia on a long-term, deep-cover mission that she was not a part of and was never briefed on.

Voltaire was their team's leader, and the only person on their team whose real name Ellie had known at the time. Brian Carter. He had told her one night in Belarus as they sat by the fire and as they both stepped over an invisible line that was strictly forbidden. The entire team knew each other on a code name basis only, all of them named after classical authors. Ellie was Pascal; the other female on the team, Faraday; there was Cicero, Dante, Virgil, Darwin. Their team's director, Mortimer, was named after the famed philosopher who edited the Great Books of the Western World. It was Mortimer, Ellie believed, who had facilitated the hits that may or may not have even been sanctioned by Ellie's government. He wouldn't have been at the helm, only a faithful hand that moved the pieces of his team to accomplish the ends of those to whom he reported.

Mortimer had sent Brian and Ellie to Belarus for three months to gather intel and conduct surveillance on Anatoly Semenov, a Russian oligarch who was wintering there and conducting a black market side business with his native country's oil reserves. The CIA had put their best two operatives up in a small cabin in the woods three clicks from Semenov's compound. To get to town or to get to the perimeter of Semenov's compound to check their cameras, wireless routers, or sound recorders meant strapping on snow shoes and treading several miles through the thick snow. The isolation meant that two people in close, snowed-in quarters soon discovered they loved each other. They had been working together for four years already and trusted each other with their lives. They worked flawlessly together, each anticipating the other's moves and decisions at times when it wasn't safe to verbalize them. So that winter, in a small hunting cabin in the mountains of Belarus, Ellie O'Conner and Brian Carter fell in love. They kept it from the Agency and, when they returned back to Brussels, continued a romance over the next year that would eventually create more stress than pleasure. They both knew they would be kicked off the team and severely reprimanded if they were caught, and, while they were the world's foremost experts on sneaking around, they both felt the increasing costs associated with the risks they were taking.

So the night he left their headquarters in Brussels for Croatia, Voltaire had taken her onto a balcony and told her they needed to end the relationship. He was right, she knew, and she had probably been a couple months from ending it herself. He just beat her to it. He left the next morning, and she tried to suppress an aching heart. She had loved him. Truly loved him. In another life they could have made it well together. But many years before, they had both made a commitment to the Agency. A commitment that meant the suppression of their own wishes and desires. When Ellie pulled the shot that night in Saint Petersburg, she went back to Brussels, and the team was immediately disbanded. Voltaire had not yet come back from Croatia when she went stateside. They never did get a proper goodbye.

As she sat in the back room of a gun range in Southwest Florida, Ellie wondered where he was now, what he was doing. She wondered if he had tried, like her, to find his way in the civilian world, or if he had stayed in the game and been repurposed by the Agency. There was no way to know.

Tyler walked back in, adjusting his hat over his eyes. "Turns out someone couldn't find the broom."

Ellie let the past roll off her and came back to the present. "Important stuff, huh?"

"Hey, brooms are a big deal. To some people." He

stepped up to his Barrett, and his eyes caught what was in Ellie's hand. "Were you digging around in my range bag? There's manly stuff in there that could hurt you if you're not careful."

She looked down the barrel and through the sites. "It's a heck of a gun," she said. "I want to shoot this next time we're out. I didn't even know you had one."

"Got it last week. It's ridiculous, Ellie. The recoil is everything you would expect."

"I've shot one before."

"Did you like it?"

"It's a little much for a handgun." She eyed Tyler and grinned playfully. "One might think that a man who owns one of these is compensating for something."

An eyebrow went up. "Hey, now…"

Ellie's phone was sitting on the table, and it buzzed at her like an impatient toddler. "Hold on a sec." She picked up the phone, looked at the number, and immediately recognized the Virginia area code.

She slid her thumb across the glass and raised the phone to her ear. "Hello?"

"Ellie. Hi."

She could pluck Ryan Wilcox's voice out of a million. Her former boss's voice was soft and had the hint of a Michigan accent. She had never expected to hear it again. Her synapses fired off while she raced through a Rolodex of reasons why he might be calling. Her tone was kind but guarded. "Ryan. Hi. Something wrong?"

"No…no," he said. "Sorry to call you like this. Nothing's wrong, but I did want to see if we could meet for a quick chat. I can come to you."

Tyler caught the reservation in Ellie's voice. "Everything okay?" he mouthed.

She put a finger up and nodded. "Sure. That would be all right."

"You're down in Pine Island?"

"Yes."

"There's a restaurant in Bokeelia, Suzie's Crabshack. I assume you know the place?"

"Of course."

"Can you meet me there tomorrow night at nine?"

She wanted to ask him for his topic of discussion, but she knew he wouldn't say anything over the phone - whatever it was. She would have to wait. "Yes. That's fine."

"Thanks, Ellie," Ryan said, then dropped the call.

Ellie slipped her phone into the pocket of the black cargo pants she always wore to the range.

"Who was that?" Tyler asked.

She chewed her bottom lip. "My old boss."

"What'd he want?"

"Didn't say. I have no idea. He wants to meet in Bokeelia tomorrow night."

"So your boss who still works for the CIA wants to have an impromptu meeting with you down *here* and won't say what it's about?"

"Correct."

"I don't know, Ellie, it all sounds very CIA-y to me."

"I don't like it either," she said.

"You know, he might be coming down here to confirm my suspicions that the Wangs are a two-person sleeper cell waiting for the right moment to pounce. Or maybe he just joined a multi-level marketing company and is hitting up friends, family, and old co-workers. It's a toss-up between the two, but if I had my guess it's the first one. Has to be."

Ellie grabbed her gear bag. "I'm going to head on out. I need to clear my mind."

Tyler came up off his stool and walked over to her, his expression more serious. "You look worried. I've never seen you worried."

"I don't know why he wants to meet. Top of the list is he wants to bring me back into the game. Well, that's the whole list. I can't think of anything else that would make sense. If he needed intel on something he thinks I know, it wouldn't go down at an island restaurant. There are channels for that type of thing. Even if he needed to step outside those channels, he has to know that I don't know anything he doesn't."

"He's a good guy, right? You trust him?"

"Yeah. Of course."

Tyler walked behind her, laid his hands on her shoulders, and started to rub. She closed her eyes. "Just relax," he said. "No reason to worry unless you think he's going to poison you or something."

She swung around and slapped him on the arm. "You've been watching too much television."

"Look, just call me if you need anything or if you want me to go with you. I can sit a ways off but be there if you want. I'm serious."

She turned her eyes to meet his. They really were the greenest eyes she had ever seen. "Thanks. That means a lot."

CHAPTER TWENTY-SEVEN

His head pounded to the obnoxious tune of a thousand kettle drums sounding off across a stratified canyon. He opened his eyes—only halfway—and, try as he might, couldn't focus past the haze that clouded his vision.

"Scccccotch," someone whispered. "Scccccotch."

He groaned and opened his eyes again, waited for the blur to fade into clarity. A large picture teetered into view: a fleet of shrimp boats sailing out to sea against the orange and purple of a setting sun. He had seen that picture before. Where? His eyes shifted to the right. The tall armor of a Spanish conquistador stood in the corner. That was the moment his subconscious screamed at him, informing his intuition where he was before he could think it. Adrenaline shot through him, and he tried to sit up. A violent panic ran through his chest.

"Shhh....shhh. Lay back down. Just rest. My couch should be comfortable enough."

Scotch winced against the pain as he tried to move.

It forced his head back onto the pillow. He stared at the ceiling and tried to get his breathing under control.

"Scotch," Ringo said slowly, carefully teasing out the sounds of each letter. His guest moaned again. "You were a hard man to find. It's been, what, six weeks since she we shared a drink together? You don't call, you don't write. A simple text telling me you are all right and would be home past curfew would have been kind enough. I called all your friends' houses and their mothers said you weren't there. Then I called all the hospitals, and they didn't have you on record. I thought the worst, Scotch. The worst."

Terror overcame pain and burned off the remaining fog from behind his eyes. Scotch sat up, blinked. Ringo sat in a white chair across the coffee table from him. One leg was crossed over another, and his fedora sat atop his knee.

"Ringo, I—"

Ringo lifted a hand. "It's okay. It's okay. We all fall off the wagon now and then. Let me get you something to drink. Your head must feel like the inside of an Instant Pot. Bloody Mary? That's what you like, isn't it?"

"Uh, yeah. Yeah, thank you."

Ringo nodded at Chewy who, in turn, disappeared around the corner.

Scotch reached up and touched the back of his head. The hair was matted to his scalp with sticky, drying blood. He looked down at the orange pillow beside him. A dark bloom of blood had seeped into it.

Ringo waved a gracious hand toward him. "Don't worry about the pillow, Scotch. It can be replaced."

Scotch nodded, tried to smile, tried to swallow and

push down the fear that was making his loins feel like water and his guts like warm grits.

"Scotch, did I ever tell you the story about when I broke my forearm?"

"No, Ringo."

"I didn't think so." Ringo looked across the expansive room and rubbed his naked chin with his fingertips. "When I was eight years old, almost nine, we lived in Pine Apple, Alabama. Not but a couple hundred people called it home. It was just my father and me. No brothers or sisters to speak of. My mother incubated me in her womb nine months and perished before they had even carried away the afterbirth. My father, he had no education and never learned a trade. He would bounce from job to job - janitor, ditch digger, newspaper delivery. Even tried frying eggs and flipping pancakes at Linda Comphrey's diner. All that work, and we still never had two dimes to rub together. I don't know what made my father an angry man. He wasn't angry when I was little. But it grew in him, like a swelling appendix. Then one day it just burst. He had come home from whatever the job of the moment was and poured himself one of these." Ringo lifted his glass. "Bourbon on ice. He was on his second glass when he went to use the head. I had decided that was a good time to try the stuff myself. My lips were coming off the rim when he came around the corner. The fire water was still burning its way down my gullet when he grabbed my belt and shirt collar, brought me above his head, and threw me into the dining room wall. He never said anything. That was the interesting part. He just picked me up and threw me down. Snapped my forearm like a dry twig."

Chewy entered the room with a glass in each hand.

Ringo smiled. "Ah, here we are."

Scotch considered Ringo's story. He had worked with Ringo long enough to know that one could never be quite sure which of his stories were true. The man was an enigma through and through.

Chewy handed a fresh bourbon to his boss, exchanging glasses with him, and extended a martini glass toward Scotch who took it and set it to his lips. He drank freely and winced as the cool liquid ran down his throat. He paused. There was no kick, no astringent bite produced by the presence of vodka.

"What's wrong?" Ringo asked.

Scotch looked quizzically at the glass. "It's...just tomato juice."

"I see. Are you inferring that I'm a poor host?"

"No." He shook his head and winced against the pain. "No. Of course not."

Ringo stared into his glass, swirled the golden liquid so the ice rattled against the sides. "The point of my story, old friend, is that you never drink from another man's glass without asking. Not unless you want to run the risk of bodily harm." He stood, nodded toward Chewy. "Come on. Follow me. I want to show you something." Chewy helped Scotch to his feet and motioned for him to follow. Andrés, who had just come out of a side room as if he had been listening, waiting for the right time, stepped in line and took up the rear. They walked toward the corner of the living room and up a narrow, winding, iron staircase that led to a carpeted landing on the next floor and overlooked the room they were just in. They walked the length of the living room before taking a right down a short hallway and coming to a stop at a small iron railing, waist high. It looked down on an empty room the size of a racquetball court. It had white bare walls all the way around, and the floor was the same red clay tile that ran through the rest of the home.

"Scotch. Have I ever given you a reason to disrespect me?"

"No, Ringo." Scotch blinked up at him, the way a puppy might when it realizes the master discovered that his slippers were torn to bits.

"If you would please, tell me the rules that I have established for my organization."

"Sell noth— "

"Number them, please."

Scotch's Adam's apple rose and fell rapidly as he swallowed dryly. "Number one: Sell nothing but cocaine."

"And that means what exactly?"

"No trafficking anything else. No guns, no girls, no other drugs."

"Next?"

"Number two: Never lie to you."

"And...number three," Ringo prompted.

Scotch took a deep breath, his chest trembling on the exhale, his lazy eye rolling down and away, as if it had just died by fear. "Number three: Never try the product."

Ringo threw his hands out. "Winner, winner, chicken dinner. Ladies and gentlemen, please tell this man what's he's just won!"

Chewy set a heavy hand on Scotch's back. "You know that this room you are looking down on is typically used as the game room. In fact, I think you and Andrés have played a few games of pool together, haven't you?"

Scotch nodded. His face was clammy.

"You'll notice that we have cleared it and that it's empty. Almost empty," Chewy corrected. "You'll also notice that the windows and doors are all gone. The last two days men have been coming and going through this place with two by fours and sheetrock and paint. Where we stand is the only entry and exit point."

Ringo spoke. "I wanted to make sure that my new guest room was suitable for *you*. Only the best for you, Scotch, old friend."

"Now Ringo—"

Ringo's smile was gone. He leaned in and locked eyes with Scotch. "You have drunk from my holy chalice without asking. You broke one of my rules and then…" He shook his head. "That boy." Ringo pulled out a cigar and slid it between his teeth, leaving it unlit.

Andrés said, "You are aware that one of Ringo's idiosyncrasies is that he sees it as a challenge to try not to relieve someone of their life in the same manner he has someone else. At this stage in the game, it makes it difficult—very difficult—to be creative. We can't shoot you or stab you or drown you or hang you or poison you. We can't even beat you."

Scotch could feel bile trying to coming up his esophagus, stinging the back of his throat.

"Chewy, this whole thing was your idea, so I will let you fill him in on his accommodations," Andrés said.

Chewy's eyes remained on the floor below as he spoke. "If you would step up closer and lean over the rail, you will be able to see." Scotch didn't move. "You must see this. We're not going to throw you over," he added.

Scotch cautiously bent at the torso and looked below.

Chewy pointed over the railing. "You'll see down there." He craned his neck. "This corner back here closest to us."

Scotch's nervous breath now wheezed through his chest. He leaned over and looked where Chewy's eyes were planted, where his finger was pointing. His throat thickened and his hands trembled when his eyes made contact with the twenty-foot snake below. It was curled into a corner and its forked tongue was flicking out of its mouth every two seconds.

"It's Ringo's newest pet," Andrés said from behind him. "A Burmese python to be exact. The snake has not eaten in six months, not since its captor pulled it out of the Glades. They can go without food for a very long time. They lower their…" He struggled to find the English word.

"Metabolic," Chewy said.

"Yes. Metabolic. They lower their metabolic rates up to seventy percent to stay alive. We gave it a small rat yesterday to bring its energy up and help it to remember what it is like to eat. By nature, pythons are gentle creatures, but this one has been stuck with a cattle prod on a low electrical setting for the last hour. So he is angry. He is angry, and he is hungry. Very hungry."

"He's hangry," Ringo interjected. Andrés smiled. Chewy did not.

"Ringo, please—"

Ringo raised a finger to Scotch's lips. "Shhh. Let him finish."

"Burmese pythons can eat small alligators and deer. I have seen a video of one eating a small hippopotamus.

It regurgitated it soon after because his meal weighed so much that the snake could not even slither away. Fascinating. It is good that you are a small man."

"No...no...please...I have a fianc—"

"You have disillusioned the citizenry, the community of this lovely county," Ringo said. "You've brought renewed and undue attention upon the nature of my business. But all this has come upon you if for no other reason than you killed that young man. How can I ever forgive that?" He came in closer, and Scotch responded with a meager whine that came off his lips.

"Now, now," he whispered and put a thick hand on Scotch's shoulder. "Let's not make this harder than it needs to be." He nodded at Andrés who came from behind and quickly shoved a large rubber ball into Scotch's mouth. Five seconds later two layers of duct tape were wrapped around to the back of his head.

Scotch yelled through the gag. It came out muffled and flat.

"This home is large, but I do have another guest, so I would prefer to minimize the noise of your intriguing demise. I have a meeting I need to get to. So if you'll forgive me for not watching." Ringo reached in, placed his hands on Scotch's temples, and kissed him on the top of his head. Scotch's breath moved loudly and forcefully through his nose, and his sweat smelled like vinegar.

"Hey...why so glum, chum? I hear the ol' Elysian Fields, Paradise, Valhalla, Heaven, you know, whatever you might be into...I hear it's quite nice." Then Ringo paused and got a far away look in his eyes. He didn't move for a while, just kept staring over Scotch's shoulder like something had just dawned on him. Then animation overtook him again, and he patted Scotch's cheek one more time. "Of course, I don't know if you'll be getting a ticket to any of those particular stops seeing as you killed that boy." He clicked his tongue and shook his head. Then he turned away.

Scotch jerked and in his panic fell to his knees, writhing violently on the ground in a vain effort to prevent the inevitable.

Ringo's hand slid along the iron rail as he descended the circular steps. Halfway down he a heard a thud and the muted crack of Scotch's legs as they broke on the hard clay tiles below. It was followed by a muffled scream, a clear mixture of pain and terror.

He smiled.

CHAPTER TWENTY-EIGHT

THE CESSNA AMPHIBIAN AIRCRAFT FLEW LOW OVER THE waters of the Gulf. The pilot had kept radio silence for the last hour since leaving Havana.

He checked his chart and made a mental note. He would put down in a small cove on the west side of the island. Crews would be there to unload, and he would be up in the air heading back to Cuba within four to five minutes.

He thought of his teenage son, Eterio, and his wife, Benita. Five more runs over the next month and his boss would help him bring his family to America. They had a happy life in Cuba, but they were poorer than the cockroaches who ate their crumbs. It had become too much to just sit by and watch his friends move the drugs and become wealthy. He had stayed out for years, but the pull of freedom had become stronger than any moral impulse that had kept him from moving drugs in the first place.

Suddenly, the lights on the front panel began to blink. The pilot frowned and checked the crucial instruments. Everything still appeared to be in working order. He looked out the window onto the black darkness of the water below, then checked his altitude again. Again, the lights went out, the plane dipped, and his breathing escalated. He pulled back on the yoke, but it didn't budge. The altitude indicator was rocking back and forth like it was seasick. A bead of sweat ran through his eyebrow and he twisted his neck and rubbed his shoulder onto his eye to clear his vision. He could feel his heart thumping.

Checking that the radio frequency was set properly, he reached for the handset. He spoke in Spanish. "Going to crash. Controls frozen. Three miles south of destination." The radio crackled but offered no reply.

"*Alguien...?* he whispered. "*Cualquiera?*" The lights from just beyond the shore twinkled in the darkness. The altitude indicator came back for just a moment and showed a reading of twenty feet. Panicked, the pilot pulled back hard, and the plane responded.

But just slightly.

CHAPTER TWENTY-NINE

At five minutes to nine, Ellie turned the El Camino left off Stringfellow Road and onto Main Street, the northmost road on the island. A hundred yards later, she pulled into the parking lot of the restaurant that her former boss had chosen as their meeting place. She stepped into the late evening air and pushed the car door shut. The sun had already descended below the water, leaving a soft orange brushed against a horizon that was gathering in more gray every moment. At this end of the island, the only lights were dim and came from the few homes lining Main Street, the Bokeelia fishing pier, the boat ramp, and the lights on the outside of the restaurant. Stars were peeking out in their eternal game of hide-and-seek.

Suzie's Crab Shack was known for its weekend nightlife and for five years running had been endowed with the acclaim of the best piña colada on the island. The inside of the restaurant was spacious, even if the ceilings were low, and boasted an outdoor bar that looked out onto the short seawall and the pier just forty feet away. But tonight it was quiet, with only a couple cars in the parking lot. A couple was sitting on the pier with their legs dangling toward the water, and someone farther out was packing up their tackle.

Ellie rounded the corner and saw the slim figure of Ryan Wilcox sitting at one of the many picnic tables used for outdoor seating. He was almost out of place; Ellie had never expected to see him again, least of all here on Pine Island.

He smiled when he saw her approach and came to his feet.

Ryan was in his late-forties - over a good decade older than she - and stood at exactly six feet in height. His brown hair was short and for the last couple years had begun to show a slight peppering of grey. It had been eight months since he said goodbye to her on the tarmac in Kabul, but it felt like a lifetime ago. Eight months in this place had a mystical way of making the past seem almost unreal.

"Hello, Ellie."

"Hello, Ryan." They reached out and clasped hands. Ryan wasn't the huggy type. He set his free hand on top of hers, a display of kindly affection she had never witnessed before. They sat down, and Ryan motioned toward a longneck. "I got you a beer if you want it."

"Thank you." The wind blew off the water and whipped strands of Ellie's hair around her face. She took a pull on the beer and set it back down. "Are you stateside now?" she asked.

He nodded. "For now. I'm going to finish up a year at Langley before going back to the field." He fixed his gaze on her in the fading light. "I miss working alongside you. I'm sorry things worked out the way they did."

"Me too," she said.

"You ever get that dog?"

"Somehow I think you already know the answer to that."

He smiled and then got down to business. "I want to clear away the obvious questions by saying up front that I'm not here to ask you to come back in any way."

Ellie felt a bundle of tension slip from her shoulders. But not all of it. "Okay. So, what is it then?" she asked.

He nodded. His eyes were calm but held something Ellie couldn't quite place. She was good at reading people, but Ryan was one she could never peg. He, like her, had been trained well. He wouldn't let her see something in him he didn't want her to see.

He stood and slipped a hand inside his open windbreaker. He drew it out and was holding a wide, but thin, manila envelope. He slid it onto the tabletop in front of the best case officer he'd ever had. "You're going to have questions."

Ellie's eyes darted from Ryan to the envelope and back to his face.

"The answers will come in time," he said softly. "I just wanted you to know." Then he walked away, disappearing around the building and into the darkness.

Ellie stared at the envelope for a long time. She took a long draw on her beer. Whatever was in there was going to change something. She just didn't know what. Ryan Wilcox didn't just call you out of the blue, invite you to meet, and then walk away ensuring that you would have questions. She picked up the envelope and reluctantly fingered the metal clasp on the back. She lifted the flap. She drew the contents out.

It was a large picture that looked to have been taken from a CCTV camera and dated last Thursday. Three grainy figures were huddled together in what looked like a subway car. They wore thick trench coats and fur papakhas on their heads. Russians, Ellie thought. She leaned in, and her eyes scanned the faces.

Then she fell apart.

She gasped, touched her lips with her fingertips while her confused eyes began to fill with moisture. "It can't be," she whispered out loud. A thousand questions poured into her mind, like a school of fish being dumped on the deck of boat. It wasn't possible.

Ellie grabbed the sides of the table and struggled to breathe.

The photo was grainy and the lighting poor, but the image of her father's face was unmistakable.

~~~~~~

A lizard, a pelican, a seagull, a stray cat, all sat along various points of the Norma Jean pier. The darkness was warm and quiet. A low hum hung in the atmosphere of the dark, early morning hours and steadily grew louder. The lizard scattered, the pelican stared, the seagull darted off, and the cat hissed as the airplane pitched toward the ocean-end of the pier and slammed into it, hurling fiberglass, pilings, fire, diesel, a cat, and one ton of Colombian-picked, Mexican-processed cocaine across a two-hundred-yard radius, all of it spraying into the sky, riding on flame.

Black packages filled with white powder bobbed along the settling wreckage, and a battered and unbreathing body floated among them.

Ellie returns in **Shallow Breeze**, *the 2nd book in this series.*
TAP HERE to get started or keep reading for a Sneak Peek.

PREVIEW OF SHALLOW BREEZE

Ellie O'Conner stood near the end of the Norma Jean pier, her belly button nuzzled against the yellow crime scene tape that prevented curious onlookers from proceeding any farther. She ducked beneath it for the third time that morning and took a few steps toward the end of the charred and fractured wood, all that remained of the last thirty feet of the pier. Three strong pilings stood almost naked out of the southern waters of Pine Island Sound, and splintered wood jutted out like broken bones. The last of the Coast Guard's thirty-two-foot Transportable Port Security Boats were moving away in the distance, leaving the DEA and the Lee County Sheriff's Office to handle the investigation.

Late last evening, as Ellie was trying to drift into sleep, a heavy sound popped through the still evening air, the vibrations of which were felt two miles up Pine Island. She had slipped on a tank top and a pair of shorts and had run a half mile to the southernmost point of the island. Gloria and Fu Wang were already there, gathered up with a handful of locals who lived a couple streets closer to the pier than Ellie did. As it turned out, an amphibian aircraft carrying a large load of cocaine had crashed into the pier and splintered into thousands of pieces. Its cargo had hurled out to every direction on the compass. One of the plane's wings had ended up in the bottom floor of the Berensons' home, the home closest to the pier. Other than that, the debris seemed to be contained to the water. Government boats had trolled the waters for the last seven hours, searching the fringes of the mangroves and shoreline for rogue kilos of cocaine. The pilot's body was found lying upside down in the water, washed up under the front half of the pier. So far, no identification had been made. No one was optimistic that it would be.

Ellie set her hands on her hips and scanned the water twenty feet below. Mark Palfrey, her partner with the DEA, drew his twenty-foot Angler close and shouted up. "See anything else?"

Ellie kept her eyes on the water beyond him. "No. I think we got everything that stuck around here. Anything else would be carried out by the current by now."

"I'm going to check the perimeter of Crescent Island again," he said. The Angler's outboard revved up and carved a wide arc through the water away from the damaged pilings before shooting out through the channel markers.

"Hello, ma'am. I'm gonna have to ask you to step back behind the tape, please." The heavy Texas accent gave him away. Ellie turned to see Tyler Borland grinning at her and holding two cups of coffee. In the last eight months since Ellie had left her role as a case officer for the CIA, Tyler had become a close friend, with tiny sensations occurring every so often that Ellie thought could be the harbingers of something more. He owned Reticle, a shooting range in North Cape Coral and could generally be expected to make Ellie laugh. After a night of no sleep, his face was a welcome reprieve. She walked toward him and ducked back under the tape.

"This one's for you. Straight up," he said.

Ellie reached out and took the paper cup. "Thanks, Tyler."

"I guess you've been out here all night?" he asked.

She nodded and took a sip. "Yeah. We're about wrapped up. We have the side of the plane and the engine, so we'll see if the serial numbers show anything."

"Think they will?" he asked.

"I doubt it. That plane probably came from Cuba, owned by someone far from there." They started walking down the pier toward The Salty Mangrove bar. "The Coast Guard spotted him on radar coming in from the southwest ten minutes before he crashed. With as much as he was bringing in on that plane, I'm sure he'll be a ghost where any identification is concerned."

"Why would his flight plan include crashing into your uncle's pier? Sounds goofy if you ask me."

Ellie smiled but ignored him. Something else was bothering her. "The fact is, he was flying around here. Here, Tyler. Not Miami or New Orleans. Seems that our miles and miles of coastline have become favorable to the wrong kind of tourists. Gas being stored near the north end of the island, Pete Wellington gone missing, and now a plane loaded with blow crashing into the pier. Folks are already furious about Adam Stark's murder.

This place is known for being laid back and quiet, not for shipments of illegal drugs by the plane load."

"Yeah, I can see the brochure now," Tyler said. "'Beautiful, iconic pier to crash into. Take advantage of this offer before it's gone forever.' How much do you think was on there?"

ALSO BY JACK HARDIN

The Ellie O'Conner Coastal Suspense Series

Broken Stern

Shallow Breeze

Bitter Tide

Vacant Shore

Breakwater

Lonely Coast

THANK YOU, DEAR READER

Thank you for joining me in Pine Island. I hope you enjoyed this story. If you did, would you please take a moment to write a review on Amazon? Even the short ones help!

Thanks so much. It means the world.

GRATITUDE

I want to thank my wife, Rebekah, and our kiddos for giving me the time to daydream and get these characters on the page. They've sacrificed much.

I have done my best to remain faithful to the remarkable culture of both Pine Island and Matlacha ["Mat-luh-SHAY"]. Like any author, I've had to take liberties in certain areas, most of all with the location of The Salty Mangrove Bar, at the southern end of Pine Island.

I want to thank Whitney over at The Perfect Cup on Matlacha (yes, it's a real place) for an unsolicited sample of his incredible chowder. Seriously, you guys. If you're ever down that way stop in and say hi to him, grab a cup of coffee. You won't find a nicer guy. Plan to have brunch there and come in the late morning hours to avoid the crowds in the winter time. Maybe give him a thoughtful review on Yelp while you're at it.

Life is short, live it well.

Jack
May, 2018

FOLLOW JACK

I truly enjoy hearing from my readers. Here are some ways to keep in touch!

To be notified of upcoming releases as soon as they come out, sign up at
http://bit.ly/jackhardinnewsletter.

Follow Jack on Facebook: fb.me/jackhardinauthor

Say hello: jack.w.hardin00@gmail.com

ABOUT THE AUTHOR

Jack Hardin currently lives in Arlington, TX, with his stunning wife and five kiddos.

He grew up in an Army family and spent half his childhood living in Germany, traveling all over Europe prior to the fall of the Iron Curtain. At nine years old he walked through Checkpoint Charlie and into East Berlin just one year before the Berlin Wall came down. He holds a 2nd degree black belt in Taekwondo, is proficient with bo staff and nunchucks, and has taught women's self-defense.

Those alone do not make him awesome, but it all sounds really cool.

Made in the USA
Las Vegas, NV
09 February 2021